# TRULY INSEPARABLE

### WANDA Y. THOMAS

Genesis Press, Inc.

# Indigo Love Stories

An imprint of Genesis Press, Inc.
Publishing Company

Genesis Press, Inc.
P.O. Box 101
Columbus, MS 39703

ISBN-13: 978-1-58571-262-5
ISBN-10: 1-58571-262-0
Manufactured in the United States of America

First Edition 1998
Second Edition 2007

Visit us at www.genesis-press.com or call at 1-888-Indigo-1

# PROLOGUE

A piercing scream shattered Nelson's dream.

"Nelson!"

*My God! That's Shelby,* he thought, bolting upright in the bed. Without further analysis, he leaped to his feet and ran across the hallway to his son's room. Seeing Shelby's tear-streaked face, panic flashed in his eyes and his temple began to throb as he rushed over to her. "What is it, Shel? What's wrong?"

Shelby held out the small bundle in her arms. "S-s-something's wrong, Nelson. Lamar won't wake up." Nelson felt his chest cave in as he took his son. He knew without looking at him that Lamar wasn't breathing.

Shelby continued to mumble through her tears. "I-I came in to feed him and when I tried to wa-wake him, Lamar wouldn't wake up. Nelson, what's wrong?"

Nelson wasn't listening. He was administering CPR to his son, blowing frantic air through the cold, stiff lips.

Lamar did not respond.

"Shelby! Call 9-1-1," he yelled, looking at her when she didn't move. "Now, Shelby!" He lowered his head again, praying and crying at the same time.

"Come on, son. Please, Lamar. Come on. Breathe! Breathe! Breathe!" He tried again.

There was no movement…

There was no sound…

There was no response.

And after several more tries, Nelson knew it was over.

He looked up at the ceiling and opened his mouth. The scream that rose in his throat never vocalized as he huddled his son's body against his. "Why, God? Why?"

Shelby ran back into the room. One glance at her husband's face and she collapsed in the rocking chair behind her, sobbing wildly. Bewildered, Nelson could only stare from Shelby to his son. The tears falling from his eyes trickled onto Lamar's motionless face. He swabbed them away with gentle fingers. What was he supposed to do? Their baby was dead and Nelson didn't know what to do.

Slowly, he walked over to Shelby and carefully laid the small infant in her arms. Then he knelt down, placed his arms around his family, and rested his head in his wife's lap.

# CHAPTER ONE

Everything looked magnificent. Trimmed in gold, holly red, and wintergreen, the room sparkled in the festive colors of the holiday season and the illumination of five overhead chandeliers. Shelby Julian Reeves held the edge of the black curtain, and her breath, in anticipation. The butterflies that had courted her stomach all day suddenly unfurled their delicate wings and Shelby felt a rush of nervous excitement. Embracing the celebratory mood, her brown eyes wandered the room, aimlessly trying to take it all in. An eleven-foot tree stood tall and majestic in the left corner of the room, its massive branches loaded down with strings of white lights, gold ornaments, and red bows. On the carpeted floor beneath its base, a multitude of empty, gold-wrapped packages reflected the twinkling lights of the tree. Miniature sleighs full of artfully cut boughs crested in white. Red berries and pinecones sat as centerpieces on round white-clothed tables. The lush and large poinsettias clustered throughout also served to line a makeshift runway down the center of the room.

Shelby released the curtain and made a mental note to send the interior design firm something special to thank them for their donation. J.R. had told her that ticket sales had increased significantly over the last two months. Maybe she should have paid more attention. But since first annual anythings didn't generally draw large crowds, Shelby hadn't given the news more than a passing thought. There had to be at least five hundred people out there, and as she listened to the loud murmur of voices, a magical feeling overtook her, the same one she felt every time she did a show. The DownTown Stock Club had its job. Soon, she would take center stage and do hers.

She turned away and came face to face with her business manager and friend, Manette Walker. Startled by Manny's abrupt appearance, she threw a hand over her pounding chest. "Girl, you nearly gave me a heart attack."

Manette gave Shelby a wry look before saying, "Shel, we've got problems."

Shelby knew her friend needed no prompting, and she waited for the tirade to begin while casually appraising the outfit Manny had chosen to wear for the evening. Instead of the black wool pantsuit Shelby had suggested, Manette wore a peppermint-striped sheath. Her accessories included a black feather boa, black gloves, red hoop earrings, and four-inch black pumps. Manny spent hours at the gym keeping her five-foot, seven-inch frame in top condition. Shelby couldn't understand why, after all that work, her friend deliberately hid her beautiful tan complexion under layers of makeup and her body under clothes that did nothing but distract from her slender figure. But at least she'd toned down the hair, Shelby thought. She directed her gaze to the slightly wild look in Manette's eyes.

"Starris just called," Manny began. "She's stuck in traffic and doesn't know how long it will take her to get here, which causes a real problem since she's supposed to model the first outfit in the show. Ty's yelling for you again. I told him that you pulled the fish skirt from the show and he's not happy. Casey won't speak to anyone because she's still sulking about having to wear the gold gown, which is not a good color for her, and Miranda refuses to get dressed because she can't find her wigs."

Shelby noted the dramatic pose struck in consideration of what Manette no doubt deemed a calamity in the making. "It will be fine, Manny."

"Fine! How can you say that, Shel? This is why I hate doing these things. Something always goes wrong at the last minute. Always! The opening number revolves around Starris. She's not here, and we fitted the outfit specifically for her. I've looked everywhere for those damn wigs and I can't find them. And if Casey throws one more black look my way, she's fired!"

Shelby laughed. "You can't fire Casey. She's donating her time this evening as a favor to us."

Red-colored lips protruded in an exaggerated pout as Manny's eyes narrowed in a glare. "I may not be able to fire her, but I can sure send her butt packing."

Shelby swallowed another bubble of laughter and took hold of the hand Manette had thrown out for emphasis. All things considered, the show had come together with relatively few problems. There had been a mix-up with the tree ornaments, but the interior design firm had corrected that mishap this afternoon. And as nervous as Shelby felt already, Manny's flair for the drama, she really didn't need. "It will all come together, Manny, so please calm down. These problems are easily solved. Jacqueline and Starris are about the same size. Go to the back and let her know that we're moving her to the first spot and to change outfits. Then give the red jumpsuit that Jacqueline was supposed to wear to Casey and tell her to get dressed. Miranda's wigs were inadvertently left at the shop this afternoon. J.R. has already sent someone to get them and they'll be here any minute."

"What about Ty?"

Shelby rolled her eyes. As much as she loved Tyrone Brooks, he sometimes made her head hurt. They had met as apprentice designers in New York, and if not for Ty, the city would have swallowed her up and spit her out. Tyrone, from a nouveau riche family, was gay and was one of the nicest people she knew. As a designer, Shelby had two words to describe his work: horribly bad. His latest offering to the world of fashion was fish skirts. The front panel displayed the head of a fish, curved slits near the side seam represented gills and he'd divided the back panel to provide an extra seam for the fish tail. The design was bad enough. Tyrone had made it worse by manufacturing the garment in two-color, fluorescent patent leather. When he'd sent the preliminary sketches, Shelby's brain had gone numb. Her opinion, though, was a singular one, because Ty's New York patrons clamored for his designs and he wanted broader exposure for his clothes. He knew Denver's fashion barometer leaned more toward casual and sportswear than fads, but they had an agreement. In exchange for his five percent stake in her boutique, she displayed a few of his samples and took advantage of the deep discount she gave by handling her manufacturing needs from his New York shop.

"Don't worry about Ty. I'll talk to him."

Relief relaxed Manny's features. "See, Shel. That's why you're in charge of this thing. You don't let anything ruffle you. Problems come up. You solve them and keep moving."

"And you shouldn't let them ruffle you either, Manny." Shelby smiled. "Now, get back there and get those women ready to go. The show starts in forty minutes."

Manny scuttled away and Shelby turned back to the curtain. She parted it and peeked out again. Her eyes swept the length of the floor once again before she assured herself that Nelson hadn't yet made his appearance. She knew he'd show up eventually. And if asked, Shelby would be hard-pressed to explain why she was looking for a man she had divorced in the first place. As silly as it was, in the back of her mind she still harbored the hope that maybe he wouldn't show up at all.

"Shel, love. I need you back here."

"Coming, Ty." With a sigh, Shelby dropped the curtain and turned to make her way to the dressing area set up for the designers and models. Yes, she was in charge, and while she'd been reluctant to take on coordinating the event, she had. And it was a responsibility Shelby didn't take lightly. J.R. had expressed his skepticism when she'd proposed the silent auction but now depended on her to put on a memorable event, one memorable enough to move the attendees to empty their wallets with a smile on their faces.

Her friends and colleagues had not hesitated to say yes when she'd called and asked for their help. Together they had organized what Shelby knew would be a dynamite show, if she could get the models to leave their egos and petty jealousies at the door before she fired every last one of them. An amused smile tilted her lips as Shelby recalled the words she'd just spoken to Manette. She couldn't fire any of them. They had all volunteered.

Nelson Lamar Reeves, Jr., took the tickets from the smiling couple, handed them an information packet and thanked them for their support of ROBY. He watched the couple until they disappeared through the double doors, his dark eyes full of longing. Those two loved each other, he thought, and they were happy. He'd been happy like that once, but that had been a lifetime ago, or so it seemed. Nelson heard a small bell ding and turned, expecting to see another couple dressed to the nines step into the foyer. He saw his friend Jordon Banks step from the elevator instead.

Jordon rushed up to the table. "Nelson. Do me a favor, man. One of the models is waiting for this thing. It has her wigs or makeup or something and I'd appreciate it if you'd take it to the back."

"Why don't you take it, J.R.?"

"Can't. I promised Cyrus an interview before the show starts and I'm running late. Thanks, man." Jordon set the trunk on the table and walked off before Nelson could respond.

Nelson stared at the small trunk. It had been J.R.'s idea to hold the fund-raiser, just as it had been his idea to organize the DownTown Stock Club and to devote most of the organization's community resources into the startup of ROBY, an acronym for Rescuing Our Black Youth. The one-year-old organization had adopted as its mission to curtail the rise of fatherless homes and the problems associated with fatherless youth. Their program targeted teenage African-American males and in addition to providing mentors, offered counseling and classes on the value of an education, proper decision-making, goal-setting and job skills. They also worked with local businesses, and once the boys completed the required classes, provided each with an opportunity to work.

Jordon Randolph Banks was an idea man who left the details to others. That is, until they had started planning the fund-raiser. For some reason, J.R. had decided to take the reins and walk this event from start to finish himself, which hadn't bothered Nelson. He'd been traveling so much he'd only had time to sell a few tickets. He did know that when asked to do the show, Shelby had said no. She had always supported anything that had to do with children with her time and money, and the last thing Nelson wanted to do was go anywhere near the back area and be reminded that she had rejected J.R.'s request because of him.

A few minutes later, Nelson stood in the doorway observing what appeared to be mass confusion. It looked as if a bomb had detonated and left the entire area in devastation. More people than he could count ran back and forth calling out names and instructions. Half-dressed men and women were being helped into clothing while assistants pulled colorful outfits from plastic bags hanging from black racks at one end of the room. A table loaded with food and beverages sat opposite the racks. At the other end of the room, a row of desks with lighted mirrors lined the walls where men and women lounged in chairs while others did their hair and makeup. Another group, all dressed in black leotards, whirled and kicked their legs in the air. And in the midst of it all, flashbulbs popped intermittently to capture it all on film.

Shelby had done many fashion shows, but Nelson had never before gone behind the scenes. Watching it all, he wondered if this was normal and if so, how anyone could pull off a show that had any cohesiveness when everywhere he looked he saw utter chaos. Seeing Jacqueline Tyler, he shook his head and began to weave his way through the clothing-strewn floor, the boxes, bags and suitcases. Reaching her, he shifted the trunk under his arm and tapped her on the shoulder. "Can you point me in the direction of the keeper of this zoo?"

Jacqueline straightened from hooking a buckle on a white boot and smiled when she saw Nelson. "Nels," she said. Then she pirouetted before him. "What do you think?"

Except for the fur trimming on the hood and cuffs of the jacket, Jacqueline was dressed from head to toe in white leather. That, however, was not what had caught and held Nelson's attention. "You look…" He cocked a brow as he sought to find the right word, "Interesting."

"It's the red stripes on my face, isn't it? I was a little concerned about that myself, but Shelby said that some designers use makeup and hair to play up or project the feel of an outfit. I don't know. It's a little wild, I guess, but she's the expert."

Nelson had stopped listening when he heard his ex-wife's name. "Shelby's here?" "Of course, she's here. Shelby put this whole show together. Didn't you know that, Nelson?"

Clearly confused, he searched vainly through the pandemonium for Shelby. "Where is she, Jacqueline?"

Jacqueline pointed to an area over his shoulder. "She's right over there, with Ty Brooks."

His size and the cluttered floor proved no obstacle as Nelson moved faster than any speeding bullet to reach Shelby. He stopped directly behind her, saw the smile break across Tyrone's face and cautioned the man with a finger to his lips. Shelby watched the smile on Tyrone's face widen, and when he smoothed the hair back on his balding head and placed his hand in the pocket of his gray double-breasted suit, she stopped talking. She had been listing her reasons for pulling the fish skirt from the show, but Ty's attention had wandered. She felt the heat of a stare singe her back and knew why. Tyrone was primping for a photographer, and Shelby knew that as soon as she turned around, the flash of a camera would momentarily blind her.

That thought annoyed her because after dodging the photographers for the better part of the day, she'd finally agreed to grant their requests for an interview with the understanding that they would not include her in any photographs taken in conjunction with the show. Steeling herself, she whirled around with the intention of giving the pushy photographer a piece of her mind. Instead of a camera, Shelby found herself staring up into the dark, impassioned gaze of her ex-husband. Her heart dropped to her feet. "Nelson!"

"Shelby," he answered with a calm he didn't feel.

She gasped and stumbled backwards, her ability to speak was lost as she stared at his well-defined build in the tailored black tuxedo. Nelson had come backstage to see her, and she smiled with the thought that he still cared. That smile soon turned into a scowl when the memories intruded and her mind tried to decipher the conflicting messages.

Nelson watched the warring emotions flit across her face and his confusion mounted. What was she doing here? Tyrone stepped forward before he could ask, and Nelson grasped the offered hand in a solid shake.

"Big man! It's good to see you again."

"It good to see you too, Ty," Nelson responded, "and thanks for agreeing to help out this evening." His gaze never left Shelby. She was thinner than Nelson remembered, but the body-hugging ivory gown trimmed in gold accentuated the curves of her willowy frame. She'd also cut her hair and the sable tresses just touched her shoulders. The shorter style didn't diminish Shelby's exotic loveliness and the luxurious, black curls he loved to run his fingers through were still there. The frown wrinkling her darkly hued face he could do without, but those eyes dusted in gold and able to reach inside him and touch his soul, he couldn't.

"How could anyone say no to my pet?" Tyrone's stare joined Nelson's. "I'd do anything for Shelby."

*I'd do anything for Shelby, too,* Nelson thought, watching pain darken her eyes. Only he'd blown his chance and she'd divorced him, putting an end to any hope he'd had of reconciling with his wife. All he could do now was soak up the image of the dark beauty standing before him to savor later when he was alone.

Their exchange gave Shelby a chance to gather her wits. She had looked for him earlier to see for herself that he was all right. But Nelson had invaded her domain, and that she would not tolerate. Conscious of the photographers who would sell their mother for a chance to capture a scandal on film, Shelby moved closer to Nelson and motioned to him with her finger. He leaned down to hear her words. His nostrils flared as the soft scent of a fruity bouquet permeated his senses. It was Shelby's scent and the scent he'd gone too long without smelling. What he did next came as a result of pure instinct. Nelson turned his head and brushed his lips against hers.

The pleasure of the brief contact surprised them both and, woefully unsatisfied, Nelson cupped her face in his hands and captured her lips beneath his. Shelby had a full and generous mouth with lips soft as rose petals, and in his haste, Nelson tried to devour all of it in one fell swoop. In the dizzying fog overtaking her ability to reason, she lifted her arms to encircle his shoulders and moved closer, close enough to rub her body against his in a blatantly provocative movement that sent a rush of blood straight to his brain. Nelson lowered his hands to span her waist and, groaning, pulled Shelby into a tight embrace and deepened the kiss.

Loud clapping and cheering shattered the moment just as a flash lit up the area around them. Shelby yanked herself out of Nelson's arms, turning her back on him as she dragged in deep gasps of air. When her breathing slowed, Shelby dropped her chin to her chest, thoroughly demoralized by her behavior. His kiss had caused a riot within her, dredging up long-forgotten passion. Sadly, she wanted more. She was, after all, a woman, and like any woman, she had wants and desires. She yearned to be held and kissed. And she wanted her husband to fulfill those needs. Impossible, considering their current situation.

Composing herself, Shelby assumed the unemotional persona that had gotten her through so many difficult situations. For the benefit of anyone who might be watching, she forced a smile to her lips, but his eyes shimmered with fury when she lifted them to Nelson again. "I don't know why you're here, Nelson Reeves, but if you ever come anywhere near me again, I'll make you wish you were never born. Now, I have a show to do and you don't belong back here, so please leave this area." Having said that, Shelby spun on her heel and walked away. Held trapped by the power of his ardor, Nelson followed her with her eyes until a crowd gathered, blocking his view.

# CHAPTER TWO

The picture appeared in the morning edition of *The Denver Post* two weeks later. Shelby didn't see it until late in the afternoon. Leaving for work, she had picked up the newspaper from her driveway and taken it with her to the shop, but her day had kept her so busy she hadn't time to remove the rubber band, let alone read any of the news.

That morning, she'd finally finished the last of the fashion show fittings and had sent the measurements off to the appropriate designers. The fund-raiser had been wildly successful and while the organization had received a great deal of favorable press, the silent auction had been the most popular segment of the evening. The average bid for each of the forty designs modeled that night had totaled $5,000, and in the final tally, ROBY had received close to $200,000. And the donations were still pouring in. J.R. had already gotten Shelby's commitment to coordinate the next show, but not before he'd agreed to move the event to a different time of the year.

The Christmas season was entirely too hectic for her. Since the show, traffic in Exterior Motives had picked up considerably, taxing the stamina of Shelby's sales staff. She had not hired additional people. Once the novelty wore off, the one-time buyers and shop browsers would return to their old shopping haunts and she didn't want to be placed in the position of having to lay off workers. To ease the load, Shelby had spent the remainder of her day helping in the store. Toward closing, the customers had finally tapered off and she'd seen her chance to take a break.

Slipping through the door that separated the ready-to-wear store from the boutique, Shelby walked down three steps into the area making up the other half of Exterior Motives. This was her personal space where she designed clothes for clients who could afford to spend a great deal more on fashion. Exterior Motives was Shelby's dream come true. Located in the Sixteenth Street Mall in downtown Denver, the shop took up the bottom floor of a ten-story building. Lavender and rose flowered wallpaper decked the walls. Delicate furniture sat amid an abundance of leafy, green foliage, gold-gilded mirrors and the pictures decorating the boutique. Surrounded by high-rise buildings, she couldn't take advantage of natural sunlight, but the sheer drapes at the large picture window and strategically placed standing lamps gave the shop an intimate appeal. She'd decorated with her female clientele in mind and was proud of the warm and inviting setting she'd created.

Entering her office, Shelby set her cup of tea down and picked up the paper. She sat, propped her aching feet on top of the desk, and leaned back to read the news. She first scanned the headlines and after folding that section, reached for the one titled, "Living." She quickly read her horoscope, flipped the page, and stopped breathing. There on the society pages for the perusal of anyone with a quarter was a picture of Nelson kissing her.

Captioned beneath the photo were the words: "Earlier this year, Shelby Reeves, daughter of noted geneticist, Dr. Martin Eugene Smith, handed her husband his walking papers. Seen here at the recent fashion show and fund-raiser for ROBY, it looks as if Nelson Reeves may have found the way back into his ex-wife's heart."

Manette dropped the telephone receiver into the cradle and pushed the toes of her brown, leather boots against the floor to roll her chair backwards toward her desk. She pivoted the chair around as she replaced a wide gold hoop in her ear.

"Have you seen this?"

Manny raised startled eyes to the doorway when Shelby barreled into her office. "Seen what?"

Shelby sat in the lemon-yellow wingback chair across from Manette and threw a crumpled ball on her desk. "That!"

Manny reached for the paper and after smoothing it out on the walnut desk glanced at the ink-smeared images and shrugged her shoulders. "Actually, I saw it this morning."

Shelby leaned forward, attempting to pin Manny's eyes with her stare. "And you didn't say anything to me. I don't understand you sometimes, Manny Walker. You're supposed to be my friend."

Manny threw up both hands. "Now, before you get started, Shel, just let me say this. What's the big deal anyway? You and Nelson have kissed thousands of times."

Shelby waved her hand in the air as if to brush the response away. "This is not the same thing and you know it. Nelson and I are divorced, and the last thing I need is to have my personal life put on public display for a city full of strangers to gawk at."

This week's hairstyle, a composition of braided twists, seemed to bristle with static as Manette took a deep breath in preparation for the interminable dispute. A diehard romantic and incessant searcher for her own lifetime mate, Manny believed what Shelby and Nelson had shared embodied true love. In her mind, they were the perfect couple, and she didn't plan to back off until one of them came to their senses. "Shelby, the only reason you're reacting this way is because you know Nelson loves you. If you're honest with yourself, you'll admit that you still love him too." She folded her arms over her chest. "Then again, maybe I'm wrong. Tell me that you don't love Nelson, Shelby. If you can do that, I'll mind my own business."

A profusion of dark lashes lowered to hide the shocking impact of Manette's words. *Am I that transparent?* Shelby worried. She hadn't thought she was wearing her heart on her sleeve and she could even say Nelson's name without sounding like a blubbering idiot. Her brow pleated with consternation. If Manny could see the direction of her heart, who else could? Her head rose to meet the challenge, and Manette's chocolate brown eyes glimmered with the dare. It was a brief confrontation. Unable to hold the stare, Shelby looked down and plucked nonexistent lint from the legs of her white, wool gabardine trousers. "I don't have to admit anything," she mumbled.

"See. You can't even say it, can you, Shelby? I knew you couldn't. If you had, you'd be lying, and that's something you don't do, out loud anyway."

Shelby's head swung up and her eyes darkened with restrained emotion. "And just what is that supposed to mean, Manette Walker?"

Rather than respond, Manny lowered a pair of long false eyelashes and took a sudden interest in her desk. Shelby watched her align the various items neat

ly, then fuss with a stack of folders until she'd straightened them to her liking. "Manny?" she prodded, a little irritated at being ignored.

Manette leaned back in her chair. The checked candy-apple red and pine-green skirt she wore rode higher on slim hips as she crossed her legs. "It means that you need to stop pretending that you have no feelings." Sensing Shelby's agitation, she lowered her voice. "The last two years have been hard, Shel. I know that. But Nelson loves you and he deserves another chance. Why don't you call him? I know he'd be delighted to hear from you."

The slight tremors working their way through Shelby's body turned her insides to mush. Manny was one of three people who knew her better sometimes than she knew herself, the other two being Nelson and her father. It was the reason Shelby hadn't been able to voice what she knew to be a bald-faced lie. She did love Nelson, but it was a love she was willing to forgo in preference of preserving her pride. To hear Manny talk, anyone would think that Shelby hadn't tried to save her marriage; she had. For months, she had stuck it out with Nelson Reeves, waiting for an indication that he still loved her. She would have taken any crumb of affection, no matter how small, and welcomed Nelson back into her heart, if he had shown some sign that he cared. What Shelby had received was Nelson's silent wrath and outright rejection.

Somewhere you had to draw the line. Shelby had drawn hers when she refused to humiliate herself by begging for her husband's love. It was a strain for Shelby to keep her composure intact and face Manny's perceptive gaze. Yet, she did, and she even managed to throw up a front that for anyone other than Manny would have camouflaged her real feelings. "Why should I call Nelson? We have nothing to talk about."

"A twelve-year history gives you and Nelson plenty to talk about. You had what every woman, including me, is looking for, Shelby. How can you throw it all away as if it meant nothing?"

Shelby had had enough. Upset, she looked away, knowing that if the conversation continued she could quite possibly break down in tears. "What Nelson and I had is over, Manny. That chapter in my life is closed and I don't want to discuss it anymore."

Manny lifted a chart on her desk and turned it toward Shelby. "Here is the staff schedule for next week. Anyone working Monday night has Tuesday morning off, and everyone is scheduled to work on Thursday, since it's the day after Christmas. I don't expect many returns, but with the after-Christmas sale, customers will flood Exterior Motives all day long. The buyers have offered to work in the store, if we need them. That doesn't surprise me since it's inventory time."

Shelby turned her attention to the chart. "Pencil me in for Thursday. That blizzard they're forecasting has me a little worried, though. If we get hit, some of these people won't make it in. And if it's as bad as they say, we'll need to call the staff and let them know that the store will be closed on Thursday."

"No problem," Manny replied, her tone indicating that she was still miffed. She pointed to a stack on her desk. "Those are the Christmas bonus checks. They're ready for your signature."

Shelby took the pen offered by Manette and began signing the checks. Nelson was the single disagreement between them. So far it hadn't altered their friendship, but having to justify herself to everyone, Manette included, had become tiresome. Still, Shelby hated to let their conversation end on such a bad note. She handed back the checks and rose from her chair. "Are you still heading home for the holidays?"

"On Tuesday. As soon as the store closes, I'm on my way to Boulder to spend Christmas with the family. I'll drive back after dinner."

"You should take some time of from this place, Manny. Why don't you stay the week? I can handle the store."

"And miss J.R.'s New Year's Eve party? No way! What about you?"

Shelby covered a grimace with a sigh. This was the second year she'd miss Jordon's annual bash. "Poppy's in New York, so there's really no reason to celebrate, and I still have a lot of packing to do. I'll probably just spend the day at home."

Manny sighed. "If I said I felt sorry for you, I'd be lying. You don't have to spend Christmas alone and if you weren't so damn obstinate, you'd pick up that phone and call Nelson." She immediately wished back the words when she saw the hurt look on Shelby's face. "I'm sorry I said that, Shel." Manette left her chair and moved around the desk to hug her friend. "Girl, you know I love you. My holiday wish for you is that you'll find your happiness."

"Thank you, Manny." Shelby glanced at her watch and turned for the door.

"Oh, I almost forgot," Manette said. "Ty called while you were out. He said he's sending Kathy's wedding dress with the belts and scarves, which are due to arrive next week."

"Do I need to call him?"

"Not unless there's something wrong with the gown, and he doesn't want to hear from you then. He said to tell Carlotta Eldridge to go and, well the first letter is an F. You can figure out the rest. He's also sending ten fish skirts and a surprise for you."

"When you unpack those skirts, find a place for them in the back of the shop, out of sight if possible."

Manette laughed. "If Ty knew what you did with his clothes, he'd take it as an insult." "Then he'd have to take it as an insult. I keep telling Ty that stuff won't sell in Denver."

"Well, all I can say is, that's your friend."

"That's right, he is," Shelby said pensively. "I could call the film commission. Maybe there's a shoot for The Return of the Fish People. If so, we could show them the perfect costume." It was a joke, but one year they had sold ten of Tyrone's space suit jumpers. The set designer had used them as props in a film about aliens that crash-landed in the Rocky Mountains.

"It's late, Manny. Let's lock up and get out of here. I'll grab my things from the boutique and walk with you to the parking lot."

Manny watched Shelby leave and waited a couple of minutes before moving back to her desk. After a glance over her shoulder confirmed that she was alone, Manny lifted the receiver and placed a long overdue phone call.

Nelson felt an obstruction lodge in his chest, impeding his heartbeat, and gripped the telephone receiver tighter against his ear. His first thought had been to let the call transfer to the message system; he should have gone with that thought.

"Did you hear me, Nels. Shelby saw the picture of the two of you in the paper and she's furious. But that's only because she cares."

He laid his presentation notes on the glass-topped desk and tried to find a quick but gentle way to deal with the latest announcement from the woman who made it her duty to keep him informed of his ex-wife's every move. Deciding on a response he hoped would speed the conversation to a hasty conclusion, he said, "I heard you, Manny, but can we discuss this later? I have a very important meeting in a few minutes and I'm still reviewing my notes."

"No," she replied, her voice tinged with exasperation. "Shelby's already put your house up for sale, and who knows what she'll do next. Now I just found out that she's planning to stay at home for Christmas. I think that you should take advantage of this opportunity and go over there and talk to her, Nelson."

He squelched a groan deep in his throat. Manny was a good friend and while he appreciated her love and concern, her little news bulletins continuously disrupted his ability to stay focused and forget that his wife had permanently removed him from her life. "Why don't you talk to her, Manny?"

"Don't you think I have? I've talked to Shelby until I'm blue in the face. Everyone has. You have to talk to her, Nelson. Shelby loves you, and if she could just hear from you that you still love her, I know she'll change her mind."

"You can't talk to someone who won't talk to you. It's over between Shel and me. She divorced me. I have accepted that, and the fact that Shelby no longer loves me. You'd do well to accept it, too."

"I will never accept this, Nelson Reeves! I swear, I've never met two more stubborn people in my life! And how I wound up with the two of you for best friends, I'll never know. You can't let her do this, Nelson. You and Shelby love each other, and I believe that love can conquer all. Don't you, Nelson?"

"No. Shelby and I are proof of that." Nelson dragged a weary hand across his forehead. "Manny, I have to go. I'll talk to you later."

"Nelson, wait!" "Manny," he replied firmly, but with sensitive caring, "I'll talk to you another time."

Nelson hung up the telephone. He swiveled his black leather chair and went to stand at the south-facing bank of windows in his spacious, contemporary-decorated office.

Absorbed in his thoughts, he looked down on the mani-cured, green golf course of the Denver Tech Center. By calendar, winter should have established its frigid hold over the city, but three hundred days of sunshine made it possible for active Denverites to enjoy their outdoor activi-ties for most of the year. The DTC, a mostly high-tech office district located in the suburb of Englewood, sat just outside the southeast edge of Denver's city limits. Englewood, along with the surrounding smaller cities, made up the larger area known as Denver Metro. Nelson's office was in the executive wing on the top floor of a brick and smoked-glass high-rise owned by Techno-tronics Cable, Inc.

"Damn," he muttered. Hanging up on Manny had been rude, and rudeness had no place in friendship. That, and the fact that she was his connection Shelby, a link he desperately needed. Only, it was galling to Nelson having to use his friend as his conduit for information about his ex-wife. Normally he would have talked to Manny, but her call had come at the most inopportune time imaginable. It was Friday, and for the last two days TTC's nine-member board of directors had been in the building conducting depart-mental reviews. Heads were rolling over the Orlando project and the company grapevine was frenetic with gossip. Rumor had it that several executives would not return after the holidays, and the employees were specu-lating on the next to go.

Nelson knew it wouldn't be him and that none of his fellow officers had lost their jobs, yet. But in twenty, no fifteen minutes, he amended, glancing at his watch, he needed to walk down that hallway totally focused on his presentation. The last thing he needed on his mind was thoughts of Shelby. Talking to Manny had effectively wiped out the weeks of self-talk he'd put himself through after seeing Shelby at the fund-raiser. Now he had to start again trying to build his immunity to Shelby. At best, Nelson could only hope to confine his wife to a place in his mind where she didn't dominate his thoughts every minute of the day. It would also be helpful if he could make that happen in the next few minutes.

The door to his office opened and Nelson turned from the window to watch his assistant breeze into his office. He moved to his desk, sat down and struggled with his internal conflict, trying to get his mind back on business.

Grace Donaldson rounded the desk and began slapping paper down in front of him. "Here are the final pages of your presentation. I've been hearing that the natives are restless, so I took the liberty of cutting it down by ten minutes. The pertinent points are highlighted and your copy is heavily marked, so just follow the route I've laid out. I've also made the copies for the board. I'll hand them out after you're introduced." Grace stopped to examine him and tsked her tongue. "Here, take this and drink it."

Nelson took the glass filled with iced tea and had no sooner taken a drink when she issued her next order.

"Stand up."

He set the glass on a crystal coaster and stood. Grace grabbed his arm and began to roll down his shirtsleeve. She turned to fish around in one of the desk drawers behind her.

"You look like a damn engineer."

"I am an engineer."

With an efficiency of skill, Grace hooked a cufflink into the buttonhole of Nelson's monogrammed, white silk shirt. "Not today, you're not. Today, you're the head of this department, not one of the boys. And I'll not have my vice president going before the board of Techno-tronics Cable looking like a damn engineer. Give me your other arm."

Nelson held out his arm and flexed his neck while Grace secured the sleeve. She straightened the navy blue and red power tie and stepped back. "Where is your jacket?"

"In the closet."

Grace retrieved the navy blue suit jacket, brushing it off as she returned to help Nelson slip into the coat. He turned around.

"Well, Gracie. Do I pass inspection?" Grace rolled her eyes heavenward, recalling her misgivings ten years prior when HR had assigned her to their newest executive. She remembered thinking, *Not another Harvard MBA.* Those brash, young upstarts thought they knew everything and wouldn't have recognized the value of her twenty-five-year work history with TTC. Nelson Reeves hadn't attended Harvard and he had recognized her worth. "You'll do," she said, giving him a smile. "Now you have about five minutes to look over the document. I'll buzz you when it's time."

Nelson watched her leave, then took a few minutes to familiarize himself with the revisions. Nothing Grace had done would throw him off and the board didn't worry Nelson; he'd been playing the game so long it was second nature to him. His mind returned to his phone call from Manny and his wife. No matter what he'd told Manny, Nelson had not accepted that his wife no longer loved him. Nelson believed that if he could get to Shelby, he could persuade her to take him back. But she resolutely refused to see him or hear anything he had to say. Somehow, he had to get her to listen, and he had to do it before she sold the only thing left that he still shared with his wife. If he couldn't, Nelson knew that the day his wife walked from their home, there would be nothing he could do or say to bring her back, and his broken heart would remain broken forever.

# CHAPTER THREE

Consciously keeping her mind blank, Shelby drove out of downtown Denver and exited on the highway. As usual, a mass of cars packed I-70. Used to the rush hour madness, she pushed the button on the CD player and hummed along with the jazz recording of Christmas tunes. The music did not improve her mood. She made herself keep time with the music, hut could summon no joy for what used to be her favorite time of the year. Somewhere along the way, Shelby had lost her Christmas spirit and after talking to Manny, dark depression had her feeling very sorry for herself. It was talking about Nelson. Shelby couldn't think about her ex-husband without sending her emotional state into a nosedive, and when she did, the loneliness rose and enclosed her heart like a tomb.

On a whim, she turned off at the next available exit and reentered the highway going in the opposite direction. Fifteen minutes later, Shelby headed east on I-225, toward the suburb of Aurora. Denver Metro held an annual contest of lights and awarded the house with the best display a plaque and a featured spot on the evening news. Most of her former neighbors competed, but Shelby had long ago learned that they didn't care about the plaque or having their house seen on television. Theirs was a neighborhood contest. The prize: boasting rights to the largest electric bill ever received for the month of December. The residents took the competition seriously and when everyone had done their best to outdo the others, the entire block looked like a giant Christmas carnival of lights.

Shelby had decided that a drive through her old neighborhood might be just the thing she needed to lift her spirits. When she turned onto her old street, Shelby drove slowly, enchanted by the colored lights, Christmas trees and other symbols of the holiday. Like a spectator at a tennis match, she twisted her head from side to side, wanting to see everything and frustrated with the moving car that kept pulling her attention from the sights. She finally parked the powder blue Mercedes and walked the long block. The festive displays did lift Shelby's spirits and her footsteps crunching on the frozen walk were more energetic than they'd been in a long time as she returned to her car. The lighter mood stayed with Shelby until she pulled into her own driveway about forty-five minutes later. She sat in the car and stared at her house. The only light came from the porch lantern, security lamps inside and the spotlights in the yard.

There would be no colorful Christmas lights strung across her rooftop, windows or doorway this year because no one was there to hang them. Nelson had always made a big to-do when it was time to pullout the Christmas boxes. He had taken his cue that "more is better" from the old neighborhood. By the time he finished, the outside of the house, the trees and the yard blazed in a myriad of colored lights and decorations.

Nestled in the foothills of the Colorado Rockies, the two-story brick and pine home sat in a forested area of Evergreen, a mountain community about thirty miles west of the city. They had moved there for the small-town atmosphere, an atmosphere Nelson had grown up in and missed. The house, surrounded by Mother Earth's natural environment, offered a panoramic view of the mountains to the west Inside, the top level had three bedrooms and a master suite they had remodeled to include a wooden deck. Pine planks lined the high ceilings and every room downstairs had an arched entrance. Their bedroom, Nelson's study and the living room held massive fireplaces. Chandeliers imported from England hung in the foyer and dining room and the house was full of light-giving windows. The house had been their dream home. The large For Sale sign standing in the yard proved that some dreams weren't meant to be.

Shelby climbed from the car and walked the winding path to the door. She entered the house, switching on every light she passed on her way to the living room. She lit the logs in the fireplace and warmed herself in the flaming heat before leaving the room to climb the stairs to her bedroom. The lights she flipped on as she moved down the hallway would shine long after Shelby had departed to the lower level and her kitchen.

Dressed in a peach-colored sheath and fluffy house shoes, she fixed dinner, then stirred the food around on her plate while reviewing the list of markeddown merchandise Manette had selected for the after-Christmas sale. When she finished with the list, Shelby looked at the plate. The congealed mess made her nauseous and she rose to dump the food in the garbage. She washed her solitary dish and fork, placed the items in the empty cupboard over the sink and headed for the living room, her thoughts a dispiritingjumble of Nelson.

Her life was a mess, Shelby decided, just as the ring-ingtelephonejangledthesilence. She hurried to the table and snatched up the receiver. The voice she heard put a smile on her face. "Mama Reeves," she cried into the telephone, crossing the room to seat herself on the couch. "How are you? And how are Dad and Terry and James and the babies and-?"

"Shelby Reeves, you calm down this minute! Anyone listening would think that we haven't spoken in a month of Sundays."

Shelby grinned, accepting the chastisement from Nelson's mother. Three days before her fifth birthday, her own mother had died at the hands of a drunk driver and her father had never remarried. She cherished her relation-ship with the only mother she had ever known and though the divorce had shocked Nelson's entire family, it warmed Shelby's heart to know that Henrietta Reeves cared enough about her to continue treating her like a daughter. "I'm sorry, but I'm so very glad you called."

"I know, honey, and we miss you, too. But before I report on this end of the family, how's that father of yours? Folks down here still can't believe that the Reeves are related to the great Martin Smith. Dad's been strutting 'round town like a peacock ever since that TV show last week. Lord, honey, I haven't seen Senior so full of pride since the day his last son was born."

"Poppy's fine and when I talk to him, I'll be sure and tell him how proud you all are of him." Shelby paused before asking her next question. "Mama, did the family attend the Christmas festival last week?"

"Lord, yes. I'm surprised Junior hasn't already told you about that."

"Well, actually...no, he hasn't." Which was why Shelby had asked. Before their divorce, they had spent every other Christmas with Nelson's family. Shelby had spent the past week nursing hurt feelings after Henrietta told her that Nelson was flying home just to attend the festival. Shelby missed her family and if asked, she might have considered going with him. It was a thought based on feelings and not reason because ex-husbands did not take ex-wives home to visit the family.

"Junior's probably been busy or I'm sure he'd have told you by now. That's no excuse, mind you. And you can believe he'll be hearing from me about that. As to the festival, the whole town turned out as usual. James took second in the pie eatin' contest. And Shel, Widow Kelly done took my blue ribbon!"

"No! Those judges couldn't have chosen her quilt over one of yours," Shelby said, commiserating with her mother-in-law.

"Humph. They surely did. I've won that blue ribbon twenty-five years in a row and this year they said the widow's quilt was better and gave me that old second-place red ribbon. Senior took second place in the whittling contest and Terry's wife took second in the fried chicken competition. I'm telling you, honey. We were just a family of seconds this year. Next year, I'm getting my blue ribbon back and I'll expect to have all of my family around me when I do. And Shelby, you should have been here to see..."

Shelby put her feet up and settled into the couch cushions as Henrietta continued to fill her in on the festival. Her attention peaked when Henrietta suddenly switched topics.

"Shelby, I don't even pretend to understand what the two of you are doing, but I do know that my children aren't happy, and it would please me greatly if you and Junior would sit down and talk to each other."

Before Shelby could think of an appropriate response, she heard scuffling noises in the background and prepared herself for the commanding voice of Nelson Lamar Reeves, Senior.

"Etta, give me that phone. Shelby Reeves, I want you and Junior to stop this foolishness and get that D-thing fixed. Except for my favorite girl, my whole family was here last week, and I have no trouble saying that I don't like this. No sir, not one bit."

"I'm sorry, Dad, and I'll try to visit soon. But Nelson and I have been apart for more than a year. It's okay to say the word *divorced.*"

"Shelby, if you and Junior are D'd, then that means you ain't married, don't it?"

"Yes, but—"

"And if the two of you ain't married, then that would mean you ain't no more my daughter than the man in the moon, don't it?"

"Dad—"

"And if you ain't my daughter, then why am I talking to a perfect stranger on this here telephone?"

Shelby cracked up. The Reeves' logic was at work again and as with Nelson, Junior, she knew it was useless to argue with Nelson, Senior.. The family refused to acknowledge the divorce and weren't of a mind to be convinced otherwise. "Okay, Dad. I see your point."

"That's what I want to hear, perfect stranger. Junior should have told you about the festival, brought you home. Think I'll have a chat with my son about the way he's treating his wife."

Shelby talked with her in-laws for thirty more minutes. By the time she hung up, she was feeling pretty good again. Talking about Nelson with his family didn't bother Shelby the way it did with other people. Maybe it was because they didn't stand in judgment of her. Then again, may be it was because they gave her so much sympathy and she liked playing the role of the innocent victim. With nothing else to do, she picked up the remote and turned on the television. HBO was showing a halfway decent movie and when it was over, she channel-surfed, hoping to find something else that would catch her interest. Turning off the television, Shelby picked up a book and read until her eyes started to hurt.

Finally, at midnight, when she knew she couldn't stay awake another minute, Shelby closed the book and banked the fire. The lights stayed on as she climbed the stairs, praying that the horrible nightmare would not come again that night.

In the living room of his executive suite, Nelson sat on the functional couch tapping a white envelope against his thigh. He knew the contents. The chairman of Technotronics had glossed over the offer right after making glowing remarks to the board on his presentation and complimenting Nelson on his leadership, management skills and team player attitude. It was a dream offer and one that should have excited Nelson. It didn't because he had no one to share the moment with. All Nelson felt was a sense of emptiness as his thoughts centered on past promotions celebrated with a bottle of champagne and a night of good loving with his wife.

Leaving the office, he'd wanted to see Shelby so badly, he'd driven downtown and parked his Bronco in one of the lots. Nelson sighed. He'd stood outside the boutique for almost thirty minutes and hadn't caught a glimpse of her. His stomach rumbled and Nelson glanced at the carton of Chinese takeout he'd picked up on the way home. It sat on the table, its aroma tempting, reminding him that he'd skipped breakfast and lunch. He made no move to pick up the food. Instead he stared at the carton and thought about his situation.

Calling his parents or his brothers was an option. It was one Nelson wasn't too eager to pursue. While all would offer congratulations and applaud his latest accomplishment, they would also inundate him with questions about Shelby. He'd had no answers for them last week and had none for them this week. It had been several months since the divorce and his family was still in an uproar. Reeves did not divorce; "till death do you part" was the eleventh commandment and Nelson was pretty sure he could find it inked into the family Bible right under the first ten. His divorce was the first in the family and as the male, his parents expected him to rectify the situation, sooner rather than later. Until he did, he would remain in the doghouse, regardless of his professional achievements.

Nope, Nelson thought. He'd tell his family about the promotion, but it wouldn't be tonight.

His stomach burned with the thought of how much he needed Shelby. Last week, the company physician had told him that he was a prime candidate for an ulcer if he didn't get a handle on the stress in his life. Nelson dismissed the advice as useless. His life revolved around Shelby, and how was he supposed to get a handle on his wife when she refused to cooperate? What had happened to the two of them was tragic and Nelson couldn't help remembering the events of that ghastly night and the months that had followed. When his eyes became shadowy with tears, he whisked them away impatiently. Nelson didn't want to remember. Not remembering was the only way he could get through the daily rigors of his life. Yet he could not think of Shelby without the memories, and it was the memories that brought on the self-condemnation of knowing that he had failed.

His insides shifted, not with hunger, but because he knew he hadn't lived up to his responsibility. His marriage had deteriorated and the blame rested solely at his feet. Shelby had depended on him, and his inability to protect his family had resulted in his losing them. In Nelson's eyes that made him less of a man, an intellection that had immobilized him until he'd voiced his feelings to his father.

"Plain stuff and nonsense, Junior," his father had said. "You are a man, son. One of the best I know, and I ain't too proud to say that I'm the one who raised you. You have to remember that anything worth having is worth fighting for, and my daughter is waiting for you to fight for her."

He had tried to fight for his wife, but his fight had begun too late, and only after months of self-recrimination, guilt and doubt over the conduct that had caused Shelby to leave him in the first place. Grim lines formed at the edges of Nelson's mouth and the muscles at the back of his neck bunched with tension. He rubbed at them with his eyes closed. He'd been thinking about Shelby so much his brain was heading toward meltdown. But he had to figure a way out of the mess he'd made of their lives and get his wife back.

It was after midnight when Nelson stopped wrestling with his thoughts and rose from the couch. He tossed the envelope on the table and picked up the carton of food. Walking to the kitchen, he saw the blinking light on his answering machine. The thought that Shelby might have called sent a small ripple through Nelson until heartache hammered him with the truth. Shelby wouldn't call him, and he didn't care about the other messages. He turned away, and after flinging the carton into the garbage, made the dismal walk down the hallway to his bedroom.

4:05 A.M. The glowing red numerals seemed to mock her in the darkness as Shelby sat on the edge of her bed and tried to bring her breathing under control. The nightmare had interrupted her sleep again, putting an end to what had begun as peaceful slumber. For more than two years she'd tried to be strong, tried to accept and tried to go on. She'd clung to the long-dimmed voices that had assured her things would get better and that she would survive. She had survived, but in the process of holding body and soul together, Shelby had lost everything.

Before the fashion show, she had finally gotten to the point where she could sleep through most of the night. In the five weeks since the show and seeing Nelson, the nightmares had returned and strengthened their grip on her mind. They were the reason Shelby had decided to put her home on the market. She needed a fresh start and by selling the house, she hoped to finally begin to put the painful memories behind her.

Though she had retired only four hours earlier, Shelby knew there was no point in trying to go back to sleep. Her schedule was jam-packed and, despite her fatigue, she had to make herself ready for another long day at the boutique. She would check over Kathy's gown, due to arrive that day, but didn't try to fool herself that Carlotta would accept the gown without a fuss. She'd returned the garment for alterations so many times that Tyrone was threatening to pullout what little hair he had left. She also needed to start on Felicia's gown. Felicia Phillips was a nominee for Best New Artist at the Soul Train Music Awards. The ceremony would soon be upon her and Shelby wanted her friend to look extraordinary. She had some ideas, but needed to get them sketched out or she'd never complete the dress in time.

That meant Manny and the sales staff would have to handle the last-minute Christmas shoppers without her help. Her schedule would take all of her day. Before any of that, though, Shelby needed to make her daily trek, a trip she took every morning to help her get through the day. She forced herself to rise and went into the bathroom, bypassing the sunken tub in favor of a hot shower. She stood under the sluicing water until its warmth stimulated her body to life. After toweling off, she pulled on a soft mint, fleeced robe and headed downstairs, turning off a few of the lights that had burned through what had been her night. In the kitchen, she brewed a pot of coffee and sat at the table with her cup.

Dwelling on the nightmare would only cause immense sadness. Her thoughts turned to Nelson, because it was in the mornings that she missed him the most. His sonorous voice had always awakened her and his playfulness had sent her off each day with a smile. Nelson had been her source of happiness, and now there wasn't much in her life to smile about. She focused her stare on a rectangle on the wall. Before she'd packed it away, the lighter yellow space had held a wooden plaque made by Nelson in his workshop out back. He'd cut and varnished the wood from a pine tree, then burned in a message that read, "You are to me what the sun is to the day and the moon is to the night. As the earth without the sky would cease to exist, I cannot exist without you. I'll always love you, Shelby Julian Reeves-endlessly forever and a day."

Staring hard at the spot, her eyes blurred as Shelby silently repeated the words composed by Nelson. Later, when she had a chance to think about what happened next, Shelby would attribute her reaction to lack of sleep and her earlier bout of depression. But for the first time since the night her life had fallen apart, Shelby Reeves buried her face in her arms and cried.

# CHAPTER FOUR

"Ho-ho-ho! Merry Christmas!"

Arms crossed, Shelby stared at the lofty, red-suited Santa. The baritone timbre she recognized and now wished she'd been less expeditious in opening her front door. Looking through the peephole, she had thought it was her neighbor coming to collect the box of toys and the check-her donation to the children's home. Already there was a foot of snow on the ground, and just beyond the man on her porch was a thick curtain of fog and white. How her neighbor planned to get into the city and back without getting stuck was a mystery to Shelby.

"Merry Christmas?" Though the greeting was now a question, the black eyes banked by thick lashes never lost their sparkle.

The ringing telephone held off any response Shelby might have made. She glanced toward the living room and back at the Santa. She should answer that, but she didn't want to leave the man standing on her porch. The beard wiggled into what Shelby assumed was a smile and he leaned against the doorjamb. His loitering pose appeared blandly sedate but inside his stomach churned, for fear she would send him away or call the police. Dropping her arms, Shelby shuddered, more from exasperation than the cold, and went to answer the telephone. It was her neighbor, calling to tell her that his trip into the city was off. She hung up quickly after suggesting that their donations be used as birthday gifts and rushed back to the front door.

Santa stood straight and waited for an invitation inside. When Shelby resumed her silent appraisal, he figured he wasn't going to get one and stepped forward. The unanticipated movement had Shelby stepping back. Before she could react, the door closed and Santa entered the pinewood foyer. He stamped black-booted feet on the Persian rug, lowered his large green sack to the floor, then stood letting his eyes soak in the five foot, nine-inch woman he loved. He remembered thinking how much thinner Shelby looked when he'd seen her last, and the bulky, periwinkle blue sweatshirt hanging off her right shoulder gave credence to that thought.

The sharp pang jabbing at his chest reminded Nelson that he was responsible for the somber pain he saw reflected in her eyes. Shelby looked so lost and helpless, his stomach tightened in a battle to override his guilt, leaving Nelson with a strong desire to take his wife into his arms and never let her go. Instead, his hand rose to rub a spot over his heart. Nelson hoped what he was about to do would remove the haunted look from Shelby's eyes forever.

As Nelson stood pondering his next move, the vibrating effect of his deep voice shivered its way through Shelby. This man, unsuccessfully disguised as Santa, could still set her body to tingling with one word. The Santa suit covered one of the handsomest men this side of the Mississippi River and one who could still make her heart fluctuate with only a glance. The white wig hid thick, wavy hair in a color that reminded her of dark, wet sand. The curly beard covered a chiseled face of burnished brown and cheeks that dented with deep dimples when he smiled. If Shelby had been in a better mood, she might have laughed when she saw that the red pants didn't quite meet the ankles of his six-foot, seven-inch frame.

Nelson had always been unpredictable. During their time together, it was a trait she had learned to live with. What had Shelby stumped was why he had come to the house. Why on today of all days when she'd been feeling down in the dumps? It was as if he'd sensed that she needed him. The thought made her want to cry again.

Nelson saw the trembling bottom lip and made his decision. Shaking with emotion, he removed the hat and wig, pulled Shelby into his arms and buried his face in her neck. When she tried to remove herself from his embrace, he held her tighter against his body.

"Let me go, Nelson."

The despondency he heard in her voice lanced his heart. Knowing he'd have to abide by her request, Nelson squeezed Shelby again, then reluctantly released her. She stepped away from him and in the refuge the distance provided, drew on her reserve of emotional strength. It wasn't fair that Nelson still looked so good to her or that her yearning to be back in his arms was amplifying while he blithely toyed with her emotions. Nelson did not have the right to be here, and she no longer had the right to seek comfort in his arms. Shelby pushed back the emotions she was an expert at hiding and lowered her lashes, concealing his gauge to her feelings. If Nelson looked into her eyes, he'd know she was defenseless and still vulnerable to his charms, an advantage he could not have. If he did, she'd never get rid of him. Under the guise of arrogance, Shelby took a stance that said she was strong enough to resist anything Nelson could throw at her.

Her shoulders lost their droop in favor of an aligned, inflexible column. She raised her head and brandished a chin tilted at a stern "don't-mess-with-me" angle. Her lashes, however, stayed down, fanning the high cheekbones and draping the glare she directed at him while placing a hand on her waist. "Why are you here, Nelson? Until it's sold, this house is mine and you aren't allowed anywhere near it. I know your lawyer explained that to you."

Nelson saw the audacious facade for what it was, a poor attempt to provoke him by bringing up an issue Shelby knew would set him off: their home. Nelson quickly concealed the spark of annoyance that flickered in his eyes. Shelby was trying to engage him in a quarrel, and he hadn't come all this way to argue.

"It's good to see you, too, Shelby Reeves," he responded, his voice intentionally light and accompanied by a humorless smile. Nelson turned away, picked up his sack and headed for the living room. Standing in the archway, he surveyed the elegantly decorated space. Furniture upholstered in deep cream and mulberry pinstripes sat on a thick carpet matching the berry shade. Tables and other furnishings, fashioned from pine, gleamed in the firelight. His entertainment center, positioned on a far wall, still held his assemblage of high-tech toys and Shelby's large collection of plants, her little friends she liked to call them, sat flourishing in their African-designed pots. The cream-colored drapes were open and large bay windows gave view to the picturesque scene outside.

Warmth came from the flames in the grey stone fireplace, but the love and devotion that had provided the room's ambiance had gone the way of their marriage, mostly due to the stacks of cardboard boxes lining the walls.

Shelby loved Christmas but Nelson couldn't locate one decoration indicating her awareness that tomorrow the holiday would arrive. While he hadn't expected to see the outside of the house trimmed, he had thought there would he something commemorating the season inside the house. Driving over, he had felt invigorated at the thought of seeing Shelby. But the room was little more than dismal, and as Nelson moved farther inside, his chipper mood lost some of its edge. He set his sack on a box and glanced toward the fireplace. Well, at least there was a fire; the rest he would take care of in short order.

Shelby had followed Nelson and stood just behind him, trying to read his reaction to the packed boxes from his body stance and the set of his shoulders. Nelson had spent the months before their separation ignoring her. Apparently he intended to keep up the practice this evening. Watching him, her imagination took flight. She saw her body stretched out along the length of his, a hairsbreadth away from pressing together with a necessity he alone could induce. Shelby was so into her fantasy she had stripped Nelson bare and her hands were traveling along his spine. When he turned abruptly, the illusion faded and Shelby felt heat in her cheeks. She dropped her eyes to the floor, a little anxious he'd caught her staring at him.

"Excuse me, Shel.'"

Nelson moved by her when she stepped to the side and Shelby watched him go out the front door.

"Good-bye and good riddance," she murmured, heading for the foyer to lock the front door. He threw it open, narrowly missing knocking Shelby from her feet. He entered the foyer dragging a seven-foot tree. Pine needles skittered across the polished wood floor as he turned for the living room, unmindful of the trail of snow he left behind in his wake.

Shelby took a deep breath and ran after him. "Now you wait just one damn minute, Nelson Reeves! What do you think you're doing? You can't just barge in here and make yourself at home anymore. This is my house! You get out of here! Do you hear me, Nelson? I said, get out!"

Of course, he heard her; Shelby was screaming at the top of her lungs. Undaunted by her outburst, Nelson unbuttoned the red jacket and slipped it off his broad shoulders. He tossed the coat on the couch, then dug into his sack and pulled out a tree stand. His eyes strayed to Shelby and Nelson visibly winced when he saw her complete misery.

"Sweetness, please don't be upset. I'd like to do this for you…for Christmas. Okay?" He didn't wait for her response. He began traversing the room, looking for the perfect spot to place the tree.

Shelby was so angry tears formed in her eyes. She stood rigidly, her hands fisted at her sides. Why was Nelson doing this to her? Why now, when he knew they had nothing left? She turned away knowing she had no means to stop him and moved to the stairs. She sat on the step and lowered her head to her knees.

In the living room, Nelson braced himself. Upsetting Shelby was not his intent. But what could he do? If she hadn't gotten that restraining order and insisted on that stupid divorce, he'd still have a marriage and he wouldn't have to feel like an intruder in his own home. He'd only signed the papers because of the jail sentence they'd held over his head. At the time, the whole process and Shelby's desire to remove him from her life had disillusioned him.

But he loved Shelby and refused to give her up just because a judge had decreed them divorced. He had a plan and enough love for both of them until Shelby realized that she still loved him, too. Nelson squatted in front of the tree and plugged in a string of lights. In trying to stand up, he found out how crippling unresolved guilt could be and since he was halfway there, Nelson lowered himself the rest of the way to the floor. He hadn't prayed or stepped inside a church in more than two years and it took a few minutes for him to get started. Then as if comforted by a gentle hand, Nelson finally closed his eyes and sent up a heavenly prayer.

"Go to Shelby." In acknowledgment of the silent command, Nelson rose to obey. He sat on the step beside Shelby and tried not to react when she moved three steps above him and turned her head away. Nelson hung his head and his hands. "Shel?"

She didn't answer.

"I know you don't want me here. But I need to be here, Shel, even if it's only for a little while. Please don't send me away."

Shelby heard the desperation in his voice and steeled herself not to weaken. "No, Nelson," she replied. *Just go away,* she added silently. *Please!*

"Shel, it's Christmas. This used to be our favorite holiday. Yours and mine." Nelson edged his body up one step as he spoke. He turned and laid his head on Shelby's knees. "Shel, please. Can't we have one last Christmas together?"

Her hand came down to rub his head; Shelby wasn't aware that she'd moved. "Nelson, why are you doing this? It's over. It has been for a long time. I wish you would accept that and move on with your life. I have." Shelby sighed wearily. "Baby, don't make this any harder for us than it has to be."

Nelson stiffened. Shelby had called him "baby," an endearment he never thought he'd hear her express again in reference to him. That she had said it, and with affection, had to mean that Shelby still felt something for him. And if she still felt something for him, then he still had a chance.

When Nelson raised his head and stared into her eyes, Shelby knew his next words would be persuasive enough to crack her shell and find the path to her heart. She held his gaze and concentrated, not on Nelson, but on maintaining her stringent determination not to relent.

"Shelby, you know how much I love you. When we got married, you promised me till death. Well, neither of us is dead and I don't want it to be over between us. I love you and I've never stopped, not for one single second. Our love is worth fighting for. Please, give me one more chance. I promise I'll do whatever you ask of me."

Nelson fell silent, his gaze watching the tear that trickled down her cheek. *I love you, too, Nelson,* Shelby thought, closing her eyes to break the spell. He was waiting for a response she couldn't give him. Even if she could, her voice would be a wavering murmur of barely audible speech. She saw his hand lift toward her face and, without replying, rose and climbed the spiraling staircase. At the top, Shelby turned and rested her hand on the polished pine banister. She looked down into the black eyes that could still make her heart do flip-flops. *Why didn't you say these things to me months ago, Nelson, when I needed you,* she asked in silence. *If only you'd been there for me, like you promised.*

"I'm sorry, Nelson. It's too little, too late," Shelby finally managed, her voice full of underlying emotion. Before he could say anything else to change her mind, Shelby turned away and walked down the hallway to her bedroom.

She didn't doubt his sincerity. Nelson had never played mind games. He had spoken from his heart and Shelby knew he meant every word. Once, she had believed Nelson and that nothing could come between them. But Shelby no longer believed. When it had really counted, Nelson had let her down, and the pain she carried would be with her for the rest of her life.

Entering the room, Shelby sat on the bed. Her eyes wandered over the pictures crowding the dresser and the nightstands. Each one represented a significant event in her life and brought on a barrage of memories. She reached for a gold-framed photograph and stared at the picture, her mind continuing to recall occasions she hadn't thought about in a long while. The smile on Nelson's face couldn't have shone brighter, hers either.

It was the first picture they had taken as a family: her, Nelson and their son.

Shelby lowered herself back onto the bed, the photograph held securely in the fold of her arms as the tears began to fall again. Nelson Lamar Reeves III had been a beautiful baby, the most perfect child any parents could ask for. Why had he been taken from them? What had they done wrong? And why hadn't Nelson been there to help her through her grief or shared his pain with her? The nightmares were a perpetual reminder, and as the questions continued to float through Shelby's mind, she couldn't help remembering her time, a lifetime it seemed to her, with Nelson Lamar Reeves, Jr.

Downstairs, Nelson rose from the step and briefly considered going to his wife. He returned to the living room and sat on the striped couch, aiming his eyes at the large picture window. Outside, a howling wind gave aid to the layers of clouds dumping their load of white over the towering, dark peaks of the Colorado Rocky Mountain range as early winter darkness began to settle over the foothills. Nelson watched the heavy snowfall shroud the night with an illumination bright enough to be mistaken for daylight.

This wasn't the first time Shelby had walked away from him and he hadn't honestly believed that one desperate speech would win her over. Words meant little to Shelby, unless backed by action. His days of courting her in college had taught Nelson that. It had taken a long time and much patience to convince Shelby that she belonged with him. Her eyes had shown him something else, but Nelson was too afraid to hope that Shelby might still love him. He picked up a throw pillow, settled back into the couch cushions and just as Shelby was doing upstairs in their bedroom, let the memories of their time together wash over him.

# CHAPTER FIVE

*Twelve years earlier it had started with...*

"Do you have any idea how long I've been trying to meet you?"

His abrupt appearance startled her and Shelby sat stock still, waiting for the deep rumble to complete its travels through her system. Her body usually alerted her when he was around. Today, he had snuck up on her and this time had managed to get so close there was no use pretending he wasn't there. Not that she could. Nelson Reeves had a presence so overpowering it demanded recognition. Her eyes moved from her sketchpad to his white-sneakered feet, then wandered slowly up the long and lean trail until her eyes met two deep dimples, then further to the radiant smile competing with the early September sun.

"I know who you are, but we haven't been properly introduced. I'm Nelson Reeves."

Nelson extended his hand. With hesitation, Shelby placed her hand in his. He gave it a gentle squeeze and released it.

Shelby already knew Nelson. The man was like a shadow: every time she turned around he was somewhere close. His stare could knot her stomach from across the room and was so concentrated she found it hard to breathe under the intensity of his gaze. In the mornings, he sat across the street on the hood of his Bronco waiting for her to leave the dorm. She'd gotten so used to seeing him that when he wasn't there, she worried until she saw him again.

And Shelby saw Nelson everywhere she happened to be. Her classes provided her only relief. Whatever Nelson was majoring in didn't parallel her courses. But whenever it looked as if he'd decided to approach her, Shelby had shot him a glacial warning, freezing him in his tracks. And yet, when she did find him staring at her, Shelby didn't understand the curious and unfamiliar feelings that coursed through her.

Nelson looked around and quickly sat on the bench beside her. He peeked over her shoulder and said, "You're very talented."

"Thank you." Shelby started to close the portfolio.

Nelson touched her arm lightly. The scant breath he drew was barely noticeable when his hand met velvety softness. "May I?"

She shook her head no, but he wouldn't be put off so easily. It had taken too long to get this close to Shelby. Only implacable determination kept him from pulling her into his arms and kissing her senseless. While that would satisfy his immediate desires, it would do nothing for his long-term goal. Today, he wanted her to acknowledge his existence. "Why not, Shelby?"

"It's not something that would interest you, and I have to go."

Her voice, a lyrical whisper, he thought, flowed through Nelson like a musical refrain. He removed the pad from her hands and said simply, "I'm interested."

By the time it occurred to Shelby that Nelson had managed to trap her, he was looking through her drawings. Fashion was a matter of individual taste and her designs ran the gamut from blunt lines and austere tones to free flowing panels and colorful hues. She had confidence in her ability and preferred not to hear the placating lip service some felt obligated to give her. Nelson flipped the pages so fast, she knew he had no appreciation of what he was seeing, and, disappointed when he reached the end without comment, she held out her hand to take the case back.

Nelson slanted Shelby a glance and opened the portfolio again. Then, as if he had all the time in the world, he studied each sketch in detail and voiced his opinion before moving on. His comments were insightful and straightforward, without reservation or flowery speech. If Nelson didn't like something, he said so plainly and told her why.

He did care! Shelby was so happy she wanted to hug Nelson, and clasping her hands together in her lap was the only way to squash the thought. It also helped her listen attentively to what he was saying, for a minute. His immersion in her work was so gratifying, Shelby found her mind straying from his words to involve itself in an assessment of him.

Since she didn't really know Nelson Reeves, it wasn't the man she disliked so much. It was the image of the man and the hysteria that erupted every time he entered a room. Nelson played basketball and in the college ranks had risen to star status. Women flocked around him and an entourage followed him constantly, hanging on his every word as if he were some sort of deity. No man deserved that kind of adoration and Shelby had made a point of ignoring him whenever he showed up on the scene.

Today, he displayed a quiet strength of character and possessed a reflectiveness of thought that both surprised and appealed to Shelby. Confused, she tried to make sense of what was happening. She couldn't; Nelson had taken over her mind completely. She still had thoughts of escaping him. Yet her opinion of him was rapidly changing. Maybe all he wanted was her friendship. Shelby didn't think so. The man had way too much sexuality to confine himself to that role. Her gaze fell to his hands. They were solid hands, with long, nimble fingers that could probably handle her body as skillfully as they handled a basketball. Shocked when she realized the trend of her thoughts, Shelby fidgeted on the bench and looked away to the pale blue and cloudless sky.

"Now this one, I really like," Nelson remarked, bringing her attention back to him. "It's simple and classic, and this neckline shows some skin, but not too much. I think you would look good in this, Shelby. The red color doesn't fit, though; it's too bright. Maybe an aqua…no, a deep emerald green would work better, and put some of those little shimmery things in the top."

Shelby smiled, pleased with his observation. She leaned closer and tried to view her work from his perspective. Breathing deeply, a whiff of his tangy cologne clogged her nose and the smell of Nelson jolted her senses to life. Moving heat inched its way up her body as acute awareness glided over Shelby. She willed her heart to stop jiggling and her dry mouth to speak. "Lit-little shimmery things?"

Nelson laid the pad in his lap and looked down at her. He needed to see her eyes and the color always hidden from him by distance or the dark shades. In her eyes, he would see her true feelings about him. What would Shelby do if he removed the glasses from her face? There wasn't a chance in hell he'd do it and Nelson filled his hands with the portfolio again.

"Yeah," he murmured. "You know, those things that sparkle in the light. Little shimmery things."

Shelby tried to ignore the warmth creeping over her and looked at the sketch. She saw that Nelson was right, and if she added a weave of gold threads through the bodice-little shimmery things he'd called them the gown would come to life. She looked up at him wonderingly and instead of telling him that she agreed with his comment, remarked unnecessarily, "Well, that's the last one, that's finished."

Nelson handed hack the binder. "You're good…"

It was an effortless compliment, but his words kindled a disturbing commotion inside Shelby. "Thank you. I'm going to be a fashion designer."

Nelson heard the hopeful inflection in her voice and smiled. He had aspirations, too, and if he had his way they would achieve their goals together. "It's your dream, huh?"

"It is, and one I've worked toward for a long time."

"Well, I'm not a betting man, but I predict that one day you'll be famous."

"I don't want to be famous."

Something in her voice made Nelson sit up and take notice. "I don't think you'll have a choice, Shelby. Talent, if pursued and recognized, will sometimes bring on fame whether you want it or not. I'm not a fashion critic, but I know you're good. Once people find out how good, word will spread and before you know it, fame will be staring you in the face."

"Not me. I happen to know that being famous is not what it's cracked up to be. My designs will be limited and exclusive and I'll only take clients who value their privacy. I want my family to enjoy a normal, quiet life. And you know what else?"

Shelby wanted a family. Nelson scanned his mind for a way to get her to see him as husband material. "No, what?"

"One day, I'll have my very own boutique. Of course, that's after I graduate and spend five years in New York learning the business firsthand."

Five years? The revelation jarred Nelson. When he had planned their life, he hadn't considered that Shelby might leave the state. *Idiot, she doesn't know about your plans,* he thought, and after acknowledging that fact, a troubled Nelson tucked the information away to deal with later. His attention swung back to Shelby, and as he listened, a side of her personality he had not seen turned up and intrigued him. The more Shelby talked, the more ebullient her face and hand movements became. Before long, she appeared so wound up, Nelson expected her to leap off the bench.

"I've always wanted to design clothes," she was saying. "When I was little I made outfits for all my dolls using a needle and thread and any scraps of material I found around the house. Poppy bought me a sewing machine when I was twelve. He said he was tired of stepping on the needles I left in the carpet. I think he was proud—"

Shelby stopped speaking and brought her fingers to her lips. An inquisitive shadow lit her eyes as she looked at

Nelson and wondered what had compelled her to open up to him.

Don't stop, Nelson wanted to say when he saw the shutter come down. Shelby had allowed him a peek inside her world, but now he was back on the outside. Nelson wanted back in, but like a fish out of water, felt himself floundering in a sea of ineptitude. Why was this so hard for him? He wanted to know everything about Shelby and he couldn't think of a single thing to ask. Talking to her about fashion was easy because her drawings had given them a topic on which to converse. Left to its own devices, his brain had drawn a complete blank.

He had not experienced a woman who rebuffed his advances until he'd met Shelby. It also made him jealous of the other men who swarmed around her. She wouldn't let him get within ten feet, yet other men she welcomed with open arms. Thinking about it brought on the anger that often swept through Nelson whenever he saw her court of male admirers. None of them seemed to hold Shelby's attention more than the others and therein lay his problem. Instead of one, Nelson felt that he had to compete against the whole pack, and he hoped she hadn't noticed how much she unnerved him. "You were saying," he prompted.

Shelby shrugged. "It was nothing."

"Oh." Nelson heaved a sigh and drummed his fingers on his thigh. "Those men that hang around you, are any of them…who is Poppy?"

"My father."

"Oh. Well, I play ball."

"I know."

Nelson's brows lifted. "Do you go to the games?" "No. Everyone on campus knows who the jocks are." *Especially the egocentric ones,* she thought.

Hearing antipathy in her tone, Nelson said, "I take it that you have something against people who play sports?"

Shelby set the drawing pad down and gathered the other implements of her art. She placed them with meticulous care in the straw bag by her side and rose from the bench. Nelson stood, too, and watched her adjust the binder under one arm. She was stalling, and that made him even more impatient for her answer. Shelby tilted her head back to look up at him.

Only this time, she really looked at Nelson. The clap of thunder that followed solidified his attributes in her mind. It became evident to Shelby, in the lucidity of the moment, why her mind was sending mixed signals. Nelson Reeves had it all: commanding height, childlike charm, drop-dead looks and devastating sexual appeal. In his seductive gaze, she finally discerned what Nelson saw when he looked at her. She was the desirable woman in his eyes and the one calling out for his kiss.

That thought was quelling and Shelby gave herself a mental shake and scolding in denial. Nelson played ball and was undoubtedly looking for a career in the pros. He was good, fame would follow. Any notions she'd had of further association with Nelson Reeves evaporated from her mind. Nelson Reeves was not for her.

She retreated a few steps away from him, removing herself from the magnetic current of his allure. "Not really," she replied in answer to his question. "I just prefer more serious-minded folks."

As prepared as he thought he was, her comment caught Nelson by surprise and he threw back his head and laughed. Shelby didn't think she'd said anything funny, but his laughter gave her the diversion she needed to undergo another readjustment in her thinking. Talking to Nelson was one thing; her body's amorous response to his was quite another. It was time to take her leave before he figured out that he affected her in ways she dare not think about.

"I see," Nelson said when he'd caught his breath. He continued to smile, the mirth easing the tension he'd felt earlier. "I know you have to go, Shelby, but I like talking to you. Will you go out with me on Saturday?"

"No!"

She'd stated the word so emphatically, Nelson knew he was back at square one. "Will you tell me the reason why?"

Shelby slung the straw bag over her shoulder and started moving away from him. "Because you're still trying." Still backing up, she lifted her hand in a half wave. "Good-bye."

Shelby hurried up the sidewalk to her door. At the door, something made her stop and turn around. When she did, Shelby realized what it was. Mentally, they had connected and Nelson's pull was growing stronger. Her mind told her to go back to him and with each passing second the suggestion grew louder. Shelby had a hard time suppressing the urge, but managed to regain her control. She had to focus on her goal and Nelson was a temptation she had to avoid if she didn't want to be blindsided by something she wasn't ready for. Not responding to him was difficult, and Shelby knew she would probably regret it later, but the smile she sent Nelson's way right before she ducked inside the building was dazzling.

Nelson did not follow Shelby. The swaying hips were mesmerizing, and he stared at the svelte figure with long legs until it disappeared behind the door. *Damn!* he thought, *that was one pair of lucky blue jeans.* Nelson sat on the bench again before anyone passing got wind of his inability to move and the reason. He'd gotten further with Shelby than he ever thought he would. They had touched, talked and that last smile she'd given him was still making the rounds through his heart. All good signs to Nelson's way of thinking. One day, though, Shelby Smith would do more than smile at him, much more.

Three weeks later, Nelson dropped down on the orange blanket beside Shelby. "Coach sure laid into me the other night."

Shelby lowered her psychology book, a potato chip poised to enter her mouth. Here you are again, she thought, hardly able to believe that Nelson had followed her. It was her own fault, and in hindsight, attending the basketball game hadn't been a good idea. But she had and trying to forget those long, brown legs in those little shorts had been like trying to forget her name. Since then, Nelson had stepped up his campaign to get her to date him and since eluding him on campus or anywhere else in Ft.

Collins was impossible, Shelby had made the sixty-mile drive to Denver.

After a week of dark skies and snow, it had turned into a beautiful day. Shelby sat under a tree on the south side of City Park, the side claimed as theirs by a youthful generation of African Americans many years before. Restricted entry gates and police roadblocks had long ago halted the cruising, but hadn't stopped the soulful beat of the music or the colorfully-garbed people enjoying the balmy weather.

It had taken a while to dissuade several other men on the prowl, and although Shelby felt her irritation with Nelson rise, his persistent pursuit had left a dizzying impression on her heart. A part of her wanted that curving slant of a mouth to kiss her; he other part warned him off. In the resulting confusion, Shelby could only fix Nelson with a curious stare. "What?"

"After the game a few weeks ago, Coach blasted me with both barrels."

If this was a riddle, Shelby didn't get it. She frowned, watching a spiral of yellow leaves being blown across the brown grass by an unusually warm November breeze. "Nelson Reeves, what on earth are you talking about?"

Nelson smiled, and the brazen stare he always laid on her seemed to ignite her soul. "I'm talking about you, Shelby Smith. Coach cussed me up one wall and down the other, and you are the reason. Why didn't you tell me that you would be at the game?"

The expression on his face was so expectant, Shelby couldn't help giggling. A few moments later, the sound of her laughter died as she continued to study Nelson. There was no mistaking the look she saw in his eyes and her eyes widened with the discovery.

Nelson couldn't possibly be in love with her. She'd given him no reason or encouragement to have any feelings for her at all. Pushing the thought from her mind, Shelby covered her nervousness with a flippant remark.

"Why are you blaming me? It's not my fault you're a terrible basketball player. If you're having trouble on the court perhaps you should spend less time following me and more time in the gym."

Nelson's jaw clamped together. "More time in the gym! Girl, I do not need to practice. You're talking to the star player."

"Really," Shelby responded, unimpressed by the size of his ego. She laughed at his wounded look. "If you're such a star, then why did the coach have to cuss at you?"

"Because of you," Nelson gritted out, his frustration on the rise. Shelby laid her book down on the blanket and picked up her lunch sack. She removed a peach, biting into it as she pulled her knees up and wrapped her arms around her legs. Chewing slowly, she gazed at Nelson. "Feel free to enlighten me, Mr. Reeves, but I fail to understand why you insist on blaming me for your faulty technique on the basketball court."

Nelson would have responded, but he couldn't pull his eyes away from her mouth. Those lips were so full and right this minute covered in peach juice; he wanted to clean them with his tongue. How many nights had he fantasized about pressing his lips against hers? Unable to resist any longer, he removed the peach from Shelby's hand and tossed it over his shoulder. He placed his hands around her waist and lowered her to the blanket.

Fitting his mouth to hers, Nelson explored Shelby's lips with agreeable politeness until he heard her gentle sigh. Deepening the kiss, he used the tip of his tongue to massage her mouth, seeking entrance. Her lips parted and as Nelson dunked his tongue inside, searing heat drenched his body in a fine sweat. Mounting desire discharged in simmering waves and Nelson closed his eyes with a groan. Shelby had tantalized him to the point of no return. Her warm, sweet lips and wanton response were an invitation too good for him to refuse.

Shelby didn't understand what she was doing.

She responded to Nelson's kiss with passionate fervor, letting his lips draw out a depth of feeling and emotion she never knew she had. Her mind petitioned her not to succumb to the sexual desires Nelson's mouth awakened in her and for a moment, Shelby waged a fight. Too many of her girlfriends had gotten pregnant and had to give up their dreams. That wasn't going to happen to Shelby. Yet her pounding heart was treacherous and denounced the wanderings of her mind. Hugging him to her, Shelby ran her hands up and down Nelson's back, savoring the feel of the tightly packed muscles.

Nelson roughly tongued the inside of her cheeks, then worked his way down to her neck where he treated Shelby to smooth, delicious licks until her trembling body arched in encouragement. His hands drifted under her top and she panted her pleasure when his fingers teased her breasts until the tips enlarged like ripened fruit. His heart raced and alarmingly close to losing control of his body, he broke free of her lips.

Breathing harshly, he cradled her face in his hands. "Stop baiting me, sweetness; you won't win. For weeks, your body language has said one thing. Your response to our first kiss tells me a different story. The only thing saving you today is daylight and the people congregating in this park; otherwise we both know what would happen. So, fight if you must, Shelby. I am not going away."

When Nelson removed her glasses, his heart stopped. The sound of a heady alarm filled his head as he stared, fascinated, into the honey-brown eyes of Shelby Smith. Enthralled and reeling with wooziness, his hand slowly reached up to her head. He ruffled his fingers through the silky black ringlets; his mouth found hers again. "Because one day, Shelby Smith," he whispered against the moist softness of her lips, "you are going to be my wife."

The bubble carrying her away burst and Shelby crashed back into reality with a thud. Shelby pulled out of Nelson's reach, gathered her things and rose to her feet. "You're nuts." She walked off, leaving him sitting on the blanket.

Nelson jumped to his feet and ran after her. "Shelby, wait!"

She moved faster, not even sparing a backwards glance. She had to get away. Nelson Reeves had obviously lost his mind.

Nelson not only caught up with her, he passed her and blocked her path, circumventing every effort she made to move around him.

Frustrated, she stopped. "If you don't leave me alone, I'll scream and every cop in this park will be here in seconds."

Seeing the alarm rising in her eyes, Nelson slowly raised his hands above his head and spoke in a quiet, pacifying voice. "Please don't do that, Shelby. I promise I'll let you go, if you'll just hear me out first."

Her eyes narrowed in a frigid glare. "No! I want you to get out of my way and I want you to leave me alone. You got that, mister? Just leave me the hell alone!"

# CHAPTER SIX

And he did. For almost a month, Shelby saw neither hide nor hair of Nelson and she began to look for him. She was doing it because she thought something might have happened to him and it concerned her. At least, that's what Shelby told herself. To think anything else would mean admitting that she missed Nelson or that she cared that he'd lost interest in her. By the end of the second week, she had stopped looking over her shoulder, thinking she was home free. That is, until the day she walked into the dining hall for lunch and ran into the unshakable resolve of Nelson Reeves.

Happy to see him, she smiled and waved. He looked at her, didn't return the smile and the brief once over he gave her before rising from his chair and leaving the room left her feeling both self-conscious and foolish.

Shelby couldn't believe Nelson had done that to her or the tears his actions caused. She moved to the line, ordered her lunch and found a table; then, no longer hungry, gathered her things to leave, or rather escape.

"How did it feel, Shelby?"

It was Nelson, and he'd come back. She sniffed and tried to will away her tears. "How did what feel?" Her voice sounded oddly hollow and flat to her ears.

Nelson straddled a chair next to her. "How did it feel to have me snub you even though I obviously saw you enter the room?"

"Not good," she admitted. "Where have you been for the last three weeks?"

"Why? Did you miss me?"

Shelby shook her head no and Nelson looked at her, brow arched, for what seemed a very long time. His expression wasn't hostile, but it wasn't friendly either, and a little intimidated by his stare, she blurted out, "Why did you do it, Nelson?"

"I wanted you to feel a little of what I've felt these past weeks." Nelson's face softened and immediately changed to misery. He lifted her hand and kissed the back of her fingers. "Shelby, don't believe that because it's not true. I'm sorry if I hurt you because it's something I never want to do in life. It just took a while before it finally sunk into this thick skull of mine that you don't want to have anything to do with me. The truth is that I've spent the last three weeks trying to forget you. I can't, Shelby. You know how much I like you, don't you, sweetness?"

"Yes," she said, trying to match his grave tone while finding delight in the pet name.

"Is there any hope for us, Shelby? Do you like me, even a little?"

She nodded. "But—"

"No buts," Nelson interrupted, back into a happy mode. "Starting right now, you and I are official."

Shelby considered his comment and the quick mood change. "Does official mean we're boyfriend and girl-friend?"

"Boyfriend and girlfriend?" Nelson laughed. It was a nice laugh and floated over her like Asian silk, just like his voice. "That's a quaint phrase, Shel. I haven't heard it since junior high school."

Embarrassed, but not deterred, Shelby forged ahead. "You know what I mean. Are you saying we're a couple?"

"Are you asking if you're my lady?"

Shelby sighed expansively. "Yes."

"Do you want to be?"

She shrugged. "I don't know. I'm not sure what being your lady means."

Nelson first wondered if Shelby was being facetious, then realized that she was dead serious. "Shelby, I know you've had a man, er, boyfriend before."

"I had one once," she answered matter-of-factly.

"Once? If you're trying to pull my leg, Shelby Smith, forget it. Too many men hang around you for me to believe that."

"What you believe is your affair."

Nelson searched her face as if trying to ascertain the truth. "Okay. What did it mean with this boyfriend that you had once?"

The dark gaze, so penetrating and hypnotic, was also open and honest She felt herself wilting and fought to rally back. She lost the battle and against her will the words tumbled from her mouth. "We were in high school and for us it meant dating and a lot of kissing. He was good-looking and popular and, as I remember, could talk me into doing anything. Well, almost anything, and he probably would have gotten that except that I met another girl who was pregnant with his child. After that, having a boyfriend wasn't very important to me."

"High school, Shelby? Though I'm sure the experience seemed important at the time, it happened what…four or five years ago? A little long for it to still have an impact on your life today, don't you think?"

Nelson's assessment was a direct hit and Shelby wisely chose to ignore the latter part of his statement. "Now, you want to know how old I am."

Leaning forward, Nelson propped his chin on the back of his fists. "I know how old you are," he said, then waited for the shutter to come down. When it didn't, Nelson knew he was making progress. Shelby had a quiet calmness about her that contradicted the suspicious look she gave him before glancing away. He waited patiently while she wrestled with a response. Positively shaken and trying not to let it show, Shelby let curiosity get the better of her. "You do?"

"Yep," he said with casual ease. "You're twenty-three. Your birthday is April fifteenth and you're a native to the state. You want to be a fashion designer and have already spent a year in Paris honing your natural talent. While your class load here is heavy, you've maintained a 4.3 GPA. Your father is Dr. Martin Eugene Smith, noted geneticist whose discovery of the FAT gene will one day put the billion-dollar diet industry out of business. Your mother is deceased and you are an only child. You don't like sports, well, basketball anyway, and you're somewhat of a loner when you can lose the crowd." He gave her a self-satisfied smile. "Want to hear more?"

No, she did not! Nelson had done his homework and Shelby knew where he'd done his studying. "Not really. The newspapers and an admirer in the office, right?"

"Yep. Now as pretty as you are, Shelby Smith, why has no other man wanted you?" "I didn't say that. I said, I had a boyfriend once."

Nelson shook his head. "Well, now you've stumped me. Either all the men you've known are nuts or it must be you. Is it you?"

"I'm not gay, Nelson. But I do have something I want to accomplish and men tend to shy away from girls who would rather hit the books than the bed."

Nelson whistled. "That's pretty heavy, Shelby. Personally, I think you're generalizing and I also think that you should grant me the opportunity to prove you wrong."

Shelby smiled. "By being your lady, right?"

"Right."

"What do I have to do?"

"You know that bed thing?" She nodded. "Well, you wouldn't have to do that until you're ready, but I figure we'll get around to it before we're married."

*Monumental* was not a big enough word to describe his ego. It came, no doubt, from having people worship the ground he walked on. "Why me?"

"Because you're beautiful."

"Is that the only reason?"

All humor left Nelson and his eyes stroked her ebony-hued face. "No. I know you won't believe me when I say this, Shelby, but I've been in love with you ever since my eyes first touched you."

*That has to be the king of come-on lines,* Shelby thought with a frown. "Nelson? How many women have heard those words from you?"

"If you're worried about my reputation with the ladies, don't be," he quickly assured her. "It's just that: a rep, and comes with the turf. I play ball, hit the books and occasionally hang out with the guys. That doesn't mean I haven't dated other women, because I have. But I've found the woman I want, if she'll give me a chance."

"You can have a date." Her response caused him apparent distress. Concerned, Shelby laid her hand on his arm. "What's wrong, Nelson? I thought my answer would please you."

Nelson's expression turned plaintive. "I am pleased," he said in a grumpy voice. Shelby stared at his expression mutely. He had the worst look of pleased she'd ever seen in her life.

Nelson saw the bewilderment in her eyes. This wasn't at all how he had envisioned this going. Here he was talking about marriage and Shelby...well, she wasn't. He made an effort to get himself together before she decided that he really didn't have good sense and left him again.

"I'm sorry, sweetness. If dating is all you're willing to offer me, then I'll take it."

Affronted by his tone, Shelby responded, "Please don't let me be the cause of your having to settle for something you don't want. I have other things to do with my life anyway."

Jesus, he was blowing this. "Shelby, you don't understand. I can date any woman on this campus and they'd be happy to go out with me-"

"Then please do," she interrupted.

He saw the obstinate glint in her eyes. "Haven't you heard anything I've said to you? You are special and I want you, all of you. Dating you would be like snatching at crumbs when it's the whole cake I'm after."

"Is that supposed to be a compliment?"

"Yes, dammit!"

"Don't cuss at me."

"If you'd listen to reason, then I wouldn't have to cuss at you!"

"If I listened to your reasons, I'd be like all the other women on this campus. You know, the ones you could date who would be happy to go out with you."

Then as if someone had decided to emphasize the fact, two women approached their table. A warm current shot through Shelby and a feather could have knocked her to the floor when she identified the emotion as jealousy. Through narrowed eyes, she watched the women stare with godlike awe at Nelson and titter bashfully for his benefit. The sound grated on her nerves.

"You're Nelson Reeves," one of the woman said, with breathless anticipation. Nelson glanced at Shelby. Just a moment ago she'd been a proud little warrior giving him what for. Now, with her bottom lip gripped between small white teeth, he saw the uncertainty in her face as if afraid of what he'd do. Suddenly everything became clear to Nelson. He'd been going about this all wrong. Shelby didn't want to hear that he loved her; he had to show her.

He looked at the women with smooth regard. "Yes, I am. Is there something I can do for you?"

The women giggled again, and the one that had spoken continued after receiving a poke in the ribs from her friend. "We just wanted to tell you that we've seen all of your games, either in person or on television, and we think you're a fantastic basketball player and one gorgeous brother, and we've been dying for a chance to meet you. We also wanted you to have this."

Appalled, Shelby stared at the little slip of paper, the girls and then Nelson. Why was she sitting here contemplating being his lady? Nelson had plenty of women. Hell, they were tripping over themselves trying to give him their numbers. She didn't need this, and she didn't want Nelson if having a relationship with him meant fighting off a sea of women to keep him. Shelby didn't like this at all and watched Nelson intently to see what would happen next.

He took the slip of paper and, looking at Shelby, tore it into little pieces. "Ladies, thank you for the compliment," he said graciously. Then, more than a little

annoyed, he added, "This is Shelby Smith, soon to be Shelby Reeves, and you are being inconsiderate of my fiancée's feelings. That I will not tolerate. And I'll thank you not to interrupt our privacy again." The women left their table with lightning speed and the dimpled smile was back in place when Nelson turned to Shelby and picked up her hand. "So, beautiful lady, where were we?"

She squeezed his hand. "Fighting." "That's right. I believe it's my turn to fire the next volley, so give me a sec to backtrack."

Shelby watched the brows come together as Nelson slouched down in his chair. Her eyes, tender and searching, filled with admiration as she took in the almost dazzling manly features. Nelson had no idea how much what he'd just done meant to her. Too many dates with immature, unfocused boys had led to her getting off the annoying merry-go-round. Nelson was no boy. He was a man, one who knew what he wanted and was honest and forthright enough to go after it.

"Nelson?"

"Yeah, sweetness," he said with an air of absence.

"I don't want to fight anymore."

His brow rose. "You don't? And I'd just thought up the perfect comeback to your last remark. But that's okay, I'll save it for our date. With you, I'm sure I'll need it."

Shelby shook her head. "I've changed my mind about dating you."

Nelson looked stricken. "Shelby, please don't say that. I didn't mean to sound ungrateful. I just wanted…no, it doesn't matter what I want. What matters is what you want."

Shelby's smile spread slowly across her face. "I want to know more about the man I'm going to one day marry."

There was silence and it seemed to stretch much longer than the few seconds it actually lasted. Nelson gave Shelby an odd look, then, as if hit by sudden comprehension, he smiled. "You're serious, aren't you, Shel?" It was almost a whisper, and he was staring at her as if his life depended on her answer.

"I'm very serious, Mr. Reeves. Of course, you'll have to allow me the time to fall in love with you. That shouldn't take too long, if you play your cards right, that is. And I'll want to know all about you, your goals, childhood, family, that sort of thing. And then, there are your views on life, marriage, kids and so forth. And of course, you'll need some time to fall in love with me and you'll also want to know those same things about me…"

Quiet settled over their table again because Nelson had silenced Shelby with his mouth. Chills that started at the top of her head spread down to her toes when Nelson drew her out of her chair and turned so that she could sit in his lap.

"Hush, sweetness," he told her. "Everything you want to know about me, I'll tell you in time. All you need to know at this moment is that I'm already in love with you, and I'm willing to wait until you realize that you're already falling in love with me."

# CHAPTER SEVEN

Shelby sat at the desk in her dorm room, doing more doodling than drawing. As the daughter of a famous scientist, she had spent many lonely days. Martin Smith had done his best to raise her, but his work had kept him so busy that often a week or more had passed before Shelby saw her father. She knew he loved her and understood the importance of his work. Yet she didn't like the glare of the spotlight or the attention focused on her because Martin Smith was her father. She had always yearned for what her friends had: a normal family life.

It was Christmas Eve and, after an early Christmas dinner with her father the previous night, he'd left for Europe and the lecture circuit. This morning, after exchanging gifts, she'd watched Nelson get on a plane to spend the holiday with his family. She looked down at the engagement ring he'd given her a week earlier. He'd asked her to go, but Shelby wasn't ready to do the family thing yet. So, depressed and having no reason to go home, she'd opted to stay in the dorm.

She flipped the page on her drawing pad, looked at the fashion magazine on her desk and began again to try to emulate the pleated skirt of the red gown she saw pictured there. A few minutes later, she laid down her pencil when something akin to singing, but sounding more like a distressing wail accompanied by a plucking noise started outside her door. It took her a full minute to recognize the largely off-key voice as Nelson's and the chafing twang as his attempt to play the guitar while he mutilated Christmas carols.

Shelby ran to the door and tried to open it. Nelson stopped playing and pulled it shut. Shelby sat on the floor and listened to him serenade her. To anyone else, the concert was probably a clear case of disturbing the peace. To Shelby, it was the most beautiful music she'd ever heard and she sat on the other side of the door feeling both stupendously honored and oddly sad. Family was important to Nelson and for a solid month he had talked excitedly of his trip home; he had given up that trip for her.

Thirty minutes later, the singing stopped and she opened the door. Nelson rose to his feet, stepped inside the room and looked down at Shelby as if he could see inside her very soul. She withstood the scrutiny and knew in that moment that he had taken possession of her heart.

"What happened, Nelson? Why are you here?" He set the guitar down, took her hand and pulled Shelby to his chest. "Not now, sweetness," he murmured, closing his mouth over hers. Melting under the power of his kiss, her lips parted. He took advantage of the open access and set off a fire inside Shelby that she knew would never die. Raising up, Nelson observed her for a few moments more, then said, "We need to talk." Taking her hand again, he led them to the bed and, after first seating her, sat beside her. Leaning forward, he clasped his hands in front of him and stared at the floor.

All manner of thoughts ran through Shelby's mind as she observed his inner struggle. The quiet stretched into minutes and she frowned. Maybe Nelson didn't want her anymore and he was trying to find a way to tell her. As disheartening as the thought was, Shelby nevertheless steadied her nerves in preparation for the announcement. This wasn't the first time she'd suffered disappointment and it wouldn't be the last.

Nelson blew out a breath and raised his eyes to hers. "Sweetness, I haven't been completely honest with you." She opened her mouth; he put a finger to her lips. "Hear me out before you say anything because what I have to say will lead to the most important decision of your life, our lives." Shelby watched him warily and when she felt her body tremble, she looked down at her hands. Courage, she thought, schooling herself. Whatever Nelson had to say, she could take it. "Shel, you know that the NBA draft is coming up in a few months. Coach has already informed us that J.R. and I will probably be taken in the first rounds and Jordon plans to take whatever offer he gets." He paused before continuing. "I'm pulling my name."

Stunned, her head snapped up. "What?" "I'm not going to enter my name in the draft, Shelby." "But why? I thought you wanted to play professionally."

"Not really. The only reason I play is because I enjoy it so much. It was also my ticket to college." Nelson rose from the bed and knelt down in front of her. "Shelby. I'm an engineer. Telecommunication is the wave of the future and Denver is the cable capital of the world. This is where I want to work and live, and I've already accepted a job as a systems engineer at one of the local cable companies." Nelson grinned from ear to ear. "So you see, I am a serious-minded individual." Shelby stared at him, speechless. "Say something, sweetness."

What was she supposed to say? His plans had changed; hers had not. On the morning following their graduation, she was headed for the airport and the bright lights of New York City. Shelby placed both hands on his shoulders. "Nelson, I'm not sure what it is that you want me to say, but you know that I'm going to New York."

"But you don't have to do that now. I knowhow much you hated the thought of being a basketball player's wife. I'm an engineer, Shelby, and I'm staying right here in Denver. You don't have go to New York. We can get married now and you can open your boutique."

"That's not the plan, Nelson. I've already accepted the apprenticeship in New York. This is a chance to hone my craft and it's an opportunity that I won't let slip away."

His eyes turned stormy. "What about us, Shelby? You said you loved me, and I can't wait five years for you to be my wife. I want us to get married now."

"Five years is not that long to wait if you truly love someone."

"Yes, it is. By the time you come back and open your shop, I'll be an old man. And I'd like to have some kids before than happens."

Shelby laughed. "You're twenty-four years old, Nelson Reeves, and I can assure you that five years from now you won't qualify for Medicare."

He rose to his feet and she propped pillows at her back when he again sat on the bed. The discussion began once more and after hours of cuddling and talk, the only thing they had managed to resolved was Shelby's introduction to the wonders of making love. Pulled into a world of titillating passion, mind-drugging kisses, which had numbed her brain, and breathtaking caresses, which had blotted out everything except Nelson.

Two years and nine months later, Shelby gripped her father's arm and tried to keep her steps from faltering when they started their walk down the long, red-carpeted aisle.

Martin Smith smiled down at his only child and patted the hand on his arm. "Steady, pumpkin. Nelson's there and he's waiting for you-the most beautiful bride this world has ever seen."

Shelby returned her father's smile. He always knew the right thing to say to make her feel better. Nelson was there and he was waiting for her, just as he'd been for almost three years. She'd stayed in New York for a year and a half and she had to admit that he'd done his best to support her during the long distance relationship. But after fifteen months, they were both so despondent that when he'd insisted she set a wedding date and come home, Shelby couldn't get back to Colorado fast enough.

"Heads up, homes," Jordon said, placing a steadying hand on Nelson's shoulder. "In a few minutes, this will all be over." As best man, best friend and a fatality of the marriage and divorce experience, Jordon empathized with Nelson.

"I'm cool, J.R.," Nelson replied, even as he felt his body tremble, though not with nerves. He removed his hand from the pocket of his charcoal-gray tuxedo and turned to watch Shelby make her bridal walk to his side. Sheathed in white, her dark skin glowed against the satin and lace wedding ensemble. This was the last time she would go anywhere as Shelby Smith, he thought. The next walk Shelby took would be as Mrs. Nelson Reeves, Jr., and he could hardly wait.

For two years, he'd worked as the systems engineer at the local cable system. Last week, he'd completed the negotiations on his contract with Techno-tronics Cable as project engineer. His primary responsibility: to design the elaborate equipment needs and oversee installation in the state-of-the-art cable system to be constructed in Orlando, Florida. The cable system would introduce interactive television to American consumers and showcase the industry's latest advances. Nelson was looking forward to the challenge. At the moment, however) his mind wasn't on Techno-tronics or the cable system in Orlando. His total focus was on the woman who was about to become his wife. His wedding night and their two-week honeymoon in Hawaii ran a close second in his thoughts.

There was a haze in Shelby's eyes as her father turned her over to Nelson. "Son, this is my only child. You take good care of my little girl; as good a care as I have or you'll answer to me, young man. Understand?"

"Yes, sir," Nelson replied, wrapping a protective arm around Shelby's waist. "You have my word on that."

At the reception, Shelby stood in Nelson's arms laughing as she watched her best friend, Manette. As the maid of honor, tradition held that Manette should have been the one to catch the wedding bouquet. Three larger women vying for the honor of catching the flying flowers—a perfect arrangement of white orchids, baby's breath and pink tea roses—easily pushed the slight-of-build Manette aside.

Shelby turned to Nelson. He pulled her against his side, crushing the white satin gown. Dropping his head, Nelson kissed his wife thoroughly. "I'll always love you, Shelby Julian Reeves—endlessly forever and a day."

Four hours later, Shelby stood at the window looking down on the trees and shrubbery that surrounded the Boulder hotel. Tomorrow they would leave for Stapleton Airport and the flight taking them to Hawaii. Several floors below, their wedding party and guests continued to celebrate in the ballroom of the Victorian-styled hotel.

Nelson had noticed her waning energy and suggested they retire to their suite. The room, decorated in vivid hues of forest green and violet, had a large brass, canopied bed, which Shelby couldn't wait to try. She leaned back when Nelson's arm came around her and took the fluted glass from his hand. She sipped the liquid and wrinkled her nose, both from the tingle of the champagne fumes filling her nostrils and the tiny nips being made on her neck. She giggled when Nelson's mouth found her ear and suckled her lobe.

Nelson twirled Shelby to face him and his gaze slowly roamed her features: vibrantly smooth skin, regally high cheekbones, full lush lips and scintillating eyes all perfectly positioned on a dark canvas. Combine all that with Shelby's charitable spirit and loving heart and Nelson knew he was looking at his fantasy come to life. Shelby loved him and had given herself over to his care; Nelson planned to spend the rest of his life ensuring her happiness.

Nelson held the tip of her chin in his fingers and stared deeply into the wide eyes fixed on his. "My beautiful Shel. I love you so much it cuts off my breath to look at you. I stand at the edge of a precipice each time I take you in my arms. You inspire me like no other and with you by my side there are no heights I cannot scale. I will be the best that I can be for you, Shelby. Anything you want, or need, or think you need, tell me and I will do all I can to provide it for you. Thank you for allowing me to love you, Shelby Reeves. I promise to always be here for you and for our family, and do all in my power to prove myself worthy of your love."

Shelby's eyes brimmed and his fingers touched away her tears. She rubbed her cheek against his palm. "I love you, Nelson. I never thought I could love anyone as much as I do you. I'll try and be a good wife and I'll do my best to make you happy."

Jet eyes lightened, then darkened to a deeper shade of black, and Nelson dipped his head. Their lips met in a caress so soft that Shelby thought a breeze had touched her mouth. Nelson left her with the delectable shudders and skimmed his knuckle along the delicate line of her jaw.

"Dinner's ready, sweetness." Smiling provocatively, Shelby briskly shook her head no.

Nelson returned a disarming grin and nodded his head yes. "Food first, my sweet Shelby. Then we'll have our fill of dessert."

Arm in arm, they moved to the table, and after seating Shelby, Nelson proceeded to fill his plate. The large slivers of crabmeat were succulent. The steamed clams were chewy and were dipped in the same lemon-butter sauce as the chunks of broiled lobster tail. There were other dishes on the table, but they sat untouched as Nelson smacked his lips and ate heartily. He'd read somewhere that seafood improved prowess, not that his virility was lacking by any means. Nelson just felt he needed all the endurance he could marshal for the long night ahead.

Shelby did not sample any of the food. She had other things on her mind, most of them centered on the brass bed calling to her from the bedroom. She picked up her glass of champagne and ran a stockinged foot along the inside of Nelson's thigh. He tensed a little, but continued lifting the fork filled with food to his mouth. Shelby watched him chew, a little dismayed that she couldn't tempt his attention away from the china plate and into the bedroom. She moved her foot higher and placed it firmly against the vee of his pants.

His fork clattering to the plate, Nelson leaped up from his chair. He flung down his napkin and quickly rounded the table. Shelby had just enough time to set down her glass before being pulled from her seat and lifted into his arms.

In the bedroom, Nelson set her down, quickly stripped and threw his clothes on a chair, then stood in all his naked, brown glory, arms crossed, frowning at the fully clothed Shelby.

"There seems to be a problem here," he remarked.

"I know," she replied.

"Are you planning to fix the problem or did you just want to see me in the buff?"

Shelby shrugged. "I've seen you naked enough times to remember what you look like. By the way, you do look marvelous and I can't wait to get my hands on you."

""And?""

"And…" A sultry smile touched her lips; then hands on waist, Shelby presented him with her back.

Nelson dropped his arms and groaned as he plodded heavily toward her. He'd forgotten the dress. When he reached Shelby, his hands began the clumsy, time-wasting task of undoing the long row of small pearl buttons she had used on the back of her gown. He leaned over her shoulder and placed a moist kiss on the graceful neck. "This is a pretty gown, Shel. The prettiest I've ever seen and one of your best. But the next time we get married, I'd greatly appreciate it if you would use a zipper."

Shelby tilted her head back and Nelson pressed a kiss into the curls on top of her head. "Next time? There will be no next time, Nelson Lamar Reeves, Jr. As of today, this union is inseparable."

Nelson had the buttons on the gown halfway undone when he lost his patience and growled a low expletive. He swung Shelby around, crushed her against his pounding heart and dropped his head, taking her mouth in a blistering kiss. Quivers raced through Shelby's body when he lowered the bodice of the dress and she felt his warm, wet tongue on her bare skin. Breathing deeply, she tried to find her voice. "The gown, Nels. The gown."

Nelson stood up. His hand embraced the back of her head and brought her forward to meet the pressing demand of his mouth. Shelby wrapped her arms around his shoulders and parted her lips, granting him access. Taking his time, Nelson lingered over the humid softness inside her mouth and moved the gown higher on her legs with his hands. Shelby felt his achingly sweet caresses on her thighs and sighed as Nelson kissed a torturous trail over her cheeks, her eyes and brow line. She tried to rejoin their mouths.

Nelson evaded her twisting head and at her ear murmured, "I like the gown right where it is." Then he disappeared. Shelby next felt him moving beneath the bell of her skirt and her knees almost buckled as kisses followed the wisps of cloth traveling swiftly down her legs. She grabbed his shoulders when Nelson lifted her feet, one at a time, to fling the bunched material out to the floor. In seconds, Shelby could hardly breathe and when Nelson reappeared from beneath her gown, he sat back and pulled Shelby onto his lap. Enduring the torment of his own need for fulfillment, he laid gentle kisses on her face and held her trembling body, whispering his love until Shelby calmed.

Hugging her tightly against his chest, he growled vehemently, "I have no self-control when it comes to you, Shelby, something you know by now." His dark gaze swooped over her face again and she saw the deep craving in his eyes before he glanced away to lookdown at the wrinkled gown. "Look what I've done to your gown! Your beautiful wedding dress, Shel."

Shelby draped an arm around his neck. "I don't care about the dress, Nelson. I care about you and right now I need your help with this gown. Take it off me, Nelson, and then take me to our wedding bed."

It was a request she wouldn't have to make twice. Nelson pushed Shelby up and with a steady agility that amazed him, quickly unhooked the rest of the buttons. Desire pinged at his body as Nelson helped Shelby step out of the gown and remove the rest of her clothing. He stepped back and examined the curved hips, long legs, hourglass waist and high firm breasts of the figure he'd seen many times. Nelson opened his arms and Shelby moved into the circle that closed around her. This was where she was safe and warm and loved. This was where she planned to stay for the rest of her life.

Nelson lifted and carried Shelby to their wedding bed. A few minutes later, Shelby cried out in abandonment and her untamed response inflamed Nelson, energizing his body. Shelby was a passionate, unbridled lover and unafraid to show her feelings. From the first time they'd come together, Shelby had held nothing back, and neither did he.

"Open your eyes, sweetness," he rumbled huskily near her ear, feeling the rise of his release. "I want to see your eyes, Shel."

Nelson gripped her tightly and lowered his mouth to connect with hers as the joy of their union collided in a splintering light. Kisses and tender pats of adoration followed as they helped each other descend from the haze. Then they clung together: damp, breathless and in need of a restful respite before round two of their honeymoon night of love began.

# CHAPTER EIGHT

*Three years and two months later...*

The house smelled of bayberry and the enticing aromas filtering through the kitchen doorway. The dark maple table gleamed beneath flowered china place settings, crystal wineglasses and sterling-silver utensils. Pink tapered candles sat in silver holders waiting for a match to ignite their glow, and crystal rose-filled vases sat in various places around the dining room, completing the romantic setting.

Shelby stood at the kitchen window peering through tiny screen squares filled with water. A late-afternoon August thunderstorm had stopped only moments earlier and the sun had mustered enough strength to chase away its shield of gray clouds to reveal a colorful rainbow. She was watching the vibrant hues reproduce themselves in the water droplets clinging to the branches of the tall pine tree in her front yard, and she was waiting for Nelson.

Shelby sighed and glanced over her shoulder at the stainless-steel stove. The clock read 6:33. "Where is he?" she asked aloud, turning back to the window. Nelson usually beat her home and tonight when he was the bearer of good news, he'd apparently had to stay late at the office. No, Shelby corrected herself. Her husband was not inconsiderate. Not once had Nelson failed to call if he wouldn't make it home on time.

She'd left the boutique early to prepare a special dinner in celebration of their becoming homeowners. Of course, she was assuming that Nelson had good news. On the phone this afternoon, he hadn't said that their offer had been accepted. But Shelby had faith. They had to get that house; it had been built just for them. They also wanted to start a family soon and the two-bedroom townhouse was too small to raise children.

Her mind had just started dredging up morbid thoughts when she saw the black Lexus roll down the street. Shelby gripped the edge of the sink, so excited she could hardly stand still. She forced herself to calm down. Nelson always told her she was like a child at Christmas when her interest was up, and Shelby was going to prove to her husband that she wasn't, that she could act like an adult and wait.

She watched Nelson climb from the car and rushed to the door, then stopped abruptly and took a deep breath. She placed her hands in the pockets of the apple green and white jumper and projected what she hoped was a nonchalant pose. A couple of minutes went by, then Shelby crossed to the living room window and pushed aside lacy, white curtains.

Nelson had stopped to converse with one of the neighbors, and Shelby groaned when she saw it was Mrs. Hathaway. Mrs. Hathaway was a lovely, elderly woman and still sprightly for her seventy-odd years. With no children of her own, she had adopted Nelson and Shelby. They shared meals with her, overindulged on Mrs. Hathaway's special chocolate chip cookies, and Shelby had spent a fair amount of time in the older woman's kitchen learning how to cook. Mrs. Hathaway had also been her first customer when she'd opened Exterior Motives.

She had developed deep feelings for the older woman, but she could talk a person's ear off. Returning her neighbor's wave, Shelby smiled when Nelson glanced over his shoulder. She watched him make his excuses to Mrs. Hathaway and head for the house again. Nelson skirted a puddle, then stopped at a patch of purple and white lilacs.

"Will you get in here, Nelson Reeves," Shelby whispered when he stooped to pluck two of each color. He stood again and Shelby went to open the door.

"Hi, baby," she greeted as calmly as her nerves would allow.

"Hi, love of my life. These are for you."

Shelby accepted the flowers and Nelson hauled her against his body with one arm. They exchanged a lover's kiss; she took his briefcase and he turned for the bedroom. Shelby bit her bottom lip.

*Okay,* she thought, setting his briefcase on the table in the hall as she walked to the kitchen. *Nelson needs to unwind and he'll say something when he changes out of that suit.*

In the kitchen, Shelby hummed to herself as she transferred homemade biscuits from a hot pan on the stove to a serving basket on the counter. She dropped the fork when a loud bellow reverberated through the house and in the process of trying to retrieve it, she burned her finger on the pan.

Shelby stuck the finger in her mouth and counted to three because that's all the time it took for Nelson, draped in a hunter green towel, to come roaring into the kitchen.

She turned and fastened her eyes on the heaving brown bulk directly in front of her. When her palms began to itch, Shelby stemmed the urge to run her hands over the glistening wet skin and the intricate diamond shapes on the tiled floor suddenly became very interesting.

When she didn't look up, Nelson's spread his hands around her waist and raised her eye level. "Where is it?"

She rested her hands on his shoulders and sucked on his bottom lip until Nelson gave in to her request for a kiss. When the drawn out caress ended, Shelby uttered a guileless sigh and said, "Nels, there are clothes on the bed. I laid them out special. Won't you please wear them?"

*She did it again,* he thought. Oh, she looked innocent, but Nelson knew that Shelby had thrown his old CSU sweatshirt in the trash, again. No matter how many times he told her that it was his favorite shirt or explained the amount of time it had taken to get the jersey, with its coffee stains and ragged holes for sleeves, comfortably perfect, she didn't understand.

Shelby thought his attachment to the old shirt was stupid and had told him so the day he'd found her using his shirt as a dusting rag. He'd nearly had a heart attack. Nelson didn't care what Shelby thought; the shirt was his and she couldn't just toss it into the garbage without his permission.

"Sweetness, I've been dressed in a monkey suit all day and I don't want to dress at home. Where is my—"

"I made a peach cobbler for you," Shelby interrupted.

His eyes lit up. "You did?" She nodded. "With buttery, flaky crust?" "Lots of buttery, flaky crust."

"And bubbling brown sugar?"

"Gobs and gobs of bubbling brown sugar."

"May I have some before dinner?"

"No." Shelby looked at the stove. "Baby, put me down. I need to take the ham out of the oven."

Nelson followed her to the stove. "Shel, if you'll give me some bubbling brown sugar now, I'll wear those clothes you put out for me."

She set the ham on the stove and turned to face him. "Nelson, you may not have any peach cobbler until after dinner."

"I don't want peach cobbler." He pulled her against him and lowered his head. "I want this bubbling brown sugar."

Nelson kept Shelby in the bedroom for an hour and a half, then, amid complaints that he was starving, proceeded to step on her heels as she rushed around the kitchen reheating their dinner.

Shelby put him out, assigning him to light the candles. She was happy he wore the dress pants and shirt, but by the time they'd eaten dinner, cleaned the kitchen and watched the basketball game on television, Shelby was ready to scream.

Nelson turned her in his arms and smiled down at Shelby. He brushed his lips across her forehead. "I'm very proud of you, Shel. I know how much effort it has taken for you to wait me out. I was trying to wait for Poppy's arrival."

By this time, Shelby was almost frantic. "Nelson, please!"

Nelson kissed her again. "We got it," he whispered in her ear.

Shelby leaped from the couch, twirling in a circle. "Baby, do you know what this means to us? When can we move in? Tomorrow's Saturday. Can we go shopping for furniture tomorrow? Nelson, you're not going to work tomorrow, are you? Oh, please say no. I'll let Manette handle the store and we can get started early."

Nelson laughed as he watched his wife. "Shelby Reeves, calm yourself, woman, and get back over here." Shelby returned to the couch. "First, the closing is in two months, so there's no need to rush out to the furniture stores. We have a lot of work to do on that house before we can even think about moving in. Second, yes, I have to go to the office. We're running a fiber optics test in Orlando tomorrow and I need to be there when they fax in the results. Third, you can go to the boutique. But," Nelson said when he saw Shelby's disappointment, "tomorrow night we'll start working on plans for the house. Okay?"

Shelby snuggled against him, savoring the feel of his hard chest under her cheek. "Okay." The doorbell rang and Nelson left the couch. He opened the front door to receive his father-in-law.

"Hey, Poppy."

"Hello, son. Have you told her the good news?"

Nelson laughed. "What do you think, Poppy? That's your daughter in there."

The subject of their conversation ran into the hallway and into her father's arms. "Poppy!" Shelby drew back and looked into eyes that matched her own. "Did Nels tell you? We got the house!"

Martin chuckled delightedly. Between himself and his son-in-law there wasn't anything his little girl wanted that she didn't get. "Yes. Yes. Nelson told me, pumpkin. I can see the news was well received."

Shelby took her father's hand and led him into the living room, chattering all the way. "And we'll be closer to you, Poppy," she said as Martin sat on the couch.

He lifted his nose in the air and sniffed. "Smells like cinnamon, brown sugar and, if I'm not mistaken, perhaps slices of juicy peaches." Martin looked at Nelson, who threw out his hands.

"Don't look at me. Shel did the cooking tonight."

Martin couldn't hide his surprise. "My little girl?" He took Shelby's hands in his. "Tell the truth now, pumpkin. Is that really peach cobbler I smell? Did you bake my favorite treat? Or is Nelson covering for you again?"

Shelby preened with pride. It was no secret that cooking wasn't exactly at the top of her skills list. During the first months of their marriage, Nelson had patiently taught her how to prepare his favorite dishes. Shelby had found that cooking wasn't so hard, if you kept your mind on what you were doing, followed a recipe and took lots and lots of lessons. Besides the hours of trial and error in Mrs. Hathaway's kitchen, she'd brought a mountain of cook-books, attended several weekend courses at cooking school and had managed to become a fair cook. "I did make the cobbler, Poppy, and if you'll promise not to start with the bad jokes, I'll serve you an extra large helping."

An offer too good to resist, Martin thought. "Little girl, you have yourself a deal."

"Shel? I'd like some, too."

She turned, hands on waist. "Nelson Reeves, you've had three helpings of cobbler tonight. I'd think you'd be full by now." "Please, sweetness? You know I can't get enough of your bubbling brown sugar."

Martin tried to hide his amusement, but to Shelby's abashment she knew her father had broken Nelson's coded message. She sent her husband a glare that promised retribution.

Nelson looked at Martin and wiggled his brows.

"She baked a ham, too. And tomorrow I get to have ham stew." Martin shook his head in mock dismay. "Has she stopped experimenting with it, son?" "I think so, but the curry powder is in the trash. I don't want to go through that again." Nelson and Martin looked at each other and burst out laughing.

Ham stew was something Shelby had concocted in her first attempt to expand her culinary skills. She'd started with cut up potatoes and fried them in a light oil with onions, green and red bell peppers and various spices, then added thick chunks of cooked ham. She stirred it all together, dumped the mixture in a pot, added baby peas, a little water and slapped on a lid.

A few minutes later, she had ham stew, which she served with sliced tomatoes sprinkled with a honey mustard sauce and hot, buttered croissants. Nelson loved the dish and always cleaned his plate. The particular night in question, Shelby had thought to enliven the dish with a dash of curry powder. She had used too much. Nelson and Martin had fought each other at the kitchen sink trying to stick their mouths under the flowing tap.

"Pumpkin?" Martin said over his chuckles. "Would it be possible for me to have a ham sandwich before it goes into your stew?"

Shelby gave Nelson a look meant to annihilate. "All right. All right, both of you!" She turned and headed for the kitchen grumbling, "Men!"

Their laughter went with her, then Martin followed Nelson to the bar. "When is the closing?" he asked, taking the glass of Scotch and water Nelson held out.

"Two months."

"Well, let's see now. That will put you close to the end of October, won't it?"

"Yeah. But the house needs a lot of fixing up, Poppy, and Shelby's already said that she wants to move in by next December. I promised her I'd do my best, but it's a tough deadline to meet. The way things are picking up in this city, I'll have a hard time locating a crew I can get up there before April or May."

Concern filled Martin's eyes as they returned to the couch with their drinks. After the death of his wife, Shelby's grandparents had done their best to stop Martin from spoiling his daughter rotten. At six, Shelby had a pony, at fourteen, her own credit card, and when she graduated with honors from high school, Martin had thought the occasion deserving of a brand new BMW. Shelby was spoiled and it was his fault.

In reality, except for the pony, she hadn't asked him for much except that he spend time with her. His work had kept him away more than he'd liked. Yet, despite all the material lavishment, he had somehow managed to instill a work ethic in his daughter, probably due to all the hours she'd spent with him in the lab, the only place they could spend private time together without interruption.

"Son, I may be overstepping my bounds here and you be sure to tell me if I am. But I've given this matter considerable thought and maybe it's time for Shelby to learn that she can't always have what she wants. Now I know that I must accept my share of the blame and I do. When Shelby's mother passed, I didn't want my daughter to miss out on anything else in her life. Unfortunately, I wasn't able to spend as much time with Shelby as I'd have liked or that she deserved. I tried to make up for the lack of parental attention, but perhaps I was wrong to give Shelby everything. And perhaps it is wrong for you to continue the practice."

"All I want is Shelby's happiness, Poppy."

"I know, son." Martin placed a hand on Nelson's shoulder. "I want the same. That's my daughter, after all. And I'm not suggesting that we cut Shelby off cold turkey, only that we both hold back a little and try telling her no every once in a while."

"After all this time, that's going to be tough." "What's going to be tough?" Shelby asked, entering the room carrying a tray. Martin and Nelson exchanged glances.

"Nothing," they said simultaneously.

They spent the remainder of Martin's visit talking about plans for the house. He offered to call a friend about a construction crew for Nelson and praised Shelby for her cobbler. He also exacted her promise that she would bake and deliver a cobbler to him the following week.

At the car, he admonished Nelson again. "Remember what we spoke of earlier, son. Saying no won't kill Shelby, but it might just save you."

Nelson waved his father-in-law off and reentered the house. Later that night, when he thought Shelby was asleep, he left the bed. He trekked barefoot through the kitchen and out to the garage. At the trashcan, Nelson retrieved his beloved shirt and returned to the bedroom. Shelby heard a dresser drawer open and close. Then Nelson climbed back into the bed, pulled his wife into his arms and went to sleep.

❧

"You are not listening to me, Nelson Reeves. I want the staircase just off the foyer," Shelby repeated, stabbing her finger on the blueprints Nelson had spread out on a fallen tree stump. "I want to stand on my landing, look out these windows and see the mountain skyline."

Nelson rolled his eyes in exasperation and wiped sawdust-filled gloves across his forehead. They'd been arguing about the damn staircase for over an hour now and he had about reached his limit with his mule-headed wife. *This "no" thing is not working,* he thought, leaning over to study the plans.

With the pencil in his hand, Nelson circled a spot on the blueprints. "How many times do I have to tell you this, Shelby Reeves? You cannot have your staircase here. We'll have to tear down the front of the house and I'll have to get the contractors out here again. Do you have any idea how much more that will cost us? We have a budget and we agreed to stay within it. We closed on this property almost seven months ago and it's already the middle of May. You told me you wanted to move in before Christmas and I'm doing my best to meet that deadline. Now I think the stair-case is fine, here," Nelson stabbed the plans with the pencil, "exactly where it is. It's accessible from both the living room and the study."

Shelby wasn't listening. Having walked off, she was sitting in a clearing with her arms folded over her chest, pouting.

Nelson dropped to the grass beside her. "Shel?"

Shelby turned her head away, refusing to look at him, and she didn't respond.

"Shelby, why are you acting like this? We're way over budget on this house and you told me you wouldn't make any more changes."

She looked at him, wringing her hands in appeal. "But Nelson, we'll probably live in this house for the rest of our lives and I want our home to be perfect. I know we're over budget and that it's my fault, but business at the boutique is picking up now and I'll add more to the house account."

"You know this is not about money, Shelby Reeves. This is about our learning to stick to a budget and staying within the guidelines of the financial goals we've set. J.R. says our disposable income is too high, Shel; our spending habits too frivolous. We need to discipline ourselves. Just because we can afford to buy something doesn't mean we have to run out and do so."

Shelby slanted her eyes at Nelson. "J.R. says. That's all I hear from you anymore. Jordon Banks is our financial advisor, not the money god."

"J.R. is tops in his field. Look what he's done with the DownTown Stock Club. Do you realize how much money we've made this year alone because of J.R.?"

The DownTown Stock Club was a group of ten men of color who had an interest in owning a piece of the rock. Organized by Jordon, each man had invested an initial fifty thousand dollars and sat back as Jordon used his uncanny ability to predict the market. In just over three years, the stock club's net worth was well over seven million dollars. Jordon figured he'd need a couple more years and they'd all be millionaires.

Nelson scooted closer and put his arm around Shelby's waist. "I trust his advice completely. Besides, I thought you liked Jordon."

"Nels, I do like J.R. He's a good friend and Jolie is just adorable. What I don't like is someone else telling us how to spend our money."

"J.R.'s not telling us how to spend our money, Shel. His role is to advise. What we do with that advice is our decision."

When Shelby pushed him down to the soft cushion of grass and sat on his chest, Nelson held his breath.

"If you let me have the staircase, Nels, I promise I won't make any more changes to the house and we won't have to go on that cruise next month." Shelby leaned over and kissed him on the lips. "Please, baby," she threw in for good measure.

His arms came around her. How could he refuse his Shelby when she looked at him like that? Nelson sat up, bumping her down to his lap. Her fingers began to unbutton the red and gray plaid flannel shirt and, once undone, she rubbed the palms of her hands over his chest.

Nelson knew he was about to give in when she placed her mouth on his nipple and sucked hard. Shelby would have her staircase just off the foyer as she wanted, and next month they'd be relaxing on a boat sailing in the Caribbean.

"Okay, Shel," Nelson groaned when he felt her lips caress his chest again. "Okay."

Later, Shelby walked around inside the house, mentally making plans and taking measurements while at the same time stepping over wooden beams, rolls of wiring, Nelson's tools and piles of sawdust. She hummed to herself, not feeling the least bit guilty that she'd gotten her way with the staircase.

After all, she hadn't said anything when Nelson bought the sailboat last year, nor last month when he'd driven up in a brand new Bronco. Anything that made her husband happy, made her happy, too.

As Vice President of Engineering for Techno-tronics, Nelson drew a six-figure income and the boutique had finally begun to turn a profit. They were entitled to spend the money they'd worked so hard to earn any way they saw fit, regardless of J.R. and his advice.

For Nelson, the real monetary rewards would come when the Orlando system was on-line. Techno-tronics paid its executives well, and for a job well done, even better. However, he also liked working with his hands, and except for major renovations, was doing most of the work on the house himself.

Nelson would make her Christmas deadline; he always kept his promises. And she would keep hers, too. They wouldn't take the cruise in the Caribbean this year, but a trip to Paris was a possibility. She could position it as a working vacation and check out the new fall lines while they were there.

Shelby stopped by an unpaned window, smiling as she watched her barebacked husband use a saw on a pine plank. She wondered if she could love Nelson any more than she did right at that moment. Her body suffused in warmth remembering that a short while ago, her hands had roamed freely over those hard, rippling muscles.

Shelby's favorite activity, when she wasn't working on a new design, was making love to her husband. Nelson had primed her body to his brand of lovemaking and he left her feeling alive, completely adored and always wanting more. He was her first and, Shelby was sure, only lover in life. When Nelson stood to flex his back, she was hard-pressed to keep herself from running into the yard and attacking him again.

Nelson walked to the back of the new Bronco. He filled a bucket from the cooler they brought with them each weekend, bent forward and poured the water over his head.

Globular beads, gleaming in the sunshine, flew through the air as Nelson shook his body.

He grabbed a towel and feeling her eyes on him, looked toward the window. "I love you," he mouthed.

Shelby returned the sentiment and went to gather her things. It was time to go. As soon as they got home, she'd feed her husband, then direct him to the bedroom to share more of the loving Shelby hadn't quite gotten her fill of that afternoon.

# CHAPTER NINE

*Six years and four months of marriage later…*

A glum silence settled over the table where Shelby, Manette, Starris Gilmore, Pamela Shaw, Jacqueline Tyler and Maxie Peterson sat having lunch at their favorite downtown restaurant.

In pairs, the ladies were best friends; similar of thought, likes and dislikes, the twosomes had expanded into a larger circle of friendship, and they tried to meet every other Saturday for lunch and an exchange of the latest gossip.

"What are you going to do?"

The question was directed to Starris, a golden-skinned, hazel-eyed beauty with naturally curly auburn hair. She was an artist and a graphics designer. She'd also just revealed the troubled circumstances of her marriage to her doctor-husband, Lonnie Gilmore.

The asker, Jacqueline, was hazel-eyed herself and genuinely concerned. She was an account rep at JuneHart Publishing and had a mane of thick, auburn hair that fell to the middle of her back. Her light caramel cheeks sported dimples and a black mole graced her upper lip. She also had a boyfriend, but was beginning to have serious doubts about his commitment to their relationship.

"I was taught that when you married, it was for life. It has only been two months and I keep hoping things will improve."

"But what if they don't?" Maxie asked, pushing her fingers through a layered cap of black hair. Maxie, a paralegal and Jacqueline's best friend, had black eyes and was a shade or two lighter than Shelby. She lived with her boyfriend and had so far been unsuccessful in steering him toward the altar. "Right now, the abuse is verbal, but it's a short hop from verbal to physical as I understand it."

"I don't think Lonnie would actually put his hands on me."

"He'd better not," Pamela, best friend of Starris, stated. Brown-skinned Pam also worked at JuneHart as the editor of juvenile books for African-American children. She had brown eyes and cheek-length brown hair tinged red with henna highlights, and was a transplant to the Metro area from Detroit. "I'd hate to put a hit out on that man."

The thought horrified Jacqueline. "You're not serious, Pamela!" "Of course I am." Pamela nibbled a French fry and chuckled. "I wouldn't have the guy killed, but if Lonnie did ever touch Starris, he'd have me to deal with."

Maxie's eyes narrowed. "And the rest of us."

"Well," Manette spoke up. "I guess we can't all be as lucky as Shelby. Her Nelson is a dream. That man bends over backwards to make her happy. Anything Shelby wants, all she has to do is snap her fingers and Nelson brings it to her on a silver tray. Talk about paradise."

"That's not true, Manny. Nelson and I have our share of problems, too." And how, Shelby thought, as the conversation about Starris and Lonnie Gilmore went on around her.

When they'd discussed marriage, Nelson had said he wanted a house full of children. He hadn't said anything to her, but Shelby knew her husband had given up his hope that they would ever have them. She also knew Nelson had tired of the countless visits to clinics, sperm and egg counts, thermometers, charts and ovulation schedules. He had put his foot down when she started talking about fertility drugs.

Other than minor skirmishes, their six years together had been happy, but Shelby wanted to give Nelson a child. It had become her obsession and she was making his life miserable because of it. The thought distressed Shelby because Nelson was her world and did all he could to make her happy. Lately, she'd spent a lot of time worrying about Nelson, but had just received news that would make her husband happier than he had been in a long while. Manette was speaking when Shelby brought her attention back to the table.

"All I know is that as badly as I want a man, I'd never stay with one who was abusive, verbally or physically."

"I have to agree with you on that one, girl," Pamela concurred. "How long do you plan to stick it out with the man?" Maxie asked.

"I don't know." Starris took a drink from her glass of iced tea. "My marriage has just begun. I feel I should at least give it a chance to work. Maybe we can work out our problems."

"Well, if you don't, I know a man who would be perfect for you."

"Shelby Reeves," Manette cried. "How dare you sit here and offer up a perfectly good man to someone else when you know how long I've been looking for one."

"Calm down, Manny. I'm talking about J.R."

"Oh." Manette sat back in her seat. She'd known Jordon Banks for as long as she'd known Nelson. There had never been a hint that they would be anything more than friends, on either side. She did, however, observe Starris with a quizzical look. "You know, Shel. You could be on to something here. Jordon and Starris would be perfect together."

Starris began to choke and Jacqueline whacked her on the back until she caught her breath. "Ladies, I'm already married. Remember?"

"True, but—" Shelby left the remark open-ended.

Each of the women repeated the phrase and when it came back to Starris, she looked around the table and smiled. "*C'est vrai, mais—*" she said, perhaps rather wistfully.

"Enough of this talk about husbands and possible future match-ups," Pamela exclaimed. She pulled a white envelope from her purse. "We're way too maudlin today and I want to show you ladies this."

Maxie's mouth dropped open as she stared at the fancy lettering of the Quad-E logo. Her career choice would never make her eligible to receive one.

"I got one of those the other day," Shelby remarked.

"I did, too," both Jacqueline and Starris said.

"Well, are you ladies joining or what?" Pamela asked, noting the way Maxie snatched up the envelope she'd just laid on the table.

Shelby pushed her plate away. Her stomach was burning and she knew she probably shouldn't have eaten those radishes in her salad. Something carbonated would help, she thought, raising her hand for the waiter as she responded. "I don't know. The group doesn't really do anything for the community."

"True enough," Jacqueline concurred. "However, getting one of these means you're part of the in-crowd."

"The in-crowd?" Pamela frowned, puzzled. "What, pray tell, is the 'in-crowd?'"

Maxie crinkled her nose. "Your ignorance is showing, Pam. The in-crowd is the women of color who have made it in this city. Every October, Quad-E sends out invitations and only to a select number of women. The group puts on an annual dinner/dance and you get to meet the influential African Americans in this city. It's one big social circle of money and power. When did you move to Denver anyway?"

"I've been here for two years. Well, next month will make two years. I sent some of my things first, then made the actual move during the Thanksgiving weekend."

"She transferred to June Hart after the buyout of her company," Jacqueline added with a smile. "Pam was a keeper."

"Well, I've lived here all my life." Maxie eyed Pamela enviously. "You've been here only two years and already you've made the list."

"Sounds like a bunch of trifling, bourgeois snobs to me."

"They are, Pam," Starris said. "But only the members of the group. I'm sure those we come into contact with outside of Quad-E are real down-to-earth folk. I don't know, I've been thinking I'd join, just to stir things up. Maybe if we all join we could get the organization to actually put together an agenda and help somebody in this city."

"All?" Manette glanced at Maxie before directing her gaze to the cloudy, gray October sky outside the window of their booth. "Some of us didn't receive invitations."

The women were silent for a moment, then Pamela perked up. "I think Starris is right. The four of us should join this snooty bunch. We'll get in there and take over, then issue invitations to Manny and Maxie."

"Sounds like a plan to me," Shelby said.

"Amen," the others responded.

"Dammit!" Nelson threw his club to the ground and marched across the green. He picked up his golf ball, returned to the hole and dropped it in.

"You're cheating again." Jordon was lounging against the cart watching Nelson's latest fit of pique. Nelson reached down to swipe up his club. His demeanor was stony when he faced Jordon. "So what?"

Jordon straightened and placed his fists on his waist. "If you cheat, you'll never get a handle on the game."

Nelson didn't look up from the grass he mowed with his club. "Apparently, I'm not supposed to get a handle on this damn game, J.R. I've hit every sand trap, pond and group of trees on the course. What's my score anyway?"

Removing the cards from his back pocket, Jordon took a moment to tally the strokes. "Counting that last fit, you're twenty up."

"Twenty! How can I be twenty up when you spotted me strokes?" Jordon laughed.

"Because you've hit every sand trap, pond and group of trees on this course."

Nelson grunted and grumbled his way back to the cart. He shucked his club into the golf bag, climbed inside the cart and looked at Jordon. "Let's go. We've only got three more holes before you're done trouncing my butt into the ground."

By the time they'd completed their golf game and retreated to the clubhouse for beers, Nelson's mood still hadn't improved.

Jordon studied his friend. "You can't be the best at everything, Nelson." "The best! I'd settle for getting somewhere in the vicinity of a hole one day. The convention is next month and with the way I play, I'll probably be sued for knocking someone senseless with one of my golf balls,"

"There's no use being pigheaded about this, Nels. You still have racquetball, tennis and of course…"

"B-ball!" They both yelled, and slapped hands. The thought of his skills on the court brought a smile to Nelson's face. He still had the touch and proved it every time the guys got together for a game.

Leaning back, Jordon folded one long leg over the other and picked up his bottle. "I have an idea I want to run by you, Nels. It concerns the stock club's community outreach programs."

Nelson tipped his bottle at Jordon. "Shoot." "Well, basically we have two. The scholarships and speeches at the high schools." "I know, I'm speaking at two schools next week."

"That's all cool and everything, but here's what I'm thinking. I'd like to see the club start a mentor program for at-risk youth, specifically young, black males who seem to have nothing better to do than hang at the mall and make babies they have no means of supporting. I want to take ten of these kids out of the mall, give them our undivided attention and direct them toward more productive pursuits. If we're lucky, we might get them to take an interest in their future."

Nelson's brows drew together. "I like it, J.R., but other organizations have big-brother programs. I think if we're going to start a mentor program, we should go one better."

"How so?"

"Well, if we want the kids to focus on their future, we can't bring them in, rev them up and then drop them with no place to go. That would defeat the purpose. So, why not offer a job training program, heavy on the technical and computer side, of course, and try to find employment for the kids, too. With the right advance team, I'll bet plenty of companies would be receptive to offering intern-ships to the kids once they're trained. I'm sure I could persuade TTC to take on a couple of high school seniors.

And," Nelson added with emphasis, "maybe there's a way to tie our program in with the high schools for extra credit."

Jordon stared around the outdoor patio area, contemplating the practicality of Nelson's suggestion. "The stock club does have enough money to do something like that, but it's up to the guys. My position is this. While it's a good idea, it's something we should look at for the future and if we decide to expand in that direction, we should also seek private funding to complement the club's. If the board approves the plan, let's concentrate on getting the first ten kids interested."

"Yeah. You're probably right. What would you call the organization? The DownTown Stock Club isn't really an appropriate name for a mentor program." "I don't know," Jordon replied. "I haven't taken the thought process that far."

Nelson sat up and leaned forward. "What about ROBY?"

"ROBY?"

"Yep. Reclaiming Our Black Youth. Has a certain ring to it, don't you think? Or we could use, regaining, refurbishing, reinforcing, reinstating or regenerating."

"Hold it, Nels. Any one of those is cool. Listen, can you drop by the crib today and give me a hand pulling together the proposal?"

"Yeah. Shel's hanging with the girls."

Jordon knew by the tone of Nelson's voice who was behind the bad mood he'd displayed earlier. His eyes were sympathetic when he looked at Nelson. "You and Shel still fighting?"

Nelson's hands played with his beer bottle, sliding it from side to side. "There wouldn't be any fights if Shel would back off this fertility thing. I put up with the rest of it, J.R., but I have to draw the line somewhere. I ain't doing it, man. I'm not going to wind up on some talk show with two sets of twins and triplets trailing behind me. I'll take my kids one at a time."

Love sure could kill a brother, Jordon thought, his expression dubious. Having witnessed past attempts, he had serious doubts about Nelson's ability to take a stand with Shelby. However, unlike his own ex-wife, Shelby was not deceitful or vindictive. Nelson knew exactly where he stood with his wife. Jordon finished his beer and threw some bills on the table. "Well, I'm sure the two of you will work it out. You always do. Hey, did I tell you I'm getting a new career?"

"Again! Man, how many jobs will this make, and what about my finances?" "Four. And I'll still be your financial planner. I'm joining a band—lead sax for Fantasy."

"That group playing at the jazz club downtown?"

"Yep. Been practicing with them all month."

Nelson just shook his head. Jordon, like a rolling stone, couldn't seem to find a place to land. "You know, J.R., I know basketball didn't work out the way you'd hoped, but don't you think it's time to stop jumping from career to career? All women are not like your ex-wife and Gloria's dead, man. It's time to forgive and forget. Our marriage is not always a bed of roses, but Shelby's my inspiration and without her I'd be lost. Find yourself another woman, Jordon. It might be what you need to settle down."

Jordon's expression turned ruthless with anger. "Gloria may be dead, but I'll never forgive her or forget. Every time I look at my daughter, I have to face what that woman did. I'll never get caught in that love trap again; it ain't worth the heartache. As far as careers, when I find something I want to take up permanently, I'll let you know."

"Well, let's hope that's sooner, rather than later." Nelson stood up. "Let's hit it, man. We have a proposal to put together for ROBY."

The next evening, Shelby watched the candlelight dance in Nelson's eyes and knew that the moment was soon when she would make her announcement. She had kept the secret for over a month, just to be sure. Now that the doctor had confirmed their baby's due date was around the last week of May, she could tell Nelson.

"Shel? J.R. and I were talking yesterday-"

"Who won?"

Nelson frowned in confusion. "What?"

"I'm sorry for interrupting, but you didn't tell me who won the golf game yesterday."

Nelson released a low growl. "Who always wins? J.R. spotted me ten strokes and still beat my no-golf-playing behind."

Shelby examined Nelson. He would be ecstatic when she told him about the baby, but it wouldn't remove the dark smudges under his eyes or the faint lines bordering his mouth. Nelson was under enormous pressure at work and his restless nights were starting to show their wear on her husband.

Although Techno-tronics still supported the Orlando project and had high hopes for the future, the cable system was turning out to be one headache after another. Product and consumer feasibility studies had shown that Americans were ready to move into the next generation of cable. Movies on demand, the ability to skip advertising or get in-depth product information were just a few of the services loved by cable subscribers participating in the tests. However, system cost overruns were astronomical, software and hardware tests showed weekly failures and though consumer acceptance had proven viable, their price tolerance was a big issue. Nelson had been putting in long hours at the office and instead of sleeping in on the one day he'd had off in months, he'd risen early and gone to the golf course with Jordon.

"Baby, if it upsets you this much, maybe you should think about giving up the game."

Nelson stared at Shelby as if she'd lost her mind. "Give up the game! Shelby Reeves, what month is this?"

"October."

"And what month is next month?"

"Nelson, I am not an imbecile," Shelby complained. "I know the Western Cable Show is held every November."

"Then you also know what Techno-tronics does every year at that convention."

"Yes, Nelson. They host a golf tournament. But why do you have to play? You don't even like the game."

"I do like the game," Nelson grumbled. "I'm just not any good at it and playing in the tournament is mandatory, not an option. This is the last big show of the year and the company has calls out to the top decision makers in the industry. We're also courting the phone companies. Every TTC executive will be in California and on that course. Golf is the game of choice in this damn industry. Why couldn't it have been tennis? I can play tennis."

Shelby crossed her arms petulantly. "I don't want to go to California this year."

Nelson frowned. "You have to go."

"No, Nelson Reeves. *You* have to go. I don't work for the cable industry and I don't have time to spend a week in California with you this year. December is my busiest month. I have orders out the kazoo and two gowns on the easel. Plus, there's our Christmas party. And you know how J.R. depends on me to help him with the New Year's Eve bash at his house."

Nelson looked down at his hands. This was turning into an argument and it wasn't about the Cable Show, golf or her boutique. Shelby had been peevish ever since he'd told her there would be no fertility drugs in their future. It was the first time in their marriage that he had refused Shelby something she wanted. Nelson believed he had made the correct decision and had stuck to his guns when Shelby tried to persuade him to change his mind. She'd been upset with him ever since and her unhappiness wounded his heart. Nelson didn't understand what was wrong. They wanted children. Physically, they had both checked out healthy and there was no reason they couldn't have them. Shelby had been off the pill for over two years, yet they still couldn't get pregnant and the strain she was placing on him was getting to be too much.

J.R.'s marriage had fallen apart and someone had once jokingly said that if he and Shelby made it through seven years, their marriage would likely last a lifetime. Nelson wasn't too sure what the statement meant, but he knew that he had to stop the fights with Shelby or they wouldn't make it. And he intended for them to do just that, not only for the seventh year, but the eighth, ninth and all the years that followed.

"Sweetness, come here." Shelby rose from her chair and moved around the table. His arm encircled her waist and brought her down to his lap. He kissed the corners of her eyes. "These beautiful brown beams are snapping at me again and I want you to stop it and smile for your man. I love you, little woman, and I'm sorry for yelling at you, especially when you prepared such a delicious dinner for me." Nelson pulled her close for a hug. "But you are going to California, sweetness. I can't be away from you for a whole week. Besides, don't you want to hear your husband's speech at the technical session?"

"Nels, we've been apart before, for weeks at a time. When I traveled for the boutique and your trips to other conferences and Orlando and…"

"And I didn't like it, Shelby Reeves. That's why you have buyers now and I travel only when necessary. But let's not talk about that right now. I want to tell you about the club."

"The stock club?"

"Yeah. J.R. wants to start a mentor program." Nelson then told Shelby about the plan for ROBY and the proposal he and Jordon had prepared. "I think we can raise the additional funding, but J.R. thinks it's too soon to get that heavily involved. What do you think, Shel?"

Shelby kissed his cheek. Nelson would truly love working with the kids. She also knew it would be his way of making up for not having children of his own. She had gotten sidetracked with talk of the cable show and it was time to tell Nelson. "I think it's a wonderful idea and if anyone can pull it off, it's you and J.R. But I also have something to tell you."

"What, Shel, another record-breaking month at the boutique?"

Shelby decided to ignore Nelson's comment. She knew he supported and was proud of her. Exterior Motives was doing a booming business. Her designs for casual winter wear and ski outfits were taking off, especially with the Aspenites. Some traveled from their mountain chalets to downtown Denver just to have her design something special for them, and she was starting to experiment with eveningwear.

"No, my husband." Shelby framed his face with her hands. "I want to tell you that after more than two years of trying, Nelson Lamar Reeves, Jr., you are finally going to be a father."

Reality ceased to exist for Nelson as the significance of Shelby's words sank into his brain. "What did you say, Shelby?"

She picked up his hand and placed it on her stomach. "You and I are going to have a baby."

Nelson's hands found her waist and, holding on to Shelby, he rose from his chair. "We're going to have a baby? You and me?"

"Yes, Nelson. We're pregnant!"

After a shout of joy, Nelson pulled Shelby to him and squeezed her tight, then released her abruptly. "I'm sorry, little fellow," he said, rubbing his hand over her stomach. He hugged Shelby again and after wetting her face with kisses, gathered her up into his arms and carried her to the living room couch.

"Now tell me," he said after lowering himself and settling Shelby on his lap. "When will my son be here?"

"Son! There's a fifty-fifty chance that our baby will be a girl, you know."

Nelson shook his head. "A son is always the firstborn in a Reeves' household. It's a tradition dating back several generations."

A little dismayed by that revelation, Shelby laid her hand aside his face. "But what if we have a girl, Nelson?"

He smiled with happiness. "Then you and I will start a new tradition and fill our daughter's life with joy and love." Shelby sighed contentedly. "But," Nelson added, "I'll bet you a dollar that you're carrying my son."

Shelby giggled. "You're on, Nels. And when I win this bet, I'll expect a cash payment."

# CHAPTER TEN

*Nine months of pregnancy and counting…*

As Shelby quickly flicked through the clothes on the circular metal rack, Nelson watched her, his smile anything but modest. Shelby had made most of her maternity clothes and the outfit she had on today was one he particularly liked. Her thick hair had grown longer and fell down her back like a wavy, black ribbon and her dark skin had the maternal glow that favored all women with child.

Two-inch yellow buttons secured the shoulder straps of a vibrant lavender, handkerchief styled top. The shirt, tied to one side and knotted, left plenty of room for the bulge where his son resided at the moment She also wore matching linen pants and flat yellow loafers, and the sight of her intoxicated Nelson's senses.

Shelby was his pride and his passion, and carrying his child, the most gorgeous creature on earth. When a rush of excitement stirred his body, Nelson overpowered his urges. At this stage in their pregnancy there wasn't a thing he could do to satisfy his craving for Shelby.

Cravings, Nelson thought with remembered fondness. He had read that cravings waned after the first couple of months. Shelby had gone from ice cream, to red licorice, to salted peanuts and lately had a gluttonous appetite for watermelon.

But that was all right. He'd buy a mound of watermelons if it would cheer Shelby. For nine months, she had been a real trouper, through the backaches, the swollen feet and the weight gain. However, their baby was a week overdue and Nelson had been the victim of his wife's sulky, temperamental mood swings. It was why he'd suggested today's shopping spree, hoping to see a return of the happy smile that, until this week, had graced her face. His idea had worked, too. Shelby had caught credit-card fever and when the bills came, he'd gladly pay them.

Shelby smiled, removed a small, plastic hanger and Nelson's smile faded when she held up the footed romper. "Baby, what do think about this?"

Nelson glanced at the outfit and sent his scowl out the window of the exclusive baby boutique and into the warm June sunshine.

"Nels! What do you think?" Nelson looked at her and folded his arms over his chest.

"It's pink." Shelby sighed impatiently. "I know it's pink. What I want to know is, do you like it?"

"It's pink and it has flowers allover it."

Shelby placed her hand on what used to be her waist and tapped her foot, wishing she had something with which to bean her husband upside his stubborn head. "And what's wrong with pink and flowers?"

Nelson's frown deepened. "Pink is for girls and you're not going to dress my son like a girl."

"Don't you think it's time to drop this macho attitude, Nelson? Things have changed since you were a baby. Today, it is perfectly acceptable for boys to wear pink."

Nelson snorted. "If I listened to you, the next thing you'd tell me is that it's perfectly acceptable to put bows and ribbons in my son's hair. No pink!" He leaned over the basket and began removing Shelby's other selections. "And no lavender and no flowers or prissy little hearts, diamonds, or butterflies." He turned to a rack of clothes behind him and held up a navy blue and green outfit. "Do you see this, Shel? Trucks! And here's one with baseball bats and gloves. This is where you should be looking, not that rack this store is trying to pass off as unisex clothing. We are having a male child, Shelby Reeves. If I let you dress my baby in that pink, flowered getup, my son won't know he's supposed to be a boy. No pink!"

Shelby watched the maroon polo shirt covering his chest heave with his breathing. When the ultrasound revealed three months earlier that their baby was a boy, Nelson had whooped for joy. That night, he'd demanded his dollar and the next day had come home loaded down with boxes and bags. After making her promise not to enter the room until he finished, he'd gone directly to the nursery. A week later, he'd led her up the stairs and opened the door.

In an amazed daze, Shelby spun in a slow circle taking in the room. Nelson had stripped the nursery walls of the pastel blue, yellow and aqua wallpaper she'd hung the month before. In its place, he had painted the bottom half of the walls to depict a green grassy field, complete with baseball diamond. The top of the walls and the ceiling sported a blue sky with white fluffy clouds and a five-inch strip with sports symbols separating the two areas. The white furnishings he'd decided to keep, but the bedding, lamp shades, wall hangings and other accessories had all been changed, replaced by primary colors of red, blue and green. The appliqués were pictures of things that, in his opinion, a male child should have around him.

Shelby had wanted to be angry with Nelson, but he'd done such a good job and wanted her approval so badly that she'd hugged him and told him that she liked it. And truthfully, she did.

Until now, Nelson had been tolerant of the clothes she'd chosen for their child. She knew he didn't like some of the outfits, but since he hadn't said anything, Shelby had put them in the basket. She looked at Nelson from beneath her lashes and her lips began to twitch. When it came to his son, her husband was a male chauvinist. Shelby couldn't hold back the giggles. The giggles soon turned to full-fledged laughter.

"Why are you laughing at me?"

"Be-be-because." Shelby leaned against the table, holding her stomach, incapable of talking over the loud sounds of her merriment.

Nelson gave her a withering glance and stalked away to another rack of clothing. She watched him go, laughing so hard she almost tipped over.

Shelby suddenly grabbed her stomach and tried to callout to Nelson. "Nels?" Pain muted the volume of her voice.

Across the store, Nelson couldn't hear her and Shelby knew she couldn't call any louder. She eased herself to the floor, parting her lips to inhale and exhale air. She tried not to panic, but she was going into labor and she couldn't get her husband's attention. She didn't want to have her baby in the middle of a store.

Shelby held her stomach in her hands, rocked forward and tried to concentrate on the breathing exercises she'd .learned in Lamaze class.

"What are you doing down there?"

Shelby tilted her head and panted at the blue jeans-clad legs in front of her face. "Nelson…the baby…is coming."

Nelson heard the shallow breaths and hunched down, immediately in sync with what was going on. Shelby's labor had started and she was about to lose it. He grabbed her hands and pulled a stopwatch from his pocket. "Sweetness, listen to me. Everything will be okay. Just don't panic, Shel. All right?" Shelby closed her eyes and nodded. "Sweetness, we need to time the contractions. Remember?" Nelson kept his voice strong, hushed and low. It was time to have their baby and he couldn't let Shelby see how scared he was. There was no telling what would happen if she did. He focused on her eyes, willing Shelby to trust him.

Inside, his nerve endings crackled and popped, his muscles turned watery and his mind got lost in the wind tunnel in his head. *My son's coming,* Nelson thought, right before his brain liquefied. Barely perceptible puffs left his lips as Nelson started panting right along with Shelby. He stopped, somewhat confused, when he heard a voice he knew wasn't his conversing with Shelby, and became even more confounded when he realized that it was his voice.

"You let me know when the next pain hits," he told her, "and I'll start the watch." Shelby gripped his fingers and a tear splashed on the back of his hand. "I don't…want to…" Shelby stopped to catch her breath. "I don't want to have our baby…here."

Knowing he had to get it together before their crisis turned into a major fiasco, Nelson held her face in his palms. His eyes begged Shelby to calm down and trust that he would make everything all right.

"You will not have our baby in this store." He sat on floor beside her. "That's a promise." He took Shelby in his arms, then helped her down so that her head lay in his lap. Nelson stared at the watch while stroking her hair and wondered how he could be so calm in the face of what might very well become a catastrophe.

"Now don't you forget to let me know when the next contraction hits and while we're waiting we'll breathe together. Come on now, little woman. Do it with me. Breathe in," Nelson said, filling his lungs with air, "and out."

Fifteen minutes later, Shelby wobbled to an upright position. "I think it's okay, Nelson. I don't think I'm in labor."

"We're going to stay right here until we're sure. So do me a huge favor, Shelby Reeves, and lay down and breathe."

"It's been a long time, Nelson. How many minutes have passed?" "Fifteen. But that doesn't mean anything. The pains can start again any time now." Nelson looked up from the watch when Shelby began trying to rise from the floor. "What are you doing, Shelby? You're in labor."

She drew in a breath of fortitude and said, "It's been too long, Nels. I think it was false labor. Come on, baby. Let's go home."

Nelson put the watch in his pocket. He rose and helped Shelby to her feet. "Are you sure? About the false labor, I mean?"

"I think so. We read about it in the book and the topic was covered in our Lamaze class."

Nelson curved his arm around her and started for the exit. "Shel, you were great back there."

"You were, too. I guess those Lamaze classes really work, huh?"

"Yep. Some of the best money we ever spent."

"Sir!" A saleslady ran toward them. Nelson and Shelby stopped. "Here are your bags." Thinly penciled brows rose in question. "I guess your wife didn't see anything she liked?"

Nelson looked down at Shelby. "Can you wait here for me, Shel. I'll just be a minute."

Later that night, Shelby moved around the nursery putting away the purchases she had made for the baby earlier that day.

When she picked up the pile of clothes Nelson had bought at the baby boutique, Shelby smiled. Everything she wanted was there. Everything that is, except the pink, flowered romper.

"Come on, sweetness. You can do this. I know it hurts, Shel. If I could lie in that bed for you, you know I would, but we're almost there, sweetness."

Shelby turned pain-glazed eyes toward her husband. "Just shut the hell up, Nelson Reeves. I'm tired of hearing your voice. What do you know about it anyway? You're not the one lying in this bed trying to pass a bowling ball between your legs."

Nelson pressed his lips together and counted to twenty in an effort to maintain his patience. Their Lamaze teacher had told him to expect this, but Shelby was pushing it. She'd been insulting him all day and he only wantedto help her.

"Shel, I don't feel it's necessary for you to speak to me this way. I'm trying to help you." He reachedout his hand to rub Shelby's stomach.

She slapped his hand away. "Did I ask for your help? You're the reason I'm here in the first damn place."

Nelson raised his hand again, then let it drop when he saw Shelby's lethal glare. "Don't you dare touch me, Nelson Lamar Reeves!"

Nelson expelled a deep breath and rubbed his tired eyes. This was nothing like yesterday. At the store, when they'd thought Shelby was in labor, they had worked together as a team. Shelby had awakened at two in morning, and this time, it was the real thing. Shelby had been in labor for over thirteen hours and Nelson was just about at his wit's end. How much longer was this going to take, he wondered. He really, really needed to know because he wasn't sure how many more of his wife's insults he could handle.

*Those damn Lamaze classes were a waste of good money,* Nelson thought. Shelby wouldn't cooperate and she sure as hell wasn't listening to him. Part of the reason was that she had almost dilated to ten centimeters and the nurses had cut off her pain medicine. The other part Nelson didn't want to think about, considering it had to do with him.

He pinched the bridge of his nose and since Shelby wouldn't let him coach her, Nelson coached himself. *Okay, Reeves. You have to remember that this woman doesn't mean any of the things she's saying to you. Shel loves you and you love her. One day, you'll both look back on this experience and laugh.*

As Nelson said these things to himself, he knew they would one day look back on the experience, but he was pretty sure he wouldn't be laughing.

The baby's heart monitor emitted a long, loud beep and Nelson jumped to his feet as two nurses entered the room. Breathing heavily, he watched them help Shelby turn in the bed. He couldn't stop the tears from stinging his eyes when he saw the terror on Shelby's face.

"I'm here, Shelby," Nelson whispered. "Sweetness, I'm right here."

"It's okay, Mrs. Reeves. The baby got tired of lying on that side. But it's all right now and it shouldn't be too much longer."

The nurses left the room and Nelson rushed to the bed. He put his arms around as much of Shelby as he could.

"I love you, Shel."

"I love you, too, Nelson."

Three hours later, Nelson looked up from the tiny bundle in his arms and smiled at his wife. His Shelby had done well. Nelson Lamar Reeves III was seven pounds and twenty-one inches of perfection, and Nelson wanted to shout his happiness from the rooftop. His beautiful wife and little man were doing fine and everything they'd gone through was worth it. Lamar, as they'd decided to call their son, bore a striking resemblance to his darkly handsome, white-haired grandfather. Nelson looked at his father-in-law and smiled.

"Shel did good, didn't she, Poppy?"

Martin replaced the card he'd been reading in the green-stemmed holder stuck in the large vase holding two dozen pink roses from Nelson. Flowers and plants from friends and work associates filled the room. "I couldn't agree with you more, son. My first grandchild already resides in a place in my heart along with the two of you. And as much as I love Lamar, I'd like to take this opportunity to make the two of you aware of my expectations for a couple more just like him. I'd also like to put in my request for a grand-daughter next time. Now, today is the seventh of June. If we give Shelby until August, I believe I can have my grand-daughter in just under a year. What do you think, son?"

"I think that now that we've finally gotten it right, it should be a cinch to fill that request. Right, Shel?"

"I think the two of you should grant me a moment's rest and time to enjoy my firstborn before asking for additions."

"Okay, Shel, A moment's rest, then we'll start working on that sister for Lamar," Nelson said with a chuckle. He kept a firm arm around his son as he rose from the rocking chair and moved to the bed. Nelson passed the sleeping baby to Shelby and sat down beside her.

Shelby kissed her baby's cheek and cuddled him close. "Oh, Nels. Look at him. Lamar's the most gorgeous baby ever born and you and I made him. Isn't it wonderful?"

Nelson looked down at his family. "Yes, Shel. It's wonderful."

*September…*

"Mooom-my."

The teeny hand making the delicate taps on her face woke Shelby and she smiled, but didn't open her eyes.

"Mooom-my. Wake up."

Shelby hummed a groan. "Go back to bed, my little darling. Mommy needs to sleep." She pulled the covers over her head.

The covers lifted and the taps on her face continued. "Mommy, I'm hungry."

Shelby frowned in mock irritation. "You're always hungry, Lamar. Tell your daddy to feed you."

Nelson had a hard time holding back his laughter as he tried to keep his deep voice sounding light and childlike. "If you don't wake up right now, Mommy, I'll tell Daddy and he won't be very happy with you. Besides, Daddy doesn't have any milk."

Shelby opened her eyes. "Well, that's true, little man. So, I guess it's me that will have to feed you." She sat up and arranged three pillows behind her back.

Nelson kissed her on the nose and laid Lamar in her arms. "Good morning, sweetness."

"Good morning, baby."

"How does my little woman feel this morning?"

Shelby gave Nelson a stern look. "Now don't you get started, too. I can only take care of one hunger at a time."

Nelson slid down in the bed and propped his head on his hand, watching as Shelby settled his son at her breast to nurse. Lamar latched on immediately and suckled greedily. Thoroughly fascinated, Nelson observed the feeding process. It had become his favorite hobby and the wonders of Shelby's body still amazed him.

His son was healthy and strong, largely due to the milk produced especially for him by his mother's body. Shelby's milk hadn't come in right away and for a week he'd gotten to feed Lamar from the bottle. As much as he had loved the experience, Nelson knew it wasn't quite the same.

"I must have really been out of it because I didn't hear Lamar this morning," Shelby said, smoothing a knuckle over her son's soft cheek.

"That's because I got him about thirty minutes early." "Nelson, how will we ever get this child on a schedule if you keep interrupting his sleep?"

"I know. But I didn't wake him this morning, Shel. Honest. Lamar didn't wake up when I brought him into our bed and he was asleep until ten minutes ago. We changed his diaper, then came and woke you."

The story sounded credible. However, Shelby wasn't sure she bought the tale. Nelson had taken to being a father like a duck to water. Officially, he was into the tenth week of a twelve-week maternity leave, although he did go to the office for a few hours each morning. At home, Nelson did everything and had relegated Shelby to the position of baby dining car, which meant she got an awful lot of rest. She had come to depend on Nelson and wasn't sure what either of them would do when he went back to work full-time.

No matter what Nelson was doing, he kept his son nearby. In the kitchen, Lamar sat on the counter, securely strapped in his rocking seat, as Nelson prepared meals and talked nonstop. They kept up their conversations through bath time, diaper changing, house cleaning and laundry. When he wasn't busy, Nelson sat for hours playing with and talking to his son. They had a bond so strong that when Lamar heard Nelson's voice, he wiggled and bumped in her arms until his father took him.

At bedtime, they again allowed Shelby into the male circle. While she nursed Lamar, Nelson read from one of the many storybooks he'd bought before his son's birth. Her private time with her son came during the two o'clock feeding. After nursing Lamar, she rocked and sang to her baby until he drifted off to sleep, then crept silently back to bed and snuggled up against her husband.

As a friend, lover, husband and father, Shelby knew that she couldn't have gotten a better man than Nelson Lamar Reeves, Jr. And after everything he did to ensure her happiness, he deserved to sleep through the night.

She leaned forward for Nelson's kiss, then he rose from the bed and pulled on his robe. "Seriously, Shel. What do you want for breakfast?"

"I don't know." Shelby switched Lamar to her other breast. "I'm really hungry though." "How about pancakes? Or I could make some bacon, eggs and toast?"

The offer of pancakes made her mouth water, but Shelby shook her head. When Nelson made pancakes, the mess he made in the kitchen was horrendous, and she knew he had plans to go to the office. "I'll take the bacon and eggs. They won't be as much trouble."

Nelson's gaze glowed with love. "Nothing in this world is too much trouble for you or for my son."

# CHAPTER ELEVEN

Nelson shut down his memories and rose from the couch. As much as he wished it, remembering would not bring back his son. And his wife remained upstairs and away from him. That, however, he could do something about, but later. He had things to do and the sharp bite of Shelby's rejection hadn't quite worn off. His hand lifted to his chest when something new squeezed his heart. Loneliness, he thought, trying to identify the emotion. Loneliness, he knew about. It had been his constant companion during his year away from Shelby. This was different, though, and more painful because with Shelby in the house he wasn't alone; yet Nelson had never felt more alone in his life.

Agitated, he went to the large picture window, cupped his hands behind his back and stared through the frosted pane at the raging blizzard. A fierce and unforgiving wind gave no deference to the mighty blue spruce pines standing guard in his yard. Its funneled blast bent their tops as if they were no sturdier than a toothpick. Aspen tree branches, crusted with ice, quaked in the blustering gales and swirling expanse of ivory flakes falling from a dark and nebulous sky.

Trembling with guilt, Nelson watched the tempestuous storm sweep the land and tried to direct the thought he could not stop. After the death of their son, he had treated his wife horribly. He had tried to be a pillar of strength and instead of turning to Shelby for comfort, he had used his job as solace for his grief. But the hurt hadn't gone away and his pain had turned into a black anger that he'd directed at Shelby, the doctors, the world and even God for taking his son away.

He remembered the weeks Shelby had automatically risen for Lamar's two o'clock feeding and the flowers she brought home every day to place at his tombstone the next morning. He remembered the many times she'd asked him to go with her and how he had refused, unable to make himself visit the place where his son's body lay cold and decaying in the earth. The thing that stuck most in his mind was that Shelby had never cried. Somehow, she had continued to function: going to her boutique, creating new designs, and even trying to take care of him. That she could do that when he could barely hold himself together had made him the angriest of all. If only he'd gotten up that night, maybe his son would still be alive. If Shelby had only called him sooner, he might have been able to do something. If only—If, if, if—

Nelson sighed in dejection and turned from the window. His eyes slowly roved the room and the cardboard boxes, a stark and visual reminder of all that had happened between them. "Too little, too late." The phrase became a chant that marched across his brain, its accusatory tone growing louder with each replay. Joined by remorse, the resulting negative energy clamored at his body, seeking a physical outlet. Nelson moved back to the tree and forced himself to begin decorating its branches.

He knew how badly he'd hurt Shelby, but emotionally crippled by his son's death, he hadn't realized the extent of the damage he'd done to his marriage until it was too late.

After all he'd been through, Nelson hadn't been prepared to lose his wife, too. He hadn't thought he could. Deeply embedded in his soul, past the guilt, past the blame, past the anger, past the pain, Nelson had expected Shelby to wait for him. He swiped his eyes when tears blurred his vision and continued decorating the tree. He was the man, and a man didn't shift the blame when he was clearly in the wrong. All he needed was time with Shelby to fix the wrong, and in seizing the moment, Nelson planned to win back everything that had once belonged to him. He stepped back and viewed his handiwork. It bothered him that the tree fell far below his usual standards, but it would have to do, and he had to decorate the rest of the room.

Upstairs, Shelby tucked away her memories and propped a large, square pillow behind her back. She pulled another into her lap and crossed her feet at the ankles. By all appearances, she seemed to be in calm reflection. However, those who knew her well would know how deeply upset she was and that the bright sparks in her eyes meant that she wasn't far from losing the tenuous hold she had on her emotions. Even if she had successfully hidden her feelings from him, she knew that Nelson would not leave. He'd sit downstairs and doggedly wait her out for as long as it took. As tired as she was, mentally, physically and spiritually, Shelby knew there was no way she could make him go away. She was also honest enough to admit that his being in the house, while disheartening, also had a calming effect as if a broken link had been soldered and fixed.

Did she really want Nelson to go? The question came unbidden and Shelby leaned her head back, closed her eyes and tried to clear the turmoil from her mind by taking deep, calming breaths. The technique didn't work. Nelson's impassioned plea had touched Shelby, and in a way that provided a balm to the wound she had carried since she'd packed her bags and left him. But it hadn't diminished the pain of losing her son or lessened the hurt Nelson's rejection had caused. After the funeral, Nelson had ignored her and until recently had not touched her since the night their son died.

Shelby hadn't cared about the sex. The daze she'd walked in since that horrible night had yet to lift, and she had had enough to deal with trying to get through the day without going insane. But she had cared that Nelson had totally withdrawn from her and that she couldn't tell her husband how much she needed him. It was not supposed to be that way between them. Nelson had promised to love her for always and when they had needed to draw on the strength of that love and comfort each other through the worst tragedy imaginable, his love had vanished.

And since she hadn't been able to talk to her husband, she'd gone to the only place where she could find comfort: the cemetery where she sat and talked to her baby. Only then had she been able to go to the boutique and numbly move through another twenty-four hours. She had tried to get Nelson to go with her on her daily visits. Pulling weeds and the other little maintenance things she did while talking to her baby helped her get through the day. He flatly refused to go, so she'd stopped asking and he'd rebuffed every other attempt she made to comfort him. Since Nelson wouldn't allow her to help him, she had basically left her husband alone and had started working late hours at the boutique to escape his silent wrath.

Sometimes Shelby felt as though Nelson blamed her for their son's death. She blamed herself, so maybe he was right. If only she had been a better mother. If only she had gotten up sooner, she could have done something to help her baby. If only—If, if, if—The thoughts attacked her every single day.

Shelby lifted her head and rubbed her eyes. Wearily, she rose from the bed and went into the bathroom to splash cold water on her face. She patted herself dry and thought about the son she'd had for only a short while.

After the autopsy, Lamar's doctor had tried to speak to them. As soon as he'd pronounced the diagnosis as SIDS— no known cause of death, Nelson had leaped from his chair and left the room. She had apologized to the doctor and followed her husband. Neither had gone back.

SIDS: Sudden Infant Death Syndrome.

As far as Shelby was concerned, it was just their way of saying that despite all their knowledge and the advances in medicine and medical technology, they had no idea what had killed her son. And she ached for her baby; her arms ached to hold Lamar. She wanted to rock him, sing lullabies to him and feel the soft downiness of his skin next to hers. Shelby knew she'd never hold Lamar in her arms again, and in leaving Nelson she had vowed to live without love. But havoc had rained within her in the moments when their eyes had met and held. She'd wanted to pretend that nothing had changed between them. She'd wanted to sink herself into the warm, protective circle of Nelson's arms and let him make everything the way it used to be.

Shaking her head sadly, her eyes sought his picture on the dresser. Nothing on this earth could change what had happened to them, and running away had only forced her to relive the everlasting anguish of losing her son and her husband. Still, the familiar tug was there and Shelby tried to fight her feelings. It was like swimming upstream against a flood and she gave up the fight, knowing there was no way for her to win. She loved Nelson, pure and simple, and he'd finally said the things she'd waited so many long and silent months to hear before she'd lost faith in him and gone on with her life.

How could she give Nelson another chance when just his being in the house was almost more than she could handle? If their love wasn't strong enough to see them through the crisis of their son's death, how long would it be before something else happened and Nelson broke her heart again? If she believed again, how long would it take for her heart to heal a second time?

Her jewelry box sat beside Nelson's picture and the walnut case drew her eyes. Shelby rose from the bed. At the dresser, she opened her jewelry box, removed her engagement ring and held it in her hand.

The stone weighed a mere half-carat, but what the ring represented, not the size of the stone, mattered much more to Shelby. Lifting her head, she stared at her reflection in the mirror.

The woman staring back at her bore the same face as the one she'd seen this morning and yet she was different. The woman in the mirror hadn't forgotten the good times she'd shared with her husband. She hadn't forgotten how exciting it was to be with Nelson or how happy being with him made her. She also knew that he hadn't thought twice about dressing in that Santa suit and driving out to see her.

Looking down, the flash of Nelson's diamond was so overpowering that, without thought of what she was doing, Shelby placed her wedding set on her finger. As soon as she slid the rings in place, the calming influence she'd sought earlier enveloped her. Her eyes glowed as she stared at her hand. The rings felt right and she felt stronger; it was time to stop hiding in her bedroom. It was time to go down and face Nelson Reeves. Her thoughts turned pensive. This didn't have to be a confrontation. She wanted to see Nelson and he wanted to give her Christmas. If they both tried, maybe it was possible to set aside their differences and enjoy each other's company for one last time. One night of happiness wasn't too much to ask, was it? And with that thought, Shelby crossed the bedroom and stepped into her closet.

Downstairs Nelson had been busy and now paced the floor. He stopped and looked toward the archway. If this was going to work, they at least needed to be in the same room. Nelson headed for the door. He was just about to place his foot on the step when he looked up and found Shelby staring down at him. She was wearing rose lounging pajamas, her favorite color and his when she wore it because of the things it did to him. He saw the tentative smile she gave him and wondered if Shelby remembered.

Looking at her, Nelson thought that he caught a glimpse of the love she'd once had for him. It was only a hint of a moment and passed so quickly Nelson wasn't sure he'd seen it at all. Probably his imagination working overtime, showing him something he so desperately wanted to see. Then again, who could say for sure? Nelson made quick work of rearranging his features into what he hoped Shelby read as placidity.

"I was coming up to make sure you were okay, Shel,' he said, trying to keep his voice even, wondering if his pounding heart sounded as loud to her as it did to him.

She moved to the top of the first stair. She knew what she was doing to Nelson and it pleased her. The silk pajamas she wore by design, and they were having the desired effect. His attempt to hide his reaction was admirable, though uselessly humorous; Shelby didn't let it show. Nelson was reacting to her as a woman and after so long, how good it felt to know that she could still turn a man's head, even if that man was Nelson.

Shelby descended the steps and Nelson kept his gaze glued to her swaying hips. Shelby's effect on him had always been immediate and apparent, but he had to be discreet until Shelby gave him permission to lose himself in her again. They would come together, and when they did, there would be no regrets and no accusations. When they made love, Shelby would want him just as much as he wanted her.

At the bottom, he held out his hand. Shelby placed her small one in his and joy flirted with Nelson's heart. Her touch, light, warm and soft as a sun-kissed wind, recklessly melded inside him as Nelson led Shelby into the living room. He stood back, watching as she slowly traipsed the room.

Red berries clung to the large boughs of evergreen looping the fireplace mantle. Two large poinsettias flanked each end, and in the center of the shelf sat a small nativity scene. The table in front of the couch held a scented, red candle circled by a green holly wreath, and a figurine of a black Santa surrounded by children reaching for his bag of goodies stood next to it. More poinsettias garnished the side tables, and the lights he'd strung around the doors and windows blinked on and off in a colorful array.

From the archway, Nelson's gaze followed Shelby, his mind playing with the thought that maybe the love he'd seen in her eyes had been real. Then nervousness took over. He should have gotten more decorations. He should have done more to make the room look like Christmases past. Nelson watched as Shelby stopped to inspect the tree and worry clamped his jaw tight. What was she thinking? Why didn't she say something?

"Too little, too late." No, Nelson thought. His effort might be sadly lacking, but it was not too late. He just needed to know what she thought about the room even if only to say that she hated the tree, she hated the room and she hated him.

Nelson's head swam with that last thought. Never before had he thought that Shelby might hate him for what he'd done to them. Anger, he'd expected, even rejection. Why hadn't it occurred to him that the only thing Shelby could feel for him now was—*Stop!* The word blared as a warning inside in his head. Maybe she didn't wait for him because she—*Stop!* It was an atrocious thought, one he didn't want, and one counterproductive to what he needed to do and feel for Shelby.

Imprisoned by guilt, Nelson found that he couldn't let it go or erase the implication that it might be true.

His body jerked, and feeling the sharp, jagged pokes of his conscience, Nelson battled valiantly to keep his head. He couldn't let guilt take away his dream of being with his wife again. Drawn by the attraction he'd never been able to manage, Nelson stepped closer, anxiously, instinctively seeking exoneration in Shelby's nearness. What he got was the light scent of her perfume teasing his nose and a reminder of the sleepless nights and erotic dreams that had plagued him every day of their separation.

Standing so close, the sight and smell of Shelby only served to spark the perpetual desire that had smoldered too long unattended. A mere look would never satisfy his craving to fill his hands and body with hers. Nelson wanted to put his arm around her waist, but knew one touch and spark would burst into flame. He restrained himself and instead inhaled deeply, letting her familiar smell grant an absolution, of sorts, that relieved him of his burden…at least for one night.

He glanced around the room again. The decorations, while adding a festive air, hadn't done much to remove the sterile aura and Nelson felt the need to apologize. "I'm sorry, Shel, but this is the best I could do at the last minute."

Shelby turned to him. "What about the top, Nelson? We need something, don't you think?"

Nelson moved to his green sack. He reached inside and brought out a white box. "I've got that covered, too." He handed the box to her.

Shelby lifted the lid. A white angel lay nestled inside the folds of glittering silver paper. The figurine was pretty, but she couldn't work up the same feeling that she'd had for their angel.

Nelson felt her disappointment and knew she was thinking about their angel, the one he'd given to her when they'd celebrated their first Christmas as a married couple. But the ornament had been broken when they moved into the house. He had scoured the mall looking for another and hadn't found one that even came close to what they'd had. He removed the box from her hands, took out the figurine and tried to make light of the moment. "I know it's not our angel, Shel. But look, she has silky hair and a porcelain face just like ours and her dress is…"

"Nels, don't," Shelby whispered. She moved to stand by the fireplace. "It's not like ours. It could never be like ours. Our angel was special and nothing will ever replace it."

"Shel, I tried to find another, but I couldn't. Please don't be upset. It's Christmas Eve and I want you to be happy. So tell me what to do, sweetness. Tell me how to make you happy."

The shutter keeping him out slammed closed before Shelby turned to stare into the fire. Nelson saw her body sag and his heart beat with regret. His request had been unfair and poorly timed. It was too soon for Shelby to answer that question. The chasm in their relationship was much too wide for him to expect a tree and a few baubles to make a difference. Nelson crossed to Shelby. He placed his hands in his pockets, knowing that the last thing she wanted was for him to touch her.

"Sweetness, it's awkward between us, isn't it?" He smiled a little smile. "You know something, Shel? I never thought I'd ever feel clumsy and inept with you again. You were my baby, my beautiful baby and now I don't even know what to say to make you feel better."

"Why did you come?" Her question sounded as frail and weary as Shelby felt.

Nelson's reasons were clear in his mind. He'd come because he'd finally listened to his messages. He'd come because this was the last chance he'd have to be with Shelby alone, and he'd come because he wanted, so badly, for his wife to forgive him and take him back. They were selfish reasons and not ones to give Shelby. Their relationship had always been honest and Nelson knew he had to rely on that honesty now. "I came because I need you, Shel, and thought…that you might need me, too."

The tears only Nelson had the power to make fall came. Shelby furtively wiped them away. Despite what she'd felt earlier, she knew it was time to take a stand. If she didn't, Nelson would open her up and expose her for what she really was: a fraud.

Shelby stepped away from him, her gaze on the yellow-blue flames. "You shouldn't be here, Nelson."

"But I want to be here, Shelby."

"Oh. So this is all about you, huh?"

"No, Shelby. This is about love, our love. And a chance that maybe we can salvage what we once had and start again."

Her fatigued state, the emotional ups and downs of the last few hours and days and Nelson's being there all fell like lead to the pit of her stomach. Backed into a corner, Shelby did the only thing she could do. She lost it.

"Love! Why is that the only thing that concerns anyone? What in the hell is so all-fired important about love anyway? You and I were in love; did it help us?" Shelby went on to answer her own question. "No! When I needed you and your love, you weren't here. So what do you want now, Nelson? Oh, that's right. You want to start over. Well, we can't start over, because it is over. I might love you, Nelson Reeves, but I certainly don't need you! And since I didn't invite you here, you can leave the same way you came in."

Nelson watched Shelby rant and rave, and heard only one thing: she loved him. Everything else she said was immaterial. He started to approach her and stopped when he saw the daggers shooting at him. "Listen to yourself, sweetness."

"Don't call me that."

She saw the effect of her words before he quickly concealed the damage. Well, he'd hurt her plenty of times. It was only fair that she strike back for once.

Nelson felt a sense of impending doom before he remembered that Shelby did love him, and knowing that made all the difference in the world. "You have a right to be angry and I won't try to convince you otherwise, Shel. However, let's try and set our differences aside and just enjoy the evening. Okay?"

After her little blow up, Shelby's anger had already deflated. She hadn't meant to get so angry, and certainly hadn't meant to let Nelson know that he still claimed her heart. Now that he knew, he would never give up. When she didn't answer, he let the matter drop. After barging in on her this evening, he was still here, and that would have to be enough. Patience, he counseled himself, convinced now that he could bring her around.

Shelby looked at the angel, then as if resigned to the inevitable, she held out her hand. Nelson looked into her face and saw a blank page. Her face was devoid of emotion: no joy, no happiness, no sadness, nothing.

Whatever she felt, she wouldn't show him, not that she needed to. Everything she felt, he felt in spades. He harnessed his need to hold her close and whisper that he would make everything right again and placed the angel in her palm.

Shelby crossed to the tree and looked over her shoulder. "Will you help me put it on top?"

Stoically, Nelson moved forward, reminding himself that they would have to take the evening one step at a time. Reaching her, he placed his hands on Shelby's waist and lifted her up. She was halfway up when she suddenly looked down. "Nelson! Put me down."

He set Shelby on her feet and watched her run from the room. Nelson didn't move, wondering what had happened in a split second to put elation in her voice. When she called, he followed her path. All he could see when he reached the top of the stairs was the bottom half of her legs and bare feet with pink toenails.

Protectively, his hands reached out to steady the attic ladder. "Shelby, what are you doing?"

"Wait a sec, Nelson," she said, her voice muffled. "There it is!" Shelby looked down, excitement lighting her face. "It's still here, baby."

"What, Shel? What are you seeing up there? Oh, never mind. Get down and let me see."

Shelby climbed down and Nelson went up. He peered around the attic. "Shelby, there isn't a thing up in this attic." Then he saw the box. Nelson climbed the rest of the steps. Shelby was almost skipping in place when he descended again. She took the box and hurried down the stairs. Nelson closed the attic and followed. By the time he got to the living room, she had the box halfway unpacked. He stood back and watched her. Each time she unwrapped one of their ornaments, she looked up at him and said, "Remember?"

Nelson nodded, unable to speak. When the box was empty there would be twenty ornaments, reminders of past Christmas years. It was Shelby's idea that they exchange ornaments each Christmas. She had wanted to start a family tradition and when their children reached adulthood, had planned to divide the ornaments equally and encourage them to continue the ritual within their own families. It had all started with his first ornament to her: the black angel. The death of their son and the resulting separation had caused them to miss the practice for two years, but he didn't plan to miss any more. Deciding he had to do something, Nelson walked to the tree and began pulling off the new ornaments.

Shelby looked up. "You're going to have to leave some of those on, baby. We've never had such a large tree and we don't have enough to cover the whole thing. But leave the new stuff on the back and we'll hang ours on the front."

*Ours!* Nelson savored the word. He glanced over his shoulder and his hand froze in midair; his eyes fused on her hand and his rings. He tried to remember if Shelby had been wearing her wedding set when he'd come into the house and clearly recalled that she hadn't worn anything on her finger. With hope shining in his eyes, Nelson turned back to the tree. Things were progressing nicely.

He heard Shelby get up from the floor and watched her walk to his side. Then together they hung the memories of their Christmases on the tree. When it was time to place the angel on top, Nelson again lifted Shelby in the air. This time when he set her down, he did place his arm around her waist, and for a few minutes they stood together staring at the tree.

Shelby broke contact first. She moved from his arm to the window. There were two reasons she felt the need to move. One, Nelson was making her feel things she hadn't felt in a very long time, and two, Nelson lived in Englewood and the drive from Evergreen would be long and strenuous. If they shut down the highway, he'd have to make his way home using side streets. If he didn't leave now there was the distinct possibility that he'd have to stay right where he was. The thought of spending the entire night with Nelson in the house was so unnerving, Shelby wrapped her arms around her body to halt the shivers moving up and down her spine.

"The snow's coming down a lot faster now, Nelson, and it's dark. This has been fun and I thank you for the tree, but you have a long drive back to your place. Maybe you should think about making a move."

Nelson watched her fidget and debated how to respond. Shelby probably had a genuine concern for his welfare, but he felt sure it was his presence that caused her jitters. "Don't worry about it, Shel. I drove the Bronco up here and the monster can get through almost anything."

"But Nelson…"

"Don't worry, Shelby. If I do get stuck, I've always got the blanket in the back." One of his favorite memories was the day she'd mastered her fear of heights and walked out onto the bridge suspended 1,053 feet above the Royal Gorge. Following the natural high of that feat, they'd sat at a picnic and recklessly made love in full view of the highway using the blanket as a shield. He could tell by her face that Shelby had recalled their little roadside escapade, just as he'd meant her to.

# CHAPTER TWELVE

Shelby cleared her throat and placed nervous hands in her pockets. They were talking about something, but for the love of her, she couldn't remember what. She searched her mind, then lifted her eyes to Nelson, hoping to find a clue, stepping back when sexuality, raw and powerful, met her gaze. She shifted her feet and looked away, her heart and body palpitating with heat. Somehow she had to stop this or before she knew it, she'd wind up in Nelson's arms.

"I was just thinking...well, you know how erratic the weather is this time of the year. Sometimes, it looks like we'll be dumped on and we get a flurry, then at other times when we don't expect snow at all, we have a blizzard. I think the weather reports are right this time and we're going to get a lot of snow." Shelby knew she was rambling and wandering the room, but couldn't make herself shut up or stand still. And she studiously avoided looking at Nelson. She walked over to the stereo. "Maybe we should listen to the radio. That way we can hear the weather reports and if it sounds like—"

Nelson cloaked his arms around Shelby and pulled her back against his body. He pressed the evidence of his desire into her backside and touched his lips to the skin on her neck. Shelby shivered uncontrollably. Nelson kissed the tip of her ear and she gripped his arms.

"Nelson, please don't."

He tightened his hold on her body and pressed himself more firmly into her until she leaned back against him. "I love you, Shel. I'll always love you," he said, kissing the top of her head before pressing his cheek down into the curls.

Shelby turned her head to speak and Nelson captured her mouth beneath his. The tip of his tongue moved in sensualistic play over the seam of her lips in a persuasive request for entrance. She granted a tiny crevice and Nelson knew if he wanted to kiss her properly, he would have to work for it. He pulled away and started again, covering Shelby's face with warm, tender kisses until he reached her mouth and engaged in an arousing battle of wills. In Nelson's arms, Shelby felt herself float away. She wanted this kiss, and surrendering to her needs, she leaned into Nelson's body and let his fiery passion begin melting the ice that had enclosed her heart the day he'd stopped loving her. She opened her mouth and his tongue dove inside to reacquaint itself with the splendor of kissing his wife. Having gotten that far, Nelson's hands stroked her arms, then came around her again to cup Shelby's breasts. Moaning, she twisted her body to face him, their mouths never separating. Her arms came up to encircle his neck and Nelson deepened the kiss.

Their mouths parted and, breathing raggedly, Nelson held Shelby's head against his chest. He just needed a few minutes to calm himself He hadn't meant to kiss her, not yet anyway. But hearing her sweet voice, seeing the way the rose pajamas contoured her body and memories of their lovemaking had all congealed in a powerful push that had urged him forward. Shelby aroused him like no other woman, but it was more than that. The first time he saw Shelby, he had known she was his destiny. She could divorce him a million times, but it wouldn't change the fact that they were meant to be.

Spoiled? Yes, she was and he loved spoiling her.

Stubborn? No question. They had both received a double dose of that particular trait. In one way it was good because their shared tenacity had helped them achieve their goals; the other way Nelson preferred to leave alone for the moment. And though Shelby could pout with the best of them, she wasn't selfish and generously gave of her time and herself While she had enjoyed doing things with him, she had her own interests, her own pursuits and her own identity. Shelby was a woman of substance, and Nelson knew that loving her was the easiest thing he'd done in his life. Conversely, losing her had been the hardest.

Nelson held Shelby for a few seconds more, then gently set her away from him. He had to come up with something for them to do, because if he took Shelby to bed now, they would not leave it for a long, long time. While that would suit him just fine, Nelson wasn't sure if Shelby truly wanted him or if her response was caused by the memories his being there invoked. Memories were okay, but Shelby needed to focus on now because Nelson yearned to hear his wife say that she still loved him and that he could come home. Something to do, he thought, something that would cool the embers of his desire. He looked toward the window again, then back at Shelby, mischief dancing in his black eyes. "Urn, Shel?"

"Yes," "How would you feel about taking a walk with me?"

After twelve years, Shelby knew Nelson well enough to know that look on his face, and, still struggling against the flux of passion he'd aroused in her, she glanced out the window. The wind and snow had not tapered off and she could not see a thing. She turned back to Nelson and hitched a thumb over her shoulder.

"Outside? In the dark?"

"Yeah," Nelson said with a dimpled smile. "I left something in the car." "Right," she responded. "If you left something in the car, why do I have to go outside?"

"To keep me company," he replied easily. "Now go upstairs and dress warmly. There's a blizzard outside, you know."

After voicing her misgivings, Shelby finally left the room. Nelson removed several gaily-wrapped packages from his green sack and placed them under their tree, then followed Shelby upstairs. Playing Santa had been fun, but he had forgotten that a blizzard meant snow and he didn't have a coat. He'd left some of his things at the house and if Shelby hadn't tossed them out, his ski jacket should still be in the back of the closet.

Without thinking, Nelson entered the bedroom and found Shelby naked. Starved as he was for his wife, his gaze traveled her body in slow remembrance. Adrenaline bounded into action, heightening his sensory perception as his eyes touched the high, tipped breasts and dark patch between her legs.

Nelson stood like a statue, mouth agape, wondering how he'd gone so long without making love to Shelby and how he would last until he could take her in his arms again.

Shelby moved, or at least Nelson thought she did, and as if remembering where he was, he suddenly shook his head, averted his eyes and headed for the closet as fast as his feet could get him there.

Shelby watched him until he disappeared inside the walk-in closet. It felt good to have Nelson in their bedroom and his look of embarrassment or arousal, Shelby wasn't sure which, made her smile. Inclined to go with arousal, she wondered if Nelson had noticed the pictures of the two of them scattered everywhere, but she doubted that he'd seen anything beyond her naked body. Her own earlier images of Nelson tried to find a place in her mind and Shelby quickly dispelled them. This is ridiculous, she thought. They'd been apart too long to still be on the same erotic wavelength. She sat on the bed and pulled on her clothes, forcing her mind to take a course that wouldn't leave her feeling so empty.

She'd had a ball decorating the tree with Nelson, and was glad that she'd remembered the Christmas box. Admitting that she loved Nelson had been a huge mistake, but saying the words out loud to someone other than herself meant she couldn't deny the truth any longer. Kissing Nelson hadn't helped matters and after her response, she now had to deal with reality. Nelson wanted them back together and there would be no stopping him now that he knew she still loved him. But what did she want? It was a question Shelby wasn't sure she could answer anymore.

*No,* she said in summation of her thoughts. She did know. What she wanted most in this world was peace.

Nelson gave Shelby what he considered ample time to finish dressing, and then came out of the closet. She'd covered herself in a boldly striped, hand knit, red and gold sweater and matching corduroys, but the shield of clothing did not stop Nelson's emotional landslide. His mind had seen what it wanted, and it was an effort for him to stand so close to Shelby and help her into the bulky jacket without touching her with his hands, especially with the bed so near. Later, he promised himself, trying to quiet the ruckus in his body. He gloved and hatted Shelby, wound a woolen scarf around her neck, then took her by the hand, led her down the stairs and out the front door.

Outside, Shelby discovered that Nelson really did want to take a walk and though she trusted him with her life, they couldn't see two feet in front of them. Dense woods surrounded their house and they could easily get lost. Her arms waved through the air like a windmill as the debate went into round two. "Nelson Reeves, look around you! Can you not see this snow? Can you not see that we cannot see anything out here?"

"You're just chicken, Shel. This is our home. I know this area like the back of my hand and you know I won't let us get lost. We'll walk a little way, then turn back. It'll be fun."

"Fun! Being lost in the woods during a blizzard is not my idea of fun. This is plenty far enough and I can see the lights in the house. If you want to take a walk, 'bye. I'm going back inside."

Their warm breaths came out as white puffs that froze in the air as each of them restated their position. Nelson remained insistent, Shelby adamant, and she finally won

the verbal skirmish. But the price of her victory proved
high. For Nelson, who had never been a good loser, pushed
her into a snow bank. Steaming, Shelby rose in a cloud of
white. She reached her gloved hands down into the snow
and when she stood up, formed a perfectly round snowball
that she threw with equally perfect aim at the back of
Nelson's head. Then she tried to run through the deep drifts
for the front door. She didn't get far before Nelson tackled
her and buried her in another pile of snow.

Shelby sat up, sputtering. Snowflakes clung to her
eyelashes and she tried to wipe them away with gloves that,
also being thick with snow, didn't help. Nelson pulled her
to her feet and used his mouth to clean the flakes from her
eyes.

When she could see again, Shelby laid her hands on his
chest and angled her chin upward for Nelson's kiss. When
he lowered his head, she pushed with all her strength and
sent him toppling. Only she hadn't planned on him
reaching out and grabbing her arm so that she'd land in the
four-foot drift right along with him.

"Not fair, Nelson Reeves," Shelby cried, sitting up.
"You're supposed to be down here by yourself."

Nelson pulled her back down beside him. "Ah, but
having you here with me is much more fun," he laughed,
stealing a quick kiss. He rose to his feet, bringing her up
with him. Like two children, they played in the snow until
Shelby complained of being cold. Nelson led her to the
door and watched her go into the house, then went to the
Bronco to retrieve the rest of the thing she'd brought with

him. Entering the house a few minutes later, he saw the trail of clothes she'd left going up the stairs.

"Nels, I'm freezing. I'm going to take a warm bath, so make yourself at home," Shelby called down.

He was glad she'd said it, but Nelson had planned to do just that anyway. He left his suitcase by the front door, carried the grocery sacks to the kitchen and picked up the clothes Shelby had dropped. After that, he easily found the boxes marked KITCHEN, and in no time at all, had them unpacked and the items they contained back in the cupboards. With that done, he brewed a cup of hot chocolate, added a teaspoon of brandy and carried it up the stairs. She was still in the tub and when he peeked in on her, Nelson found her asleep. He sat on the edge of the tub and studied her.

Papery thin lids and curly lashes now hid eyes that had earlier drooped with exhaustion. Her body was so slender, he knew she wasn't eating. She never did when she was bothered by something or emotionally upset. She had never weighed much to begin with and the only time Shelby had gained any weight was during her pregnancy. But when he was here, he could usually coax her out of her moods and she'd eat for him. Their romp in the snow had probably taken all the energy she had left.

Worry creased Nelson's forehead as he placed a light hand on her shoulder and shook Shelby awake. Half asleep, she allowed him to lift her from the tub and carry her into the bedroom. Nelson dried her with the towel, dressed her in a nightgown and fed her the hot chocolate. Once she finished the drink, he tucked her under the king-size, multicolored quilt and sat on the bed until her eyes closed again.

"Sweet dreams, my Shelby," he said, leaning over to kiss her temple.

She sprang up and her arms surrounded his body. Shelby gave him a fierce hug. "Thank you for today, Nelson."

She lay back down and snuggled into the pillows. He snapped off the lamp and rose from the bed. At the door, his footsteps faltered when he heard Shelby add sleepily, "I'm glad you came home, baby."

Nelson sat on the couch staring at the Christmas tree. Shelby was glad he was here and her words sent his hope soaring. He wanted to come home, not just for a few days, but permanently. The executive suite had all the accouterments to make living there comfortable, but it was not a home. It was a place to sleep when he was too tired to do anything else. This was where he belonged; everything he loved and held most dear was here. Nelson looked around at the boxes. Shelby had packed their entire life into cardboard containers with neat little labels.

The thought made him angry and Nelson left the couch. He hesitated for a moment and glanced at the door. In the morning, Shelby would be furious with him, but Nelson ripped open the first box anyway. Exhausted at three in the morning, Nelson retrieved his suitcase from the hallway and went into the downstairs bathroom. He showered, dressed and returned to the living room to make up a bed on the couch. He could have slept in one of the guest rooms upstairs, but until things changed and Shelby took him back, it seemed safer to put as much distance between them as possible.

He had just laid down and closed his eyes when he heard the sobs. Nelson lunged from the couch and raced up the stairs. He ran into the master suite; Shelby wasn't there. He sped across the hall and into his son's room and in an instant, he was at Shelby's side, trying to pull her into his arms. He couldn't because she was fighting him. Her arms flew in every direction and when she slapped him across the face and punched him in the stomach, the unexpected blows stunned Nelson for a moment and his hold on her loosened.

The eerie silence that followed terrified Nelson, and a film of moisture beaded on his upper lip as a tear ran unnoticed down his cheek. He fought down his rising paranoia and watched Shelby like a hawk, trying to anticipate her next move. Her eyes, full of accusation, lashed out at him and when she took a step toward him, he mentally braced himself. Her face, unfettered by conscious control, plainly displayed her true feelings for him and he had earned her look of disgust. Shelby had the right to castigate him for all that he'd done to her and he wouldn't try to stop her.

Standing his ground, Nelson masochistically willed Shelby to deliver the blows to his body. Reason told him that she could never mete out the type of punishment he deserved, but he wanted her to try. If she could inflict on him even a small measure of the pain he'd given her, he would let her vent her wrath on him. Maybe the action would take away some of his guilt for what he'd done to both of them.

Instead of hitting him, Shelby sank to her knees and hugged her arms tightly around her body. She rocked forward, almost in slow motion and curled into a ball. When he heard the low moans, Nelson fell to his knees and hoisted her limp body in his arms, "Shelby?" A gentle slapping at her face accompanied his urgent whisper.

Her eyes opened and Shelby tried to sit up. His arms locked around her as her next words carved his heart into tiny portions. "Why, Nelson? Why did it have to be our baby?"

His tears fell into her hair and his voice cracked as he gripped her tightly. "Sweetness. Oh, Shelby. I-I don't know."

She searched his face. Saw the pain twisting his features and knew it was the same pain she still carried inside. Nelson had no answers, just as she had no answers. Not only had they suffered the ultimate tragedy, they had also failed to help each other cope. And because of that, they had lost everything. With that thought, the dam burst again and Shelby crumpled against him, sobbing gut-wrenching tears.

Holding tight to Shelby, Nelson let her cry. Finally, he thought, wiping the tears from his own face. Shelby hadn't cried since the night she'd found their son. At the funeral, she'd stood stiffly and stared at the little white casket, but she hadn't shed a single tear. It wasn't until the casket had been lowered into the ground that the shaky state of Shelby's emotional balance became evident. She fainted, then spent a full week in the hospital recovering from self-starvation and dehydration. After that, she'd begun to visit their son's grave daily.

During the dreadful months that followed, Nelson had known there was something wrong with Shelby, but was so caught up in his own loss and anger that he couldn't help her. He hadn't been able to help himself. Nelson rose to his feet, with the still sobbing Shelby in his arms, and carried her into their bedroom. He laid her in the bed, climbed in beside her and pulled the covers over them both.

For a long while, Nelson watched over Shelby. When she fell into a deep slumber, he left the bed and crossed the hall to his son's bedroom. In a hallucinatory void, he walked around, trying to comprehend something that was incomprehensible. He had just experienced one of the most hair-raising episodes of his life and in the process validated his worst fear: His wife did hate him.

Crushed, Nelson gripped the top bar of the crib, staring down at the little bed, remembering his son's small, curled body and the little thumb Lamar sucked while he slept. Something inside his chest squeezed as the assumptions he made regarding Shelby formed a pile of rubble at his feet. He couldn't just waltz back into her life and pick up where they had left off. Too much had happened between them. Now that a blunt dose of reality had cleared his head, Nelson could readily admit that while Shelby had physically left, he had left her long before she'd walked out that door. He had forsaken his wife in every way possible and this was the result of that desertion. After what he'd done to her, how could he ever expect Shelby to forgive him?

Crossing the floor, brutal anguish followed him to the door of the bedroom. Persuading Shelby to love him the first time had been no easy task, and he had had to overcome his reservations and his fears. He had to find consolation in the thought that he was here now, and he would never abandon Shelby again. He turned off the overhead light and returned to the master suite, a little less confident and a great deal more ambivalent about his chances of reconciling with his wife.

When he climbed into the bed, Nelson wrapped Shelby in the warm cocoon of his arms. He kissed her brow lightly, then lay with his eyes open, holding on to his wife until dawn's light ushered in a new day.

# CHAPTER THIRTEEN

With a soft moan, Shelby snuggled closer to the warmth sheltering her. Waking slowly, her brows wrinkled when her mind registered that something was not right. Her eyes opened and widened when they met the dark and compelling eyes of Nelson.

He kissed her on the nose.

After the kiss, Shelby next registered the tired shadows beneath his eyes. *He's been awake all night,* she thought as guilt bore down on her. Guilt, because after scaring him half to death and sobbing her heart out on his chest, she'd slept the remainder of the night secure in the arms still holding her. She watched a frown form on his brow, but managed to smother the urge to smooth it away as she waited apprehensively for the question she knew was coming.

Nelson kissed her on the nose again. "Good morning, sweetness."

Tension eased from Shelby's body. He hadn't asked, and while Shelby wondered why, she gave the thought no more than a brief examination. She snuggled closer. "Good morning, baby."

Nelson slowly released the breath he'd been holding. Shelby had assumed he would question her about last night, and he almost had until he sensed her inner turmoil and changed his mind. When she relaxed in his arms, he knew he'd made the right decision. "And how does my little woman feel this morning?"

A smile played at Shelby's lips as she got into the game. Nelson had greeted her this way every morning since their marriage, at least until things had changed between them and he'd taken to being up and dressed by the time she'd awakened. With the opening of his eyes, Nelson was a ball of energy until he closed them again at night. Their sunrise antics and a morning jog had usually helped harness some of his pep until he got to the office.

"Your little woman is hungry." "Oh?" Nelson kissed her cheek. "And what is my little woman hungry for?"

Shelby closed one eye, pretending to ponder the question as Nelson placed tiny kisses allover her face until he reached her mouth. He drank deeply before releasing her lips.

"I think I would like some pancakes."

Nelson gave her a stem mock frown. "That, my little woman, is not the right answer." He kissed her again. "Now, what is my little woman hungry for?"

"Bacon and eggs?"

Nelson rose over her. "Wrong again, little woman."

"Waffles?"

"Nope," he replied, pinning her arms above her head with one hand; the other raised the nightgown. Dry-mouthed, Nelson stared at her chest, eager to apply his tongue to the mounds he'd dreamed about for so long, but thought he'd never see again. It was hard to maintain his control, but he called on iron will, knowing he had to play the game for a few minutes longer.

"Oh, I know," she said, as if she'd just thought of the right response. "Sausage. A nice, long, thick piece of sausage."

"Right," Nelson concurred with a smile he somehow managed to put on his face. He kissed the corner of her mouth, then flicked the edges of her lips with his tongue while the pads of his thumbs grazed the surface of each breast. Shelby gasped for air as spiraling warmth spread through her body and desire flooded her center.

"And where is the sausage, my little woman?"

Needing to catch her breath, Shelby didn't respond right away. When she was able, she said, "In the refrigerator, where else?"

"Come on, little woman," he said, rubbing his hand across the flat plane of her belly. "I know you can do better than that." He lowered his head and she squirmed under the erotic torture of his mouth. Shelby released a long, deep sigh. "Do-do you have it?" she asked with a catch in her voice.

Nelson raised his head and smiled. He released her arms. "Yep, and because you took so long to give me the correct answer, you'll have to find it."

Shelby's eyes twinkled. She placed the tip of her tongue in one of his dimples, then covered it with her lips. Leaving a trail of hot kisses to his mouth, she kissed him quickly, then laid her arm across her forehead. "Oh, Nelson. Nels, baby. I haven't the strength to go on a search for my sausage. Feed me, Nelson. Feed your little woman."

Shelby felt the tremor that ran through Nelson's entire body and watched his face transform. He was no longer smiling and she felt the heat of his desire pass from his body to hers. His eyes shimmered with it and she knew the game was over. Nelson wanted to make love to her; she had a decision to make and quickly, although Shelby knew there really was nothing to decide. She wanted her husband as much as he wanted her.

When she pushed on his chest, Nelson closed his eyes and moved off her body. He rolled to his side, his back facing her, and battled to slow his racing heart. His chest tightened with frustration, a frustration he'd been living with for almost two years. Lying in their bed beside Shelby, holding her through the night, his senses filled with her sweet scent; his need for her had grown to epic proportions. His groin ached with an almost smarting pain. He'd come so close to losing it and Nelson felt like an idiot. Why had he started that stupid game? He knew Shelby had seen his hunger for her. To hell with that thought. Nelson was long past hunger; he lusted for Shelby-and she didn't want him. Every muscle in his body contracted in protest when he felt her soft touch on his back.

"Nelson?"

He didn't move, afraid if he did he'd embarrass himself even further by letting Shelby see what she'd done to him.

"Nelson?"

It took every ounce of willpower Nelson had to answer Shelby with a steady voice, though he still couldn't face her. "What is it, Shel?"

"Aren't you going to feed me?"

Rolling to his back slowly, Nelson turned his head and looked at Shelby. She had removed the gown and lay open and naked before him. The passion sparked by their game radiated in the depth of her eyes. Shelby reached for him and Nelson quickly moved into her arms, crushing her body to his. His lips found her mouth again and somehow during the deep, long-lasting kiss, he discarded his pajama pants.

He raised his head. "Are you sure, Shel?"

"I'm sure, baby," she replied, placing her mouth on his again.

To assure him further, she pulled his head down and brushed his lips before slipping her tongue inside his mouth. They exchanged several long, hot kisses, pressing their bodies together in an attempt to get inside each other. Moaning a sigh, Nelson released Shelby's lips. He pressed his nose to her neck, sniffing her unique fragrance, and massaged his lips into her skin as he moved lower. His mouth nudged her breast before he trapped a pebbled bud between his lips and she cried out as rippling, tiny bursts of delight flowered and dispersed inside her. Her stomach coiled at his repeated touch. She felt magically, wonderfully alive again and savored the feel of his mouth on her body. That Shelby was still so responsive to his touch made his head spin and only intensified his need.

"Baby, please. Now!" Shelby cried. The divine torment of his mouth and hands had her reeling in ecstasy, but she needed more and she needed it now.

Nelson gentled his suctioning mouth and his lips tracked their way back to her mouth and he sipped the tears on her cheeks. He housed her trembling body in his arms. "Don't cry, Shel. I only want to please you."

Shelby gripped him to her, her eyes squeezed shut. "You are, Nelson, but it's been so long."

"I know, baby. It has been just as long for me, but I've dreamed about this day and you for too many nights." His voice shook with the force of his emotions. "You're like a fine wine, Shel. I took a sip and I've been in a drunken stupor ever since. I love you and being without you has been hell on earth. Let's not rush this, Shelby, not when we've gone so long without each other."

He lowered his head again and placed a series of hard, scalding kisses on her lips, instantaneously cutting off lucid thought. Her hands groped for him beneath the blankets and Nelson, already hard and throbbing, shouted her name when she used both hands to massage his manhood. He tenderly lifted her hands away from him.

"No more, Shel," he said in a throaty groan. "I need to be inside you." He placed her body beneath him. She stared into his face with passion-drugged eyes.

"Now, Nelson?"

"Now, Shel."

Nelson sank himself into her body and quickly found his rhythm. She held him tightly as they rocked together in the age old dance, easing the pain and need of not loving each other for what seemed like a lifetime. Nelson couldn't think beyond the woman beneath him. His mouth and hands were everywhere as he caressed and petted Shelby's body. She ran her hands across the hard, taut muscles of his back, reveling in the sound of his voice murmuring her name, and her shouts joined his as together they rode a rapturous tide of explosive ecstasy.

Fighting for breath, Nelson collapsed on top of her. Shelby wrapped her arms around him, waiting for the spasms to subside. He lifted himself and moved to lie at her side, but they were far from finished with each other. It had been too long to live with pent up desire and Nelson didn't know how long it would take to extinguish his blaze. Feeling himself harden, he pulled Shelby into his arms and covered her mouth, stroking his tongue in and out. When they joined again, Shelby not only accepted Nelson back into her body, but also back into her heart.

The ringing telephone in no way slowed down Nelson's movements. Whoever it was would have to wait. They had more pressing problems to deal with and one of them was pressing into his wife right now.

The answering machine beeped. "Shel, my pet. Wake up!" Shelby groaned, both from Nelson's motions within her and the voice of Tyrone Brooks.

"I know you're there, love. With that snowstorm, you can't possibly be anywhere else. Now, wake up! If this machine beeps me, you know I'll keep calling back until you do."

"What are you doing?" Nelson asked, when Shelby reached for the telephone.

"Answering the telephone." She kissed his jaw.

Nelson stopped moving. "You can't be serious. We're in the middle of something here."

"I know that, Nels. But you know Ty will keep calling until I pick up, so I thought I' d get it over with." She reached for the receiver and Nelson lowered his mouth to her chest. "Mer-Merry Christmas, darling."

"Merry Christmas, pet. You sound like you're getting a present I would have liked to get."

Shelby squeezed her eyes shut as Nelson shifted his position. "What do you want, Ty?"

"To wish you happy holidays and find out how my fish skirts are selling?" "Ty, I'm kind of busy. Let me call you back later."

Shelby heard the sucking sound Tyrone made with his teeth and knew she'd hurt his feelings. His relationship of five years had recently ended, devastating Tyrone. Shelby had given him a shoulder to lean on and knew his query about the fish skirts was a ruse. Ty was lonely and probably spending the holiday alone. He needed a friend and she was thinking of a way to apologize when Nelson took the phone from her hand.

"Tyrone. Shelby will have to call you back. We're busy!"

"Big man! How the hell are you, Nels? I didn't know Shelby was with you. Wait a minute. What are you doing there?"

"Trying to make love to my wife," Nelson rumbled.

"Then you have my apologies for the interruption, big man. Do her right though, then maybe she'll stop being so bitchy."

"You'll never change, will you Ty?"

"Not ever, big man. Listen, ask Shel how she liked my surprise, then I'll get offthe phone and let you attend to business."

Nelson looked down at Shelby. "He wants to know how you liked his surprise."

Shelby took the phone. "No, Ty."

"Ah, pet. This is *Harper's* we're talking about and maybe my big break. They want to feature my skirts and some of my other designs. I've been absolutely dying for a chance like this and this article will make Exterior Motives the most fashionable and sought-out boutique in the West."

Through word of mouth, Shelby had garnered the prestige of being one of the best fashion designers in the region. She didn't want a spread in *Harper's;* she was already turning potential clients away.

Shelby pushed her hand against Nelson's chest. "Wait a minute, Nels. Tyrone, I'm very happy for you and you have my support. But you know how I feel about undue publicity. I like Exterior Motives the way

it is and so do our clients. They don't mind the prices and they like the personal touch. I'm sorry, but you're going to have to do this one on your own."

"All right, pet. I get the message, but I had to try, didn't I? Wish me luck?"

"All the luck in the world, Ty. I need to go now. Talk to you soon."

"All right, love. Tell the big man to have one on me."

Shelby laughed. "'Bye, Ty."

"'Bye, pet."

"What was that all about?" Nelson asked, replacing the receiver.

*"Harper's* is interviewing Tyrone for their April issue. He wants to include Exterior Motives in the story."

"Maybe you should do it." Shelby's eyes darkened. "Sweetness, don't get upset. I know how you feel about that sort of thing. But if it will help Ty, maybe one time won't have an impact on the shop."

"A feature in *Harper's* will have every fashion reporter and curiosity seeker landing on our doorstep. I don't want that. The boutique is just as I envisioned it. The clientele is small and my designs are exclusive. Andyou know howI feel about the attention that comes with fame."

"I do know. But Ty is our friend and if we can use the business to help him, then I think we should at least consider it."

Shelby silenced his lips with her mouth. "Let's not talk about Exterior Motives now, Nels. You have some unfinished business to take care of right here." She wiggled beneath him as a reminder.

A long while later, Nelson moved off Shelby and gathered her close. They entangled their legs until she lay nestled between his thighs. She traced the hard line of his jaw with her finger.

"Thank you, Nelson," she whispered, planting soft kisses on his chin. "I needed to feel the fire again. Two years is a long time to go without being loved."

A convulsion ran through Nelson's body. Two years? "Shelby, are you saying—?"

Shelby put her finger to his lips. "Just know that you are the only man, ever."

Near bursting with pride, Nelson steered her head to his chest. Shelby was made for loving, and often, and he made a vow right then that she would never go without that love. Shelby deserved better than that, much better. Holding his wife close to his heart, Nelson kissed her lips tenderly and closed his eyes, letting the restful sleep that had eluded them both for two years carry them off to dreamland.

❧

Squealing with delight, Shelby removed the gold locket and sent the maroon velvet case flying. She jumped up from the floor and ran over to Nelson, who sat on the couch silently observing as Shelby opened her Christmas gifts. After throwing her arms around his neck, she placed her hands on his thighs.

Nelson watched her bouncing breasts. He had to learn when to keep his big mouth shut. Mentioning the gifts under the tree had ended the loving and ruined his plan to spend the day in bed making up for lost time. Shelby had showered and dressed in blue jeans and a top before he could summon enough strength to rise from the bed.

The violet top dipped with Shelby's movements and Nelson leaned toward her. He first used the tip of his finger to rim the neckline, then lowered the garment. Her breasts popped out. He attached his lips and suckled.

Moaning deeply, Shelby allowed his tongue's caresses on her body, but only for a few moments, then she pulled away from his mouth and pranced in front of him. She held out her new locket.

"Put it on, Nelson. Please, baby!"

His mind was not on the necklace, but Nelson rose and took the eighteen-karat gold locket from her hands. He turned Shelby around, reprimanded her to stand still and hooked the chain around her slender neck. Holding her shoulders, he bent over and kissed her on the cheek. He released her and Shelby ran to the mirror over the fireplace for a closer examination of her necklace.

Nelson looked at the little pile of gifts on the floor. Though he could well afford it, nothing he'd given his wife had been expensive: her ornament, a white church with a tiny choir inside; a bottle of her favorite specially mixed fragrance; a shorty-short, ruby-red nightgown and matching wrapper (that was for him); a box of Godiva chocolates (which she loved); and a pair of moose slippers (which Shelby would wear once and throw in the back of the closet because she liked going barefoot).

She had reacted to each one as if he'd given her gold, and Nelson still glowed with pleasure just remembering the joy in her face as she'd torn into the packages. Shelby had shocked him by giving him gifts, too. The brand new CSU sweatshirt he probably wouldn't wear. His open-ended ornament with the black saxophonist inside, he liked. But the gift that had caused his chest to expand with love was the Wilt Chamberlain rookie card, encased in gold and glass.

He'd been looking to add that card to his collection for years and wondered where Shelby had obtained it. He also wondered why Shelby had bought Christmas presents for him. She couldn't have known he'd be here today. When had she planned to give the gifts to him? Nelson smiled again and bent over to pick up the scattered paper and presents. His wife was a constant surprise. Buying the presents meant Shelby had been thinking about him, and that was the best gift she could ever give him. He stood straight when he felt Shelby's arms encircle his waist

She laid her head on his back. "Thank you, Nelson," she whispered.

He turned in her arms and saw the tears in her eyes. His eyes dropped to the opened locket. On one side was a picture of him and Shelby; the other side held a picture of their son. Nelson kissed the top of her head.

"You're welcome, sweetness."

Nelson held Shelby and kissed her lips, then groaned when the telephone rang and she left the warmth of his arms to answer it. Feeling a little deserted, he picked up paper and took it to the kitchen. When he returned, he found her sitting on the couch, staring at the pictures in the locket.

Shelby sighed and settled her weight more comfortably on the couch. She stared at the pictures and silently asked the question that never strayed far from her mind: Why? She had been taught to plan for the future, to set goals and to work to achieve them. In that, she and Nelson were alike and they had worked hard to achieve their dreams. Theirs had been the perfect marriage, and just when it had come together with the addition of their son, fate had stepped in and shattered their lives. Planning hadn't stopped the death of her son or her marriage, but it had impressed upon her how little control she had over her own destiny.

Feeling a presence enter the room, she looked toward the doorway and bit down on her bottom lip when she saw Nelson leaning against the archway. The pose was casual, but the message his eyes sent could not be misinterpreted. He wanted her to put the memories away and come back to him. She stood and moved slowly toward Nelson, watching the changes occurring in his face as she approached. Several feet still separated them when she stopped and took a deep breath. She wanted to go to Nelson; she couldn't, held back by months of rejection.

They had made passionate love this morning and had taken the edge off their hunger. But after a night of shared anguish, wasn't it natural for them to use each other to relieve the burden they both carried? She didn't want to deny what she felt anymore. No matter what lay between them, the loneliness, the darkness, the pain, couldn't Nelson see that she loved him, only him? Didn't he know she always would?

Her tension was palpable and Nelson felt the anxiety across the space. He straightened and pushed his hands into the pockets of his pants. Their eyes mirrored the questions and for what seemed like an eternity, they stared at each other. After all they'd been through together, so much lay between them keeping them apart. A short while ago, they'd come together, reaffirming that, at least bodily, they still needed each other. Did Shelby need him beyond that? Did she still want him? Nelson knew he had to rid himself of the doubts weighing him down if he wanted Shelby to take him back. And what mattered to him more than Shelby? Nothing, his mind answered. Shelby was his love, his woman and his life.

He opened his arms and she flew into them.

"I love you, Shelby Julian Reeves."

"I love you, Nelson Lamar Reeves."

Nelson lifted her from the floor and twirled her around. His mouth came down to possess hers and a low moan escaped Shelby when his tongue dove inside. He set Shelby to her feet and she lowered her gaze to his hips. Nelson never could hide his feelings for her. She had a gleam in her eye when she stood on tiptoe and flicked her tongue against the area just beneath his ear. Nelson trembled.

Liking that response, Shelby repeated the action, then pushed her hands beneath his white sweater. Her fingers fondled his nipples. The tremble became an uncontrollable quake and feeling his knees about to buckle, Nelson reached for the wall. She raised the sweater and replaced her teasing fingers with her mouth and his face twisted into a grimace. His eyes closed, then opened and Nelson glanced over his shoulder at the stairs knowing they'd never make it to the bedroom. He heard the rasp of his zipper and tensed. If Shelby touched him, Nelson knew he would explode. Grabbing her hands, he swung her into his arms and headed for the couch.

# CHAPTER FOURTEEN

"Shelby Reeves, you know I don't like raisins. Why are you putting them in the sweet potatoes?" Nelson folded his arms over his chest, frowning as he watched her pour more of the offending fruit into the pan.

"Because I like them. Just pick them out, like you always do."

Nelson grunted softly. "I don't want to pick them out. They look like little black bugs."

Setting the box down on the counter, Shelby turned to face him. "Nelson Reeves, you are acting like a child. And stop talking about my food. If you didn't want me to use the raisins, then you shouldn't have bought them."

She had him there, and Nelson didn't respond. They were in the kitchen preparing their Christmas dinner and he'd stopped chopping the onions and celery for his stuffing when he saw Shelby reached for the big red box. He smiled and picked up the knife. He'd only bought the damn things because he knew how much Shelby liked them. He glanced at her out of the corner of his eye and reached for a large celery stalk, then began to chop it into really big pieces.

Hearing the hasty speed at which the knife hit the wooden cutting board, Shelby looked up and watched him. He knew she didn't like celery and tolerated the stuff only if cut into very thin, barely seen slices. "What are you doing, Nelson?"

His face held an innocent grin when he glanced over his shoulder to look at her. "I'm chopping the celery," he told her, "for the stuffing."

She punched him playfully in the arm. "Nelson, you know I don't like celery."

The grin on his face widened. "Then pick it out, like you always do."

They exchanged laughs. They'd had this same discussion every year of their marriage. And every year, Nelson had picked black, buggy-looking raisins out of his sweet potatoes while she did the same with the big chunks of celery in her stuffing.

Nelson turned and eyed the twelve-pound turkey he'd already dressed. It was just waiting for his sausage stuffing, then he'd put it into the oven. He glanced at the clock. Making love to Shelby again had really thrown their schedule off At this rate, they'd be eating at ten o'clock tonight. That didn't bother him, though. Loving Shelby was better than any food, and he couldn't care less if they had to eat at two in the morning.

Nelson dumped his pile of chopped vegetables into the pan, mixing them with the butter until the onions were translucent and the celery tender. Dumping the mixture into a bowl that already contained the bread crumbs, sausage and spices, Nelson finished preparing the turkey and slipped it into the oven, then leaned back on the counter to watch Shelby at work.

He was in charge of the turkey and stuffing. She prepared everything else. There was only one problem with their arrangement. His wife tended to use every pot and pan in the kitchen, and he was also responsible for cleaning up the mess when she finished.

He didn't think she really needed to use every dish they owned to cook. Shelby did it on purpose. He was sure of it, but had never gotten her to admit it. He cleared his throat when Shelby reached into a cabinet for another clean bowl.

"You already have five bowls on the counter, Shel. Do you really need another?"

She smiled over her shoulder at him. "Yes. Those other bowls already had stuff in them and this one is for the mashed potatoes."

Nelson pursed his lips. "Why don't you just wash one of them?" "Because I'm not in charge of clean up. You are."

Nelson straightened and stalked her. "You do this on purpose, don't you?"

Shelby feigned a look of innocence. "Why, Nelson Reeves, whatever are you talking about?"

Nelson grabbed her around the waist and pulled Shelby flush with his hard body. "You know exactly what I'm talking about, Mrs. Reeves, and I think it's time we discussed this little arrangement of ours."

Mrs. Reeves. Mrs. Shelby Reeves. Mrs. Nelson Reeves. Hearing Nelson use her name again sounded good to Shelby's ears.

He kissed away the frown wrinkling her forehead. "What's the matter, Shel?"

Her lashes fluttered up and Shelby stared deep into his eyes. "Nothing, baby. I was just thinking how good it sounded to be called Mrs. Reeves again."

Nelson released her and stepped away. He wasn't sure if now was the best time to broach the subject. After all, he'd only been home for one night. Still, Shelby was wearing his rings again. "Shel, what are you going to do about the house?"

The question sent a cold, chilling wind down Shelby's back. That had been her real estate agent on the phone earlier informing Shelby of the three bids submitted on the house. She needed to make a decision, and while she'd like nothing better than to take Nelson back, he couldn't just walk back through the door and pick up as if nothing had happened between them. Turning away, she picked up a potato and began to peel it. She felt Nelson's arms encircle her waist and closed her eyes. He laid his cheek on the top of her head. "I want to come home, Shelby."

"You are home, Nelson."

He dropped his arms. "No, Shel. This is a visit. I want to live here again, with you."

Shelby turned around. "What happened to the boxes, Nelson?"

A guilty look crossed his face. He moved to the sink and began filling it with dishwater. "I unpacked them last night and burned them in the fireplace," he mumbled.

"Why?"

A scowl marred his face when he turned to face Shelby again. "Because I couldn't stand to see our entire life together packed away in cardboard containers. Our things belong in this house. You belong in this house and so do I. I know things aren't right between us, Shelby, but I want to try again. Our marriage was good. I tried to make you happy. We were happy, and I can make you happy again, if you'll only give me another chance.

"Losing Lamar was the first thing that truly tested the strength of our marriage and I came up short. I was angry, Shelby. So angry. We had a healthy, beautiful baby boy. Lamar wasn't sick one day of his life and no one could tell me why we lost our son. When I looked into your face, his face, all I saw was Lamar and instead of helping and loving you, I turned that anger against you. I'm sorry I let you down, Shel, and I promise I will never let you down again. Please, can I come home?"

Shelby swallowed around the lump in her throat. This was the first time Nelson had apologized to her for the way he'd acted after their son died, although he'd done everything else to keep from signing the divorce papers, even leaving the state for two months. He hadn't left a forwarding address and a private detective had tracked him down in Florida. He'd moved back to Colorado, but refused to sign the divorce papers until the judge threatened to send him to jail for contempt of court.

She'd thought Nelson would go to jail rather than sign those papers and remembered his look of defeat the day he'd entered the boutique, papers in hand. Nelson had signed his name at the bottom of the forms, left them on the counter and walked out the door without a word. This talk was long overdue.

"Nelson, if you wanted to come home, why did you wait so long?"

"I was afraid."

"Of what?" She saw the sheen of tears in his eyes before Nelson turned back to the sink. "Why were you afraid, Nelson?"

His shoulders lifted in agitation and with his eyes staring hard at the froth of bubbles swirling in the sink, he forced his mouth to form and say the words. "After the way I treated you when our son died, I was afraid you wouldn't want me anymore."

Feeling himself about to break down, Nelson threw the sponge into the water and strode quickly from the kitchen. Shelby watched him leave and turned back to the potatoes. They were not through talking, but she knew Nelson needed some time alone. She finished preparing their dinner and when everything was on the stove, went in search of her husband. She found Nelson in their bedroom, staring at a wooden-framed picture in his hands. Shelby sat beside him on the bed and laid her head on his arm.

"Lamar sure was a wiggly little thing," he said. "Those little legs of his were in constant motion. I think he would have been an early walker. What do you think, Shel?"

Shelby's heart filled with joy. So often, she had longed to sit with Nelson and talk about their baby. She needed to remember the good times, the wonderful memories created in the short span of time their son had been with them.

Nelson placed his arm around her shoulders and Shelby nestled closer, laying her head on his chest as she stared at the picture with him.

"I think you're right. Lamar was a smart baby, just like his father. Remember how we used to lay him in the bed between us and when he was hungry he'd wiggle down and attach his mouth to my breast without my help?"

A deep chuckle rose from Nelson's chest. "Yep. It was at those times that I really envied my son. You were his food source, but I couldn't help wishing that I was in his position."

Shelby sprang to an upright position. "Nelson Reeves, I cannot believe you'd say something as horrid as that. Imagine being envious of a baby, your own son, when all he wanted was to eat, for goodness' sakes."

He pulled her back down and encircled Shelby with his arm. "Don't make me out to be the bad guy here, lady. My son was getting something I could only dream about."

"Well, I think it's terrible that you were jealous of your own child."

"Jealous? Who said anything about jealousy? I just wanted him to share," Nelson responded. "Hey, do you remember that stuffed rabbit Lamar loved so much?"

"It wasn't a rabbit, baby. It was a brown pig and our son wouldn't go to sleep without it."

Nelson's brows came together. "A pig? But it had long, floppy ears and fur. Pigs don't have fur."

"Trust me on this, Nelson. It was a pig."

Nelson and Shelby continued talking about their son: his first smile, how fast he grew, how much he ate, the special closeness Lamar had shared with Nelson and the plans Nelson had already made for his future. As they talked, the cracks in their relationship began to cement and heal as the realization of what they had shared hit them both at once. After two years of living alone in their separate hells, sharing remembrances of their son worked to draw them closer than they had ever been.

Before, they had loved each other to the distraction of all else. Theirs had been a romantic, giddy kind of love, a love that, while it could sustain them through the good times, was not mature enough to handle any kind of crisis, especially the tragedies of life. They had concentrated so much on trying to make each other happy that they had missed something important.

They were happy because they wanted to be together and had made a commitment to each other. Their marriage wasn't something they had to work at; it had worked because they truly loved each other. While they did bump heads from time to time, the elements of a good marriage, communication, trust, respect, friendship and more had been there.

A few minutes of tranquil reflection went by before Nelson asked, "How long have you been having the nightmares, Shel?"

She remained quiet as she contemplated his question. She had left Nelson two weeks before Christmas the previous year. Things had gotten so bad between them they barely looked at each other. The night before, she'd found him in the study. He'd been in the room for hours, supposedly working, and the computer screen was on, but Nelson wasn't working. Bent over the desk, his head on his arms, he had been crying.

She'd never seen Nelson cry before, and his loud sobs had paralyzed her. Afraid to approach him, she'd stood in the doorway, watching and waiting, hoping he'd pull himself together. He didn't and she'd gone to her husband. She had tried to comfort him. He had screamed at her to get out. The look on Nelson's face when he'd said those words to her had struck the final blow to their marriage.

She had known that he wasn't just talking about leaving the study. Nelson wanted her out of his life. The next morning, she'd given him his wish. She had packed her bags and what remained of her broken heart, and left. She'd gone to her father's and Nelson had come looking for her that same day. When she refused to return, he'd come each night until New Year's Eve, begging her come home. New Year's Day, she'd found a letter stuck in the mail slot saying that if she wanted to return to the house, he'd leave.

She'd moved back a week later and spent the first night walking around the big, empty house filled with their things and memories of their life. That night and every night since, Shelby had dreamed about her son. Until last night, she'd always had to deal with her emotional state alone; last night, she had Nelson.

"For awhile now," she said, looking at him.

"How long is awhile, Shel?"

She stared at her pink-colored toenails. "Since I moved back into the house."

Nelson felt his guilt rise even further. No wonder Shelby looked so tired. Sleep had been eluding her for almost a year. Her subconscious was trying to force Shelby to face the death of their baby. Because of him, she'd had to do it alone. Nelson draped his arms around Shelby. "I haven't been the husband that you deserve. I should have been here for you and I wasn't. I'm sorry for everything you've gone through because of me and even sorrier that the woman I love had to endure pain caused by me. I know it doesn't change anything, Shel, but I love you with all my heart and if you can ever forgive me, I swear I'll make it up to you and I promise to try to never do anything that will cause you to hurt again." Nelson dropped a kiss on top of her head. "I don't know what else to say."

The intensity in his voice moved her and choked up with tears, Shelby squeezed her arms around his waist and buried her face in his chest.

Shelby's pulse rose as she stared down the candlelit table at her husband. She hadn't wanted to dress for d-inner, but Nelson had insisted they keep their tradition. He'd chosen a loose-fitting, red woolen suit with a band-collared, white silk shirt. The attire only served to enhance his already good looks. She wore an emerald-green gown with thin strands of gold woven into the velvet bodice that shimmered in the candlelight and a scooped neckline that gave Nelson a hint of the darkly colored mounds lying just beneath the material. Her jewelry included the locket, her wedding ring and pear-shaped diamonds in her ears.

Looking at Shelby, Nelson sucked in his breath. She was exquisite, his black china doll with honey-brown eyes. If Shelby let him come home, Nelson promised himself they would never separate again. He popped the cork on the bottle of champagne and rose from his chair to fill her glass. He couldn't resist bending over and stealing a kiss from her ruby red lips. Standing quickly, he made a speedy return to his chair. If he stayed near Shelby one second longer, he'd have that dress off her and they'd be writhing on the floor, the heat of their dinner lost in the flames of their passion.

Shelby, having similar thoughts, smiled when Nelson moved away from her. His nearness raised her temperature to feverish degrees and made her body react in ways that were electrifying. *Love makes all the difference,* she thought, and bowed her head.

Nelson said the blessing, then stood to carve the turkey. Shelby sat quietly, peering at him through the diaphanous screen created by the candled illumination. The light dappled the angular planes of his face and gave his brown skin a golden sheen. His strength radiated out to include her, and Shelby felt herself warmed by the sight of him.

Of all the gifts she'd received today, Nelson was by far the best. His vitality and energy filled the house and the laughter and love he'd brought with him had chased away the void she'd lived in for the past two years. Yesterday and today were typical of the times they spent together. Her husband was fun and she'd had so little in her life to enjoy lately. But it was more than the fun. Nelson was her soul mate and the man she would love for the rest of her life and beyond. How silly it had been to think that she could live without love, Nelson's love, in her life.

To the accompaniment of timeless Christmas tunes belted out in the rich, soulful voice of Patti LaBelle, Nelson and Shelby rose to fill their plates.

They returned to their seats and lifted their forks, then stared at each other, feeling a little adrift at sea and oblivious to everything except their love.

Her eyes beckoned him across the length of the table and Nelson picked up his plate. He moved down to sit next to Shelby and took her hand in his. "Better?"

"Yes," Shelby replied softly.

The meal was a happy affair as they remembered the humorous, loving and tense moments of their relationship. Remarkably enough, Nelson even found himself laughing as they recalled the day Shelby had given birth to Lamar and the insults she'd tossed at him. Shelby suddenly grew quiet and Nelson looked at her plate. She'd hardly touched the food and shadows had replaced the light in her eyes. "You're not eating, sweetness. What's the matter?"

She tucked her bottom lip, glanced down at her plate and back at Nelson. *Nothing's the matter,* Shelby thought, on the verge of tears. *Except that it's Christmas and it's snowing outside and I didn't visit my son today and I know how much he missed this morning. I want to tell him that I love him and wish him a Merry Christmas and so even though it is snowing, will you take me to the cemetery?* Those were things Shelby wanted to say. She took a deep breath to control the trembling in her lower body and said, "I'm not really that hungry."

Nelson didn't mention that she hadn't eaten all day or press her to say the things he saw written in her eyes. He dug his fork into the stuffing. "You know, I think this is the best stuffing I've ever prepared, Shel. Taste it and tell me what you think."

Shelby lifted some on her fork and after flicking out the celery, stuck it into her mouth. "It is good."

Nelson watched her eat more. "These greens taste a little odd, though. What did you do to them?" He put some in his mouth, screwing up his face as he chewed. "They taste kind of vinegary."

"You know I don't use vinegar," Shelby said, frowning as she put some into her mouth. They tasted fine to her, and she ate a little more just to be sure. "Nelson, there is nothing wrong with these greens." Looking up, she saw the cocked brow and sly smile. "Okay, baby. I'll eat."

"Good," Nelson said. He picked up his glass. "And, Shel. Lamar is okay and he knows how much we love him."

After dinner, Nelson led Shelby into the living room and after loading the CD player, fitted her soft, slim length against his rock-hard torso. She had eaten, but not enough to keep a bird alive, and the closeness they had found earlier was gone.

He was right here in the room with her and Shelby had taken her pain and withdrawn. His heart sank with desolation. She didn't have to carry her burden alone when she had him. "Lean on me, Shelby," Nelson whispered, surrounding her with his body. "I won't let you fall again."

His arms offered comfort, and holding her closer, he tried to pass some of his strength to Shelby. By the end of the first song, her body had relaxed. On the other hand, Nelson now had a huge problem, which he tried to hide by keeping Shelby in his arms. When another song, a long, slow love song began to play, he looked down at Shelby and saw the tiny smile threatening to break loose. Taking her hand, he led her through a dance of love so sensuous and sizzling she had trouble standing on her own two feet when the music stopped.

"Nels, are you trying to seduce me here in our living room?"

Another song began. Nelson cupped his hands around Shelby's buttocks, pulling her firmly against his pelvis and the turgid shaft straining against the zipper of his pants. His mouth trailed billowy kisses along her jaw. Shelby swaggered against him, shivering with shocking pleasure. Only this man could make her body sing with his touch. Only Nelson could love her the way she needed to be loved.

She tightened her arms around his neck, resting her head against his chest. "Nelson, oh, Nelson. The things you do to me," she murmured,

He responded by tipping her chin upward. His lips, soft as fleece, brushed against hers. The kiss he left on her nose was numbing until a trail of kisses down her cheek caught fire and ignited an inferno inside her.

"Please, Nelson," she gasped when his lips began to worry the pulse at the base of her neck.

He thrust his thigh between her legs and the dance of love continued. "Please what, Shelby Reeves." He looked down into eyes that were shimmering lakes of passion. "Tell me," Nelson whispered against her lips. The pads of his thumbs rubbed the hardened tips of her breasts through the velvety material of her dress. "Please what, Shel? Please, let's stop dancing? Please, let's make love? Tell me what you want from me, Shelby Reeves."

Shelby drew her head back, resting her palms on his broad chest Her brown eyes were shining as they locked with his and accessed the depth of his inquiring gaze. His eyes said that he really wanted to know and her mind told her to tell him. "Do you remember our wedding night, Nelson?"

He nodded and pulled her closer. "Well, I believed in the vows we took that day. And I believed you when you said that you would always be here for me and for our family. You promised to love me forever, and forever lasted a few short years. I need to know and believe that forever lasts forever."

His hands loosely draped her body as Nelson held the gaze. "For us, forever does last forever, Shelby. Don't you know that? Distance can separate us physically, but it is our love that binds us irrevocably. I know that I didn't fully appreciate what I had with you, but I loved you, Shelby. You are the most important person in my life and my commitment to you is eternal. I stand by everything I said to you on our wedding night. I have always been and will always be, here for you. Believe again, sweetness. Believe that we can have forever."

Believe, Shelby thought with her emotions running riot as Nelson's words continued to rock her. He'd said the things she wanted to hear, but Shelby couldn't let go of the niggle of doubt she hadn't quite put down. It stayed within her, warning her to keep caution at her back. Trusting Nelson again would be courting the risk of being hurt again. His words of love and commitment, and of always being there were meant for her and only her. He'd said nothing about their family, and while Shelby wasn't sure how she felt about having more children, they were still young and she couldn't rule out the possibility that one day they might have another child.

"Children," she murmured, and suddenly she didn't care anymore. Nelson was here and that's all that mattered, that and the fire he'd rekindled within her. All else could he worked out over time.

Fear, vast and deep, rattled Nelson's body. The word Shelby thought unspoken, he'd heard, and the thought knotted his stomach with anxiety.

Shelby laid her cheek over his heart and something tight seized his chest. She didn't see the look of anguish that quickly passed over his features.

Children? Did Shelby want another child? Nelson's brain zinged into action and tried to calculate the number of times they had made love. He'd been so delirious and caught up in Shelby and his need for her, wearing protection hadn't even crossed his mind. And he had none! During his shopping spree, Nelson had thought to buy everything, except the one thing he needed most: Condoms! What in the hell was he doing? What if Shelby got pregnant?

Nelson shook his head, wanting to kick himself for being so irresponsible. As much as he loved Shelby and wanted his life with her back, having another child was out of the question. No way could he live with the fear that something might happen; losing another child would kill him. They could never have more children; Nelson couldn't handle it.

He tried to step out of her arms and Shelby lifted her head. She fanned her fingers through his hair and drew his head down for a deep, wet kiss. Her teeth nipped the end of his chin and her tongue slowly rimmed the circumference of his lips. His body sent up flags of distress, unwilling to cooperate or heed his mind's command to subdue his escalating ardor. After all day, unlimited access, it dismissed his mental insinuation that he should again do without.

Nelson stifled a groan and pulled Shelby closer, running his hands down the back of the gown. He had started this and he couldn't turn his emotions on and off like a water tap. Not with Shelby and not with her softness and scent enticing him to make love to her. He was not made of steel and Nelson's need for Shelby roared through his body like a tornado. He scooped Shelby into his arms and turned for the door.

Mounting the stairs, Nelson added to his list of Christmas hopes that when he again took his wife in his arms tonight, his life-giving seed would not find its mark.

# CHAPTER FIFTEEN

"Good morning, sweetness," Nelson said when Shelby opened her eyes. He kissed her on the nose.

Shelby smiled. Relaxed in the safe haven of her husband's arms, the nightmare hadn't come and she'd slept the sleep of angels. Last night, their lovemaking had been slow and tender, a bodily unveiling of their devotion to undying love. Nelson had cherished her with his hands and mouth, thrilled her with his words and taken Shelby on a journey of love where their spirits had touched and fused again in an inseparable union. She needed no further assurance that her husband loved her, had never stopped loving her and that he would love her for the rest of his life.

Her feelings for him, imprisoned by denial for so long, she could finally release and freely admit that she wanted Nelson more than ever. She wanted him home, in their house and in their bed.

"Good morning, baby," Shelby replied, snuggling closer.

And the game began again.

Two hours later, they were up and dressed. The snow had stopped and Shelby stood at the window in their bedroom watching Nelson use the blower on the driveway. The storm had dropped four feet of winter white before blustering its way East and when she cracked the window, she heard his cheerful whistling as Nelson labored with his task. Having her husband home again filled Shelby with a warm, wonderful feeling, one she thought she'd have to live without for the rest of her life. Nelson loved her and the refrain replayed in Shelby's mind like a needle stuck on a single track of a record.

Watching him, her mood turned somber and she turned away, her fingers absently playing with the locket as she slowly traipsed the room. The blizzard had provided a protective shield around the two of them and helped keep others out while they tried to repair the seams ripped in their marriage. The last two days had been so good between them and she wished they had more time, but they didn't. Tomorrow they would re-enter the real world.

When the phone rang, Shelby rolled back her shoulders in a physical gesture to throw off her blue thoughts. Rather than answer, she headed down the stairs. Nelson would be freezing when he came into the house and the least she could do was have a warm fire and a cup of hot chocolate waiting for him when he did. The phone rang several times while Shelby was in the kitchen and she let the calls go to the machine.

Sometime later, she met a cold and tired Nelson at the front door. She removed his hat and coat and wrapped her arms around his waist, wanting to share her body heat with him. He let her, savoring the feel of her body against his as they rocked together in the foyer. He placed his hands around her face, raised her head and placed his chilly lips against her warm ones. He rippled his fingers through her glossy curls, squeezed her tight, then let her go.

"Little woman," he said, a smile crinkling his eyes. "Your man has been working his butt off for three hours and all you have for him is a kiss. Where's the food? Where's the hot ale? Where's the roaring fire?"

Shelby took his hand and led him into the living room. A fire blazed noisily in the fireplace. A tray sat on the table decorated in holiday colors of red and green. On it was a large Santa mug filled with hot chocolate topped by marshmallows, along with two turkey sandwiches, bounteous with meat, mayonnaise, lettuce, tomatoes, and sliced in half—just the way Nelson liked.

"Much better, little woman," Nelson said, kissing her.

He moved to the couch and sat down. Shelby climbed up behind him and massaged his shoulders while he ate. She ran her fingers along the strong jaw line, traced them over the high forehead and filtered them through the soft hair. Nelson hunkered back against her body, almost purring like a kitten. Sexual love and the physical gratification derived from it was great. But nothing beat cuddling with his Shelby. She could soothe and calm him with a stroke of her hand, and with her gentle fingers easing away his tiredness, Nelson relaxed and closed his eyes.

The ringing telephone broke the spell, and he lifted his body to let Shelby rise. A log split in the fireplace, sending up a shower of red and orange sparks. Through the black grill, Nelson watched the glowing spray fall and scatter across the fireplace floor. He had tried to show Shelby by his actions and tell her with words how much he loved and missed her. While she'd seemed responsive to his overtures, she hadn't yet said that he could come home. His only hope now was that he'd at least done enough to keep himself uppermost in her mind so that she would at least consider his request.

"What's the matter, pumpkin?" Martin Smith asked when Shelby answered the phone and greeted him with a less-than-cheerful Merry Christmas.

"Nothing, Poppy."

"Shelby, you're talking to Poppy. It's Nelson, isn't it?" Martin didn't wait for her to answer. "Pumpkin, we haven't talked about Nelson in a long time. But I am aware of your feelings and I know that this time of year is hard, missing him the way you do. I wish I could be there with you, little girl. I miss him, too."

Shelby heard her father clear his throat and knew there was a tear in his eye. "Yes...well, now, the two of us must buck up and go on with our lives. We have each other and for now we'll have to live with that and let it be enough."

"Poppy," Shelby interrupted softly. "Nelson's here."

Martin went on as if he hadn't heard her. "I've given this matter a great deal of thought of how we can best accomplish that. When your mother-" A full three seconds of quiet passed. "What did you say, Shelby?"

She smiled into the phone. "Nelson's here with me. He came home on Christmas Eve."

"Nelson's there!" Martin's voice boomed over the telephone. "Well, why didn't you say so in the first place, Shelby. Put my son on the telephone. Oh, and Merry Christmas. I love you, pumpkin."

With his pulse racing, Nelson took the receiver from Shelby. "Dr. Smith," he said with respectful caution.

"Dr. Smith? Since when is it my son's habit to refer to me by title." Nelson straddled a chair, his face alight with the love he felt for both Shelby and Martin Smith. He had missed his second father almost as much as he missed his wife. "How are you, Poppy?"

In their conversation, which lasted well over an hour, Martin reprimanded Nelson for giving Shelby the divorce, welcomed him back into the family, and admonished him to take care of Shelby.

"Yes, sir," Nelson said, rising from the chair. "I'll take good care of our Shel and I'll look forward to seeing you next month. Merry Christmas, Poppy."

Drying her hands on a dishtowel, Shelby walked back into the room. Nelson turned to her, his dimples prominent in his cheeks.

"Well?"

"Poppy said, 'Welcome home, son.'"

Shelby's smile was impish. "So, when are you coming home?"

Nelson stared blankly, unsure he'd heard correctly. "When am I coming home?" he repeated.

Shelby turned for the doorway. "Well, if you've changed your mind, I guess I'll find a way to live with your decision."

She was lifted from floor before she reached the archway. Nelson set Shelby on her feet and turned her to face him, holding her by the shoulders to keep her still. "Are you telling me that I can come home?"

"No, Nels. Moving out was your decision. Moving back in has to be your decision, too."

"Shelby Reeves, I moved out so that you could come home."

Shelby's lips pursed as she regarded him. "But I never asked you to leave, Nelson, and since I didn't ask you to leave, I see no reason to invite you back."

What did Shelby mean by that? Utterly confused, Nelson was about to launch into a detailed account of the events that had led to his leaving their house, then he noticed the tilt of Shelby's lips. "Little woman, you're messing with my mind, aren't you?"

"Well, since I'm a Reeves that means that I'm entitled to use Reeves' logic, too."

Nelson's lips buzzed her forehead. "I should put you across my knee."

"Now there's a position we haven't tried. Sounds like fun, though. Help me clean up the kitchen and maybe I'll let you try it."

"Don't answer it," Nelson rumbled in Shelby's ear; at the same time his legs trapped hers so she'd stay still.

The doorbell pealed again. "It might be important, Nelson. Let me up."

"The person at that door had better have an updated insurance policy," Nelson snarled, rolling to the side of the bed.

Shelby threw on a wrapper and belted the sash. "Stop growling, Nelson. I'll go down and get rid of whoever it is. Then we'll pick up where we left off."

Shelby left the bedroom and ran down the stairs. Opening the front door, questions brightened her eyes when she saw not only Manette, but the imposing presence of Jordon Randolph Banks. She opened the door wider to make room for the two people pushing their way inside the house.

Manny pulled Shelby to her in a tight hug. "Shel, you're okay." She looked over Manny's shoulder at Jordon. "What are the two of you doing here?" "I'm here because Manny called and made it sound as if you were at death's door."

Releasing Shelby, Manette turned to face Jordon. "I did not," she disputed. "I said that Shel didn't come to work today and that I was worried about her being up here alone. You're the one who insisted that we drive up here and see about her."

"That is not what you said and you know it," Jordon returned sharply.

Shelby sighed wearily and closed the door. Her friends cared enough to come and see about her and she appreciated that, but if she didn't step in and stop them, Manny and J.R. would argue the point till doomsday.

"Hold it, the both you. First of all, thank you for coming all the way out here, but as you can see, I'm fine. Second, I'm not alone. Nels—"

"That is correct. She's not alone," a deep voice stated.

Shelby whirled around to find Nelson standing halfway up the stairs. He looked over her head at the stunned faces of Manette and Jordon. Nelson jogged down the rest of the steps and took Manette in his arms. The heavy scent of Joy was cloying, but he hugged her tight, then stepped away and extended his hand to Jordon.

Jordon's movements were mechanical, and after shaking his hand, Nelson slapped him on the back. "Come on you two. Let's go into the living room. You look like you could use a drink, J.R."

Shelby started to follow the group. Then remembering her state of undress, she headed for the stairs instead. When she returned, Nelson had already provided refreshments so she sat on the couch beside him and clasped his hand in hers. By the curious looks she received, she knew Nelson hadn't said anything so Shelby took a deep breath and said, "We've decided to try again." Silence greeted her announcement until Manette screamed with joy and began chattering away as if everything in her world had just been righted.

Nelson glanced around the room, distantly listening to Manette. When his gaze swung to Jordon, he wished it hadn't because it reminded him of the things his friend had suffered at the hands of his wife. Shelby wasn't anything like Gloria Banks, but he saw the concern in Jordon's eyes and his brief glances to a spot just over Nelson's head spoke volumes. Mentally shaking off his thoughts, he tuned Manny back in.

Jordon, occupying a chair across from Nelson, scrutinized his friend. Nelson hadn't said anything to him about this reunion and he wanted some answers. When Shelby left the room to get more coffee, he looked at Manette. "Manny, will you go and tell Shelby that I'd like another piece of sweet potato pie, too?"

Manette eyed him. "Something the matter with your feet, J.R.?"

Jordon glanced at Nelson. "Manny, please."

Thoroughly put out, Manette stood up. The black leather cups on the red sweater outlining her breasts moved up and down with her breathing. "Oh, all right," she said. "I'll do it this time, but if you need more you can just forget about Manny Walker being your maid."

When she left the room, Jordon moved to the couch. "What's going on here, Nelson?"

A frown appeared on Nelson's face. "You heard Shelby. I'm moving back home." He left the couch and went to the bar.

Jordon followed and perched on a barstool. He selected a yellow, plastic stirrer from the holder and used it to tap out a beat on the black marble bar top all the while training his eyes on Nelson. "Why now, Nelson?"

"If not now, when?"

The beat on the counter increased in direct correlation with the muscle working in Jordon's cheek as he narrowed his eyes. "The bull you can save for corporate America, Nelson. Look me in the eye and tell me something. After you saw Shelby at the fund-raiser, the plan was for you to be in North Carolina until after the first of the year."

Nelson faced Jordon's stare head-on. "I changed my mind." He released a long breath and jammed his hands in his pockets. "Look, J.R. I already know how you feel about this, but I love my wife and I had to find out if Shelby could love me again."

"And?"

"And she does. Shelby loves me; I'm moving back home, and if you don't mind, I'd prefer not to hear the women aren't worth it speech."

Nodding, Jordon replaced the stirrer and stood up. "I wasn't planning on giving it, Nelson. I know how much you love Shelby, but my concern is this. The last time Shelby left, you fell apart and it took months for you to recover. What's going to happen if it doesn't work out this time?"

Nelson held out a glass filled with ginger ale. "It'll work out, J.R. This time I'll make sure of it."

Taking the glass, Jordon said, "I hope so, Nelson, because if it doesn't, I'm not sure I want to go through that with you again." He grinned. "But I will."

"How was your holiday, Manny?" Shelby asked as they worked together in the kitchen.

Manette closed the refrigerator door and set the sweet potato pie on the counter. "I think that's a question I should be asking you. I'm not the one who spent the Christmas holiday hiding in a log cabin making what I'm sure was very passionate love to my ex-husband."

Shelby's cheeks burned with embarrassment. "I swear, Manny. The things that come out of your mouth sometimes…"

Manette turned to pour steaming coffee into the serving pot. "Well, isn't that what you and Nelson have been doing?"

"Did it ever occur to you that Nelson and I may have been talking?"

"No." Manny set the pot on the tray and reached for the sugar canister. "Nelson's a hot-blooded man. You're a hot-blooded woman. The two of you have been apart for over a year. Any talking that went down in this house happened while you rubbed against each other between the sheets." She wiggled her brows. "So, how many times have you done it anyway?"

Shelby snatched the sugar canister from Manette's hands. "You know, sister-girl. I'm going to help you find a man of your own so that you can stop fantasizing about my love life."

Manette went to the refrigerator for the cream. "Fine with me. If I had a man of my own, I wouldn't have to fantasize about your love life." She turned and gave Shelby a speculative look. "Got anybody in mind?"

Shelby moved to the counter and began slicing the pie. "Not really." She placed the slices on saucers, then on the tray. "But you know, Nelson does have this friend. I don't know if you'd be interested though."

"What's his name?"

"Christopher Mills. Nelson's known him for years. In fact, they grew up in the same town. He came to visit about eight years ago and liked Denver so much, he moved here."

"What does he do?"

"He's a cop."

"I don't know, Shelby. I don't think I want to get involved with a guy on the force. That line of work is so dangerous. If we did get together, I'd just worry all the time."

Shelby groaned. Manny resisted every attempt Shelby made to set her up with a decent guy and couldn't understand why she kept ending up with losers. "But he's a nice guy, Manny, and he's settled. Christopher's been in law enforcement for over ten years. He knows what he's doing and I'm sure he doesn't take any chances. Plus, he owns a home and he doesn't have any children. I'll talk to Nelson and get his number. Then you can call him and check him out for yourself."

Manette's two-inch, fire-engine red nails waved through the air. "Forget it, Shelby. I'm not going to call a man I don't know."

"And why not? You're a grown woman, a college graduate and you have perfect command of the English language."

"That's just it. I am the woman and if a man wants to see me, then he has to make the first move."

Shelby tried to hold on to her patience. "This is the nineties, Manny. If a woman is interested in a man and wants to call him, she can."

"You've been with Nelson for more than a decade, Shelby. So that hardly makes you an expert in the dating game. Men don't like pushy women and with them in such short supply, I'm not going to do anything to hurt my chances of getting one."

Is that right? Shelby thought, watching her sashay over to the counter. Flaps of gold peeked through the pleats of the ankle length, red wool skirt as Manny moved. The word "individualistic" described Manette Walker to a T. Shelby could vividly recall other more exotic outfits, including a tiger-print bodysuit and a beer can top skirt. Even at her wedding, Manny had shown up in an altered version of the rose silk bridesmaid dress. Always one for a little flair, she had replaced the chiffon puff sleeves on the dress with a black spandex material and fur. It had taken the better part of an hour for Shelby to calm down. Judging her friend a walking disaster, Shelby had long ago thrown in the towel.

Thankfully, however, Manny's ineptitude in the personal apparel department did not transcend to the store. She could regulate an outfit to the "What's Hot and What's Not" list in the blink of an eye. She also had a heart of gold, and for her, the word *friend* held special meaning. Which was why Shelby would not give up on her. Somewhere in the world, there had to be a man who could meet her friend's needs, if Manny would just cooperate a little.

Manette handed a cup of coffee to Nelson and sat on the couch beside him. "So, Nels," she began guilelessly. "As I understand it, this house burned bright with the passion of love over Christmas?"

Nelson smiled at the gleam of curiosity he saw in her eyes. "Since you know what went on, Manny, what is it that you'd like hear from me?"

Manette rolled her eyes. "Shelby gave me the boring details. I want to hear about the love, the passion and the excitement. And get descriptive, Nels; I can take it."

"There was love. There was passion. There was excitement," he responded.

"You know, Nelson, the two of you make me sick. Here I have for best friends, the most exciting, romantic couple in the history of love and you guys never tell me anything. What's the big secret anyway?" Manette propped her chin on her fist and pushed out her lips.

"The secret, Manny," Nelson paused to sip from his cup, "is that you have to create your own romantic tale and stop trying to live vicariously through Shelby and me."

"What do you two do, plan ready-made responses for me? Shel just told me the same thing in the kitchen. But I haven't found a man who'll love me the way you love Shelby. You two have that no-holds-barred kind of love that all women dream about and that I've been looking for for a long time, Nels. It seems there aren't more like you out there."

"Thank you for the compliment."

"Well, if the two of you won't talk about your sex life, then let's talk about the game. I don't suppose you saw it, Nelson."

An avid sports fan, Nelson's eyes lit up, but it was Jordon who asked sarcastically, "What do you think?"

He received an acrimonious glare from Manette. "I don't think he did," she returned. "But I do know those Nuggets of yours are a sad bunch, J.R. They didn't just lose. They were dissed, hissed, and not missed when they left the floor. If the NBA had any sense, they'd collect their uniforms and fine 'em for trying to impersonate a basketball team."

Jordon snorted. "Bet you wouldn't say that if they had won, lady. And don't forget, you're dissing some of my former teammates."

"Oh, puh-leez," Manny replied, crossing her legs. "The only chance that team has of winning is if that ball comes with wings and can fly itself into the basket. They're a sad, sad bunch of ball players."

Bored with the debate, Shelby's eyes turned to Nelson. He sat in silent amusement observing their two friends. She moved closer and nudged his thigh with her leg. He placed his cup on the table and took Shelby in his arms, and by the time he released her lips, Jordon was feeling so uncomfortable he left the room. He returned a minute later, coats in hand. He looked first at Nelson and Shelby, then at Manette. She sat enraptured by the two people trying to mesh their bodies together in a shared kiss of passion.

Jordon waved her coat in front of her face. "Let's go, Manny. As you can see, we are not needed here."

Later that evening, Nelson walked up behind Shelby and put his arms around her waist. "Why not?"

Shelby unshackled his arms and moved to the bathroom counter. She plucked two tissues from the box and leaned over the pearl-shelled sink to remove the excess Oil of Olay from her face. Her eyes met the determined black eyes of her husband in the mirror. "Nelson Reeves, there are times when you act just like a big baby. Go to your side of the bathroom and finish drying yourself."

Nelson moved closer to Shelby, planted his bare feet firmly in the sea-green carpet on either side of her and braced his hands against the counter, trapping her. "You still haven't told me why we can't spend the day together tomorrow. We can go to the suite and get my stuff."

Electric quivers caused by the hot kiss Nelson placed on the nape of her neck rocked her body. Shelby gripped the counter but determinedly held his gaze in the mirror. "You know why."

Nelson bit the tip of her ear. "I forgot. Tell me again, sweetness."

Shelby knew she was in trouble when he lifted the hem of the turquoise teddy and brought her back against his naked form. He splayed warm hands across her breasts and she closed her eyes. She opened them again to his smile of impending victory. She lowered her eyes to the sink. No, she thought. She would not fall victim to those dimples or give in to the wonderful sensations caused by the sensuous love strokes on her body.

Twisting away, she moved across the bathroom. "We have to go to work. I do and so do you. We could have gone this afternoon and I let you talk me into staying home. I have a fitting tomorrow and I'm sure you have things to do at your office. Tomorrow night, I leave to meet Felicia and Ty in New York. You said you were going to move back home Saturday and be finished in time to bring me home from the airport."

Her eyes widened when she saw the gleam in Nelson's eyes and his long strides bringing him toward her. She held up her hand to ward him off, backing up until her legs hit the tub. "No, Nelson Reeves. This time I mean it. You stay away from me."

Nelson swept the teddy over her head and placed his hands on her waist. She balanced herself using his shoulders as he lifted her from the carpet and brought her chest level with his mouth. His tongue played with her breasts until she moaned, and when Nelson set her on her feet, his kiss was languidly long. "Let's do it tomorrow, Shel."

"Saturday," she whispered, peeking at him from beneath her lashes.

Nelson lifted her again. Dangling in the air, Shelby was in no position to stop him or hold off the tidal waves rushing in to carry her away. By the time Nelson lowered their bodies to the floor, Shelby's loud moaning had cut off any further protest.

In bed later, Nelson rested his head on Shelby's breast, half listening to what she was saying, his mind on what had happened in the bathroom. He might have struck the match, but Shelby had stoked their love to a roaring blaze, and after taking him through his paces had sent him careening in a climax so powerful, tremors still shook his body and the hand he ran with familiar motion over her belly.

How had he survived so long without Shelby? Nelson wondered, letting his eyes drift over the slim hips and long expanse of legs crossed at the ankles. He hadn't felt this whole, this complete, in a long while. A year ago, he'd foolishly watched half of himself, the most important half, walk out the door. This time, Nelson vowed to keep a firm grasp on their love. This I time, he'd hold on to the two of them so tightly that nothing would make him let go.

# CHAPTER SIXTEEN

Shelby's mind was on Nelson, otherwise she would have noticed the figure Manette had circled on the Christmas sales reports showing the tidy profit made by the store over the holiday season. Uncaring, she let the report fall to her desk and picked up her coffee cup. She leaned back in her chair and propped her feet on top of the antique desk, her fingers playing with the locket around her neck. This morning, Nelson had made her breakfast, handed her a brown bag containing a turkey sandwich and an apple for lunch, and escorted her to the car, already warm and running. He'd driven her to work and after walking with her to the boutique, headed off to his own office. Nelson hadn't been gone five minutes before she'd started missing him, and she could still feel the sizzle of his good-bye kiss on her mouth.

Nelson took good care of her, and Shelby readily admitted that she liked the things he did for her and that he cared enough to keep spoiling her. Maybe it was selfish, but the thought of Nelson moving back into the house and continuing what he'd started so long ago had made her smile. So much so, that by the time she had arrived at the shop, Shelby was grinning from ear to ear.

The grin had gotten her put out of the store after Manny told her that she was making the staff nervous. She'd left willingly. It gave her more time to think about Nelson and the magic that had swept her heart again. She set the cup down and opened the locket. From the outside, it was only a piece of jewelry. For Shelby, it signified not only everything she'd once had with Nelson, but what she could have again. She stared at the pictures inside, her heart full of happiness, wanting to call Nelson, just to hear his voice and assure herself the last three glorious days had indeed been real. Shaking her head, Shelby snapped the locket closed. Tonight, they were going to dinner before Nelson took her to the airport. What she needed to do was get her mind back on work so that she'd be ready when he got there.

Draining her cup, Shelby rose from her chair and left her office for a refill. On her way, she stopped at a mirror in the dressing area and smoothed back a strand of the hair she'd brushed back from her face and pinned in a coil at the nape of her neck.

At the boutique, Shelby wore only black or white, a decision made to eliminate the potential conflict of having to refuse a customer something she'd designed for her personal wardrobe. Today, she had on a black, square neck top that buttoned down the back. The long sleeves were velvet and featured a deep red piping. Matching piping adorned the cuffed, black leather culottes that hit her legs mid-calf, meeting the tops of a pair of black leather boots. Besides the locket, she wore a set of oval ruby earrings and her wedding set. Officially, they were still divorced, but wearing the rings seemed right somehow and gave her back that sense of security.

She crossed to an oversized, ornate, white desk that held two silver carafes. One she kept filled with a special blend of coffee, the other, hot water for tea. Next to the carafes sat a silver serving tray that held flowered china bowls filled with sugar and cream and matching china plates. On days like today when she had a fitting, she also added a tray of sliced fruit and selected cheeses. She filled her cup and, carrying it with her, climbed the three steps leading to the inside entrance of the ready-to-wear store. Sipping the hot brew, she watched her salespeople deftly handle the large crowd eagerly snapping up after-Christmas bargains.

Even with her off-the-street patrons, Shelby had a solid reputation. Customers flocked to her store, unmindful of the costly price tags, because whether designed by Shelby or ready-made, they found quality garments. Her buyers traveled worldwide in search of the clothes sold in the shop and, with Tyrone, hit New York twice a year. Everything in Shelby's shop was fashionable and she carried nothing but the best.

This year, after going over the concept of Kathy's wedding gown with Ty, she'd selected the New York inventory. It would be interesting to see how her customers reacted to her choices when they put out the new spring line next week.

Sighing, Shelby turned away and went back to her office. She set her cup on the desk and moved to her drafting table. Clearing her mind, she took a quick glance at the concept boards above her head, picked up her drawing pencil and began sketching the outline for Felicia's gown.

This was the part of her job Shelby loved most: creating. Coming up with a concept and choosing the right fabric and colors that would bring the garment to life. Her adoration of color, especially those found in the fiery hues of the mountain sunsets she'd watched from her balconies at home, were incorporated into her designs. Gowns exemplifying the sensual appeal of understated elegance and casual wear defined by classic lines were Shelby's trademark and compliments used often in describing her work. The headaches that came with fittings and alterations were inevitable. However, seeing her creations on other people filled her with pride and was enough to make her start the process all over.

The doorbell tinkled and Shelby groaned when I she heard the excessively loud voice of Carlotta Eldridge, president and founder of Quad-E. She had hoped Kathy Lawrence would come alone. She should have known better. Carlotta, the self-designated wedding coordinator, always came. Kathy was so intimidated by the woman that every fitting turned into a stress-filled affair. As the tension set in, Shelby closed her eyes in silent supplication that she would maintain her cool with the woman.

Quad-E had turned out to be even more of a disappointment than Shelby and her friends had imagined. An annual dinner/dance and a five-hundred-dollar college scholarship fund constituted the group's community involvement. Carlotta, already influential, had another agenda. In the hope of increasing her power base over the African-American community in Denver, she limited Quad-E's membership to attractive, professional women of achievement, preferably single. Then, hoping for a marriage, made sure the members had plenty of opportunities to interact with the moneyed men in town.

To their complete disgust, Quad-E was nothing more than a matchmaking service. Their plan to infiltrate the group and change things had backfired. They had faced down the woman on numerous issues, including the lack of any real community involvement by the group. For their trouble, they had all been censured a number of times.

Shelby looked up when Manette peeked her head around the door. "Queen C is here and she has her entourage with her."

Shelby returned Manette's grin with a grimace. "Thanks. I heard." She pushed herself up from the drafting table and headed for the front of the shop. With any luck at all, she could have Carlotta out the door in sixty minutes or less. She pasted a smile on her face as she stepped into the boutique.

"We've been here for ten minutes, Shelby."

Biting down on her lip was the only way for Shelby to stop the sharp retort from leaving her mouth. She moved forward. "Then I offer my apologies, Carlotta. I hope that you took advantage of the refreshments white you were waiting."

Carlotta's lips thinned. "Yes. Yes. The tea is fine, dear. However, tea is not the purpose of our visit, now is it? Kathy's gown is here?"

Shelby's smile slipped a little. With effort she managed to keep it in place. "You're right, of course, Carlotta." She turned to Kathy. "How are you holding up, Kat?"

"About the same as the last time I saw you, Shelby. I'm a nervous wreck."

Shelby was a little taken aback, because she hadn't heard more than two words from Kathy in previous visits. "You do look tired, Kathy. Maybe a few days off would help."

"I can'ttakeanytimeoff, Shel. I have too much to do."

"What about taking vitamins? I know there are some out there that can help boost your energy level."

Carlotta, tired of being ignored, clapped her hands together. "Ladies, I think you can find a more appropriate time to discuss health issues. Right now, I'd like to see Kathy in her dress and I'd like to see the bridesmaids' dresses as well." Carlotta moved to the rose and. lavender sofa and sat her considerable girth on the middle cushion with a flourish.

Shelby turned to Carlotta, somewhat confused. "The bridesmaid's dresses are not here. Only Kathy was due for a fitting today. The other dresses won't arrive until after the first of the year."

The room grew quiet. Shelby watched Carlotta's struggle for words. She was surprised at the calmness she heard when Carlotta directed her gaze at Kathy and spoke. "Then the message must have been taken incorrectly. Shelby, take Kathy and help her into her gown. The rest of you find seats."

Although she wanted to, Shelby did not respond verbally to Carlotta's command. She waved her hand toward the back of the shop. "You know the way, Kathy."

In the back, Shelby removed the wedding gown from the rack and handed the dress to Kathy. "Call if you need my help."

When Kathy stepped into the dressing booth, Shelby went to her office and dialed Nelson's number. Her patience with the high-and-mighty attitude of Carlotta Eldridge was already waning and needed a boost. She hung up after being told by Grace that Nelson was in a staff meeting.

"Shelby? Can you come in here?"

"I'll be right there." Shelby got up and went into the dressing booth.

"I don't understand this, Kathy," Shelby said a few minutes later while giving the dress a final tug. "It's only been a few weeks since your last fitting." Shelby threw up her hands, acknowledging defeat. No way was the mother-of-pearl button going to meet the buttonhole on the other side of the gown. She placed her hands on her waist when guilt stained Kathy's chestnut brown eyes. "Didn't we agree that you were going to lay off the food, at least until after your wedding?"

"I know, Shelby, and I'm sorry. It's this stress. Carlotta has me running in so many circles I can't see straight."

"I thought you were going to talk to your fiancé."

"I tried. He said that since I don't have any family, I should be grateful that Carlotta is willing to help me with the wedding."

Kathy "Kat" Lawrence was agent to some of the top women basketball players in the country. There were so few women in her chosen field that the men tended to treat them as flighty fluffs or ignore them entirely. They did neither with Kathy Lawrence. She'd already proven that she was a force to be reckoned with. When Kat stepped up to the negotiation table for her players, she didn't leave it until she'd gotten everything they'd asked for. Around Carlotta though, Kathy faded into the background, too afraid to speak up for herself. Shelby saw the tears in Kathy's eyes and knew she couldn't yell at her friend. Neither could she send the gown back to Tyrone. His crack about Carlotta might have sounded like a joke, but Shelby knew better.

They were talking about a two-hundred-thousand-dollar gown, loaded down with lace, seed pearls and shellwork. Ty would have a fit if she told him the gown was coming back. Shelby ran a practiced eye over the dress. Kathy's middle had grown by a fourth of an inch and Shelby knew she couldn't be trusted to work off the extra weight. If anything, she could depend on Kathy to keep eating, which meant she was going to have to work elastic into the gown's waist. A satin cummerbund camouflaged with beads and shells might work, she thought, just as Manette stuck her head over the door.

"Queen C wants to know what's taking so long."

Manette's flashing eyes and turned-down mouth meant she'd had another run-in with Carlotta. "The gown doesn't fit. What's eating you?"

"Apparently, my gold lamé top is not to the Queen's liking," Manette huffed. "I told her I didn't care what she thought and to mind her own damn business."

Great, Shelby thought. Now she had to smooth over Carlotta's ruffled feathers. This just wasn't her day and more than ever, she needed to hear Nelson tell her that he loved her. With one palm pressed against her temple and the other on her waist, she looked first at Kathy, then Manette. "Tell Carlotta I'll be out in a minute." To Kathy, "Get out of the dress, Kat. I'll need to take your measurements again and have the gown altered."

Shelby sighed wearily as she made her way to the front of the boutique. Nelson was right. She should have taken the day off.

As expected, Carlotta's anger over the problem with the gown had bordered on abnormal and the encounter with Manette had only added fuel to the fire. With no help from the quietly sobbing Kathy, Shelby had explained her solution of adding elastic to the waistline to give the gown more room and scheduled another fitting in three weeks.

Once she'd gotten Carlotta and her followers out the door, Shelby had gone back to working on Felicia's gown. She reached for the ringing telephone.

"Shel?"

"Felly?"

"How's the sewing biz, sister-girl?"

"It's fine. How's the song biz?"

"Great! I'm number twelve with a bullet and the Europeans adore me."

"I heard, and congratulations."

"Thanks, girl. I called to see how my dress is coming along and to make sure we're still on track for New York tomorrow."

Shelby looked down at the easel. "Funny you should ask that, Felly. I'm working on it even as we speak. What do you think about a trail of taffeta ruffles done up in a tawdry crimson red?"

"If we're going for a giant bird with a fever look, then okay." They laughed.

"I guess that means no taffeta, huh?"

"No taffeta."

"Well, how about a midnight-blue velvet, sitting off the shoulders with a v-dipped neckline and tiny bell satin sleeves. A gown that will hug your body, outline your fabulous figure and sweep the floor with its slightly flaring, flower petal hemline."

"Adornments?"

"None, except jewelry to accessorize. I was thinking diamonds and sapphires."

"Sounds gorgeous! I'll be the belle of the ball and all because of you, Shel."

After Carlotta, the compliment warmed Shelby's heart. "Thanks, Felly. I'll have the sketches finished by the time I get to New York. After we take your measurements, I'll have a sample ready in time to coincide with your return to the states in two weeks."

"Two weeks! I can't come to Denver in two weeks, Shelby. I'm booked to perform on the East Coast for the entire time I'm here." In seconds, Felicia's voice had risen several octaves, exhibiting her ability to reach crystal-breaking range, the reason for her success. "Besides that, I have two interviews, a taping for BET and they want me to do a couple of promos for the awards show. The show is over three months away, why are you rushing on this, Shel?"

Shelby swallowed hard. "Felly, I guess I should tell you that Nelson came home and I was planning to take some time off."

"What! Okay, okay. Start at the beginning and speak on, sister-girl. What happened?" "Nelson happened. Oh, Felly. Nelson loves me." "Tell me something I, as well as the rest of the world, don't know already."

"Well, now I know, too. I love him more than I ever did and he's coming home."

"Well, it's about time." Shelby heard the rustle of silk and knew Felicia was making herself comfortable in anticipation of a long talk. "I feel like I should be there with you, Shel, But I can't, so start at the beginning and tell me everything."

Shelby related the story and as she talked, a feeling of serene, internal peace began to envelop her as Felicia listened without interruption. Manette would always be her best friend, but she liked playing the role of advisor. Felicia and Starris were the shoulders she leaned on when all she wanted was to unburden herself.

"I think you're doing the right thing," Felicia said when Shelby finished, "and I'm so happy for the two of you. I wish I could be there."

"Talking to you has been a big help. Listen, sister-girl. Ma Bell is clinking in my ear and it's your pocketbook she's reaching for. Thanks for listening. When we get together for your fitting, we'll have a longer heart-to-heart."

"I can't wait. Tell Poppy I miss him and that man of yours that I said way to go."

"I will. 'Bye, Felly."

Shelby hung up and returned to the sketch.

# CHAPTER SEVENTEEN

At two-thirty, Nelson entered his office and tossed a stack of manila folders on his desk. He'd been in meetings all day long and because of Shelby, couldn't recall one thing of significance that had been said in any of them. The last had been impromptu as he'd walked down the hallway with the Chairman of the Board and successfully deflected the expected the question.

Nelson went to the windows, his thoughts divided between Shelby and the offer he'd received before Christmas. While subscribers were still down, from an engineering standpoint, the cable system in Orlando was up and running. Equipment tests had showed no failures during the past six months, and Nelson was bored. It was time for a new challenge and working for TTC in Italy was probably the answer to his dilemma. Negotiations had reached the final stages between Techno-tronics Cable and the government in Milan. The agreement would be the first of many hoped-for partnerships as TTC expanded its reach into overseas markets. Nelson had received the nod as Senior Vice President, International Operations, if he chose to take the offer, an offer he still needed to discuss with Shelby before making any decisions.

Hands in pockets, Nelson stared at the line of moving cars. This morning, they had risen to sunshine and the pristine white landscape had sparkled in its rays. The roads, however, had been a different story. Despite the maintenance crews, it would take several days to melt the piles of ice, and then only if the frigid Arctic wind that had accompanied and pushed the storm moved out of the area. As soon as the sun set, temperatures were expected to drop to sub-zero and the splash-back on the tar would freeze, turning the highway into an ice rink.

He looked at what he knew to be the smog-encircled Rocky Mountains, his mind across town on Shelby. She hadn't even left and already he missed her. But she'd only be gone for one day and by the time she returned, he'd have moved his things back into their house. He was supposed to take Shelby to the airport, but her plane wasn't leaving for several hours. If he left now, maybe he could talk her into leaving the store a little earlier than they had planned. And when they stopped at the hotel for a bite to eat, maybe he'd be able to talk her into a little something else. He returned to his desk for his keys just as Grace blustered into his office.

"Miles on one, Nelson. That storm is wreaking havoc in the Central Division and they've been dark in Emporia for three hours." "Three hours! Why the hell didn't Miles call before now?" "Why don't you ask him?" Grace responded. "He's waiting on line one." Nelson whipped up the telephone. "What's going on out there, Miles?"

"Hold on, Nelson. Things are not as bad as they might seem. We still have the locals and some of the nets, but everybody's hollering about their goddamn HBO. This storm is hell, Nelson. In the last four hours, we've been hit with snow, rain and ice. Right now, we're running on the backup generator, but I think I've also lost a modulator or maybe it's one of the amplifiers. Hell, I don't know. That's what you damned engineers are for."

"Update me on the other systems."

"Well, the blizzard is hitting Boise and Kansas City pretty hard. We've gone dark a couple of times, but the equipment is holding. Emporia is the main concern. The equipment in this system is so old, I've thought about adding superglue to the standard office supply list. The switchboard is flashing like a sparkler. I'm afraid it's going next."

Miles chuckled. Nelson didn't find the situation the least bit funny. He saw the customer service department overwhelmed with calls and Subscriber Notifications promising refunds flying out the door. The last decade had been hard on cable operators, and the FCC's determination to hold their feet to the fire wasn't making things any easier. Rulings regulating every aspect of the business, including customer hold time, service call scheduling, ownership limitations, programming tiers and rates, were almost impossible to meet. The industry was taking the heat for everything from poor customer service, violence on television, the lack of educational programming to monopolization of market accusations from the telephone companies, satellite dish providers and the broadcast networks.

Cable was infamous for the daily bad press it received, and Nelson had worked in the industry long enough to know that some of it was justified. However, much of it was not. Part of the reason was that the public couldn't seem to separate cable, which was trying to clean up its act, from the broadcast networks, which largely were not. The other reason was that the industry was not very good at tooting its own horn or marketing itself to the public. Add to those problems new technology already on the horizon and the scramble to upgrade old equipment Techno-tronics Cable had already invested millions and was in the process of selling isolated, unprofitable properties, hopefully before Nelson had to accommodate them in his capital budget.

By the time he hung up the phone, Nelson was ready to strangle Miles. Thirty minutes on the phone and they were no closer to finding the problem than when the man had called. Frustrated beyond any stretch of the imagination, Nelson had told Miles he'd get back to him within the hour. He looked at his watch and called Shelby. "Sweetness," he said, when she answered. "I've run into a snag here at work."

Shelby threw down her pencil and reached for an eraser. She'd redrawn the hemline on Felicia's gown several times and couldn't get her pencil to produce the flowing, curved edges she'd envisioned. "I've sort of got a snag here, too."

Nelson heard the tiredness in her voice. "Carlotta?"

"No. The fitting went exactly according to my expectations. Kathy has eaten her way out of the gown, again, and Carlotta is spouting hellfire and thunder. But it's nothing I can't handle. My current problem is Felly's gown, which at the moment looks like the upside down, fluted end of a crystal vase."

Nelson laughed. "Well, my snag is Miles." Shelby groaned. She knew all about Miles and the headaches he presented for Nelson and his staff. "Our storm moved East with a vengeance. It knocked out Emporia, and possibly Boise and Kansas City, and as you know, Miles, the idiot, doesn't know an amplifier from the rear end of a horse."

Shelby sighed. "I guess that means you can't take me to the airport."

*Damn,* Nelson thought, when he heard the disappointment in Shelby's voice. "I'm sorry, sweetness, and I wish I could tell you when I'll get out of here, but with Miles, who knows how long it will take to identify and fix the problem. With the condition of the roads, I'd rather you not wait on me."

"Don't be sorry, Nelson. You do what you need to do and don't worry about me. I'll call a cab and I have plenty to keep me busy until it gets here. Manny and the buyers are trying to get a jump on inventory. Since we've had to cancel, I think I'll help out."

Nelson glanced out the window. "The roads are really bad, Shel. Maybe you should call the cab now to make sure they have plenty of time to get you to the airport."

"I will. Now listen carefully, because I want to leave you with this thought. My body's so stiff after all your loving, I'm planning to take a long, hot soak in the tub when I get to New York. It's too bad you can't be there, but can you imagine my body naked and glistening with steam as I lower myself into a tub filled with hot, perfumed bubbles?"

"You little minx," Nelson groaned, feeling a rise in the front of his pants. "Now how am I supposed to go back to work?"

Shelby giggled. "I don't understand what you mean, Nels."

"You will when I get my hands on you again."

The thought made Shelby's toes tingle. "I'm going to hold you to that, Nelson Reeves."

"Good, because it's a promise and the next soak we'll take together." Nelson paused for a quick scan of the images his comment provoked. It took another few moments to bring himself back under control. "Seriously, though, Shel. I'm sorry about tonight, and I am going to miss you something terrible until you get back."

"I know, and I'll miss you, too."

"I love you, Shelby."

"I love you, too, baby."

Another line flashing on the phone caught his eye. "I have to go, sweetness." "I know. So do I." Nelson couldn't keep the concern out of his voice when he said, "Shel, call me before you leave the shop…and when you get to New York. I don't care how late it is, okay?"

"Okay. But don't worry, Nelson. I'll be fine." "It's Miles again," Grace informed him over the intercom. Nelson hit the flashing button. Most system managers had cut their teeth on various positions in the system and could fill in wherever necessary; Miles wasn't one of them. As long as everything ran properly, Miles didn't care about the hardware in his system. That meant they would have to play ABC until they lucked up on the problem. However, he wouldn't have to worry about Miles much longer. Emporia was on the sell list, and when the deal went through, Miles would be someone else's headache. The thought was consoling, but not enough to replace his unhappiness at having to give up his evening with Shelby.

"This is the last box for the night," Manny said, pushing a huge box toward Shelby. She straightened to flex her back and mop the back of her hand across her forehead. "Belts and scarves, I think."

Shelby looked down at the inventory sheet. "Fifty, two-inch-wide, gold belts and an equal number in silver according to the list. Twenty black leather, fourteen brown, five gray and two each of purple, white and tan. But there aren't any scarves here."

Manny lowered herself to her knees and opened the box. "There will be as soon as we count them." Laying the clipboard down, Shelby rose and stretched her arms over her head. She'd been at it for only forty minutes and already she was sick of inventory. She got on her knees. "Let's get at it, Manny."

Fifteen minutes later, they were done. The backroom was complete, but everything in the warehouse and on the display floor still had to be counted. Another day, Shelby thought, pushing herself to her feet.

Manny did the same and peeked at her watch. "Mind if I take off a little early, Shel? I have a date tonight."

"I didn't know you were seeing anyone, Manny."

"I'm not. This will be our first date. I'm not sure about him, but at this stage in my life, I can't afford to let any man slip by without checking him out."

"Wait a minute," Shelby said. "Is this the guy you met in the club last week?"

"Yes, it is." Manette's smile was wistful. "Who knows, maybe he'll turn out to be the man of my dreams."

"You met him in a club, Manny, and he was hanging with a bunch of guys. Does he sound like a candidate for settling down to you?"

"Not really, but if my sheets are as hot as yours tonight, who am I to complain?"

Shelby pursed her lips and frowned at Manny. "For your information, Manette Walker, Nelson is workinglate tonight so I won't be able to see him before I leave."

"You'll make up for it when you return, though," Manny murmured.

"What was that?" Shelby asked, smiling.

"Nothing. I'm just happy that the two of you have decided to give it another go. I know you'll make it this time, Shelby. And with you as a model, I don't plan to settle for anything less than what you and Nelson have."

"Maybe you can find what I have if you give Christopher a chance. At least call him and see if you could be interested. I've already talked to Nelson and I can give you his number."

Manette gathered her things. "It's not necessary. I don't want to get involved with a cop, and I hope you haven't given him my number either, Shelby."

"You know I wouldn't do that without your consent, but I hope you'll change your mind. Anyway, you be careful driving home. And be careful on that hot date of yours. I'll want details when I get back."

"Hopefully, there will be some to provide. You be careful, too, Shel. I'll see you on Monday. Good night."

After seeing Manette off, Shelby let the rest of the staff go home and locked the doors. She set the security alarm and returned to her office. Lifting the phone, she called the cab company and scheduled a car to pick her up in plenty of time to get her to the airport. Hanging up, her eyes strayed to the sketch of Felicia's gown and Shelby gravitated toward her drafting table.

She heard a horn honk, and looking up, couldn't believe an hour had passed, although she was extremely pleased with the results. Shelby quickly packed up the sketches. She looked at the phone. She didn't have time to call Nelson now; she'd phone him from the airport and let him know she was okay. She met the driver at the door and when he'd loaded her bag in the trunk, secured the shop for the night.

She climbed into the cab and buckled her seat belt as the car pulled away from the curb. It had started to snow, and watching the charming effect of both the flakes and the elaborate lights decorating the streets, Shelby felt her spirits lift. She had booked a seat on the last flight to New York so that she could share an early dinner with her husband. She had wanted to spend some time with Nelson before she left, but she'd only be gone for one day and after a year apart, did a few hours really matter?

"Pretty, ain't it?"

Shelby turned her head forward. "What?"

The man peered at her in the rearview mirror, then returned his attention to the road. "The lights. Me and the missus even brought the kids down this year for the parade. It's one of the best things about the season, the lights, I mean."

Shelby glanced out the window again. "I suppose."

"Ah, now. Don't tell me you're depressed in this season of hope. Or maybe you're one of those bah-humbug types?" Looking in the mirror again, he grinned.

"Tired is more like it. It's been a long day and I have a six-hour flight ahead of me before I can relax."

"Sleep on the plane," the man murmured.

"I'm sorry, sir, but I didn't hear what you said?"

"Name's Armand, not sir, and I said, why don't you take a nap on the plane? You flying first class? I've always wanted to fly in first class. When I retire, the missus and me are gonna take a trip and I told her that when we go, we're going first class all the way."

Talkative individual, Shelby thought. Settling in the seat, she half-listened to the driver and directed her thoughts elsewhere. She hoped Felicia would like her gown and she was looking forward to seeing Ty as well as her friend. Not only had she gotten the hemline on the dress the way she wanted, in making the changes, Shelby's creative juices had begun to flow. Satin flowers now adorned the bodice and in between the long stems and petals, she'd added blue netting where the caramel color of Felicia's skin would show through. Not too much, but enough to draw attention to her fantastic body and flaunt sex without the sleaze.

Putting away her thoughts, Shelby noticed that Armand had stopped speaking to concentrate on his driving. Looking out the window, she saw why. They were on the highway and the light snow wetting the streets of downtown had turned into a swirling mass of ice and fog on the highway. Now that she was paying attention, Shelby felt the tires slipping as they tried to grip the road. Suddenly fearful, Shelby grabbed the edge of the seat with hands that had turned ice cold as Armand lost his battle to steer the vehicle. The car slid several feet before he regained control, and Shelby released the breath she'd been holding. For the next few miles, Armand remained quiet, concentrating on peering through the windshield where poor visibility met his gaze.

Typical of Denver, the snow let up a couple of miles later, leaving the fog behind. Another mile or so and the fog dissipated, too. "Scared me for a minute," Armand remarked, referring to the earlier mishap.

She heard the lingering tinge of panic in his voice "Yes," she agreed. "Me, too."

The plane came out of nowhere, and before Shelby could form another coherent thought, the cab swerved, knocking her sideways, and she felt the jolting impact of another car. She felt several more hard bumps before the cab slid forward, hit the guardrail and flipped on its side.

Flares, flashing lights and sirens marked the area and Christopher Mills, a tall, good-looking man of medium build, pulled his Jeep to the side of the road and climbed out. His sharp brown eyes quickly scanned the area, and after noting the various players doing the jobs they had been trained to do, he walked over to inspect the scene of the accident. He cuffed the collar of a black leather jacket against the wind and snow, placed his hands on his waist and shook his head in amazement.

By his count, there were at least fifteen cars involved in the crash. A large truck had skidded through the guardrail, but not before its back door had opened and spilled the barrels it contained onto the highway. Most of the other cars would need major repair work, but it looked as if most of the people had walked away dazed but unharmed. His eyes turned to a yellow cab. It lay on its side, its back end crushed. *Whoever was in that car probably didn't make it,* he thought, walking over for a closer look.

"Mills. Glad you're here, man."

Christopher looked down at his partner. "Any fatalities?" "Two, we think."

"What happened?"

"From what we've able to piece together from the witnesses, a small charter plane came out of nowhere. The driver of the cab must have thought they were going to be hit, and in trying to avoid the low-flying aircraft, he swerved into the next lane. That set off a chain reaction of metal on metal. We've got some broken bones, but except for the two fatalities, the others walked away with minor bumps and bruises. They've already cut the roof on the cab and pulled the driver out; he's one of the dead. There was a woman in the backseat and they're still trying to get to her. Since she's not moving, we think she's dead also."

Christopher looked away to another ambulance slowly weaving its way through the debris. It stopped in the middle lane and they stepped out of the way when its occupants jumped from the vehicle and ran over to the yellow cab. He watched them pull the woman's limp body from the car and place her on the stretcher. Moving closer, he looked down. A raw chill ran the entire length of his body when he recognized the bruised, still face of his friend's wife, Shelby Reeves.

# CHAPTER EIGHTEEN

As the first yellow rays of sunshine peeked over the horizon to shine on the mountain peaks far in the distance, Nelson's eyes opened. The events of the last few days rushed through his mind, and his arms closed tighter around Shelby's soft body.

So close. He had come so close to losing her that Nelson didn't know if he'd be able to let this woman, whom he loved more than life itself, out of his sight. Realistically, he knew it was not possible to keep Shelby by his side twenty-four hours a day, but it didn't stop his mind from trying to find a way to accomplish the impossible feat.

Shelby had lain in a coma overnight, and when she'd awakened the next morning, the doctors had kept her for another day. Other than some scrapes, cuts and a couple of bruised ribs, she was fine. Wearing the seat belt had saved her life. It had been Christopher who'd noticed Shelby's scant breathing and alerted the medical personnel. He'd also ridden in the ambulance taking her to the hospital so that she wouldn't be alone. In Nelson's mind, Christopher Mills had risen to hero status and he didn't know how he'd ever repay his friend.

Shelby resisted her mind's effort to pull her from the dream. She wanted to stay in the enchanted place, a place where she was happy, a place where she felt loved and warm and safe. Nelson was there with her, adding to her joy. His arms were around her and the kisses she felt on her face aroused her to heights of passion Shelby never knew existed. In this magical place they had found their love again and Shelby held on to her dream and to Nelson, never wanting to leave.

Nelson stroked his hand over the curve of a dark and supple hip. That there was less of Shelby to love caused Nelson a moment's concern. He didn't dwell on the thought, focusing instead on the rightness of having his woman back in his arms.

His hand moved to her back and continued the caresses, easing Shelby from the realm of slumber. She wiggled her body closer against him and Nelson felt a vital part of himself come to life, and harden with desire.

After letting her recuperate for most of the day, last night they had joined in desperation, their passion borne of a need to hold tight to what had almost been taken away. Their touches had skirted heated skin; wild limbs had competed for closeness as each tried to show the depth of their love. After a long night of urgency, Nelson had plans of indulging his craving at a more leisurely pace this morning. Shelby loved him and nothing would ever cause her feelings to change. That thought alone fanned the intensity of the heat sequestered in the lower half of his body. He reached into the bedside table drawer for a foil packet, then nudged Shelby's mouth with his lips. "It's time for you to wake up, sweetness."

Shelby heard his voice, so deep and so near. She felt the arms embracing her body and the muscled hardness beneath her. She opened her eyes and encountered jet black orbs where desire flamed anew. Happiness bubbled up inside her. The magical place was real. Nelson was here and he was holding and kissing her as if he'd never let her go.

Shelby grabbed hold of his shoulders as Nelson deftly reversed their positions and nudged her thighs apart with his knee.

"No foreplay?" she asked with a teasing smile.

Nelson centered himself at her entrance. "No foreplay."

"No loving, sweet kisses? No—"

Nelson thrust forward, invoking a sensual moan from Shelby. "I love you, Shel," he murmured against her mouth. "And I swear I'll spend the rest of my life showing you how much."

The shower they took later was refreshing, though heated by much more than the water flowing from the tap. It seemed they were still making up for lost time and a mere glance or touch would set their hearts to racing and their arms to reaching for each other. Utterly satiated, but well aware that their passion could swellat anytime, Shelby lifted her fork and sliced through the western omelet Nelson had prepared. If they were to keep up the morning's sensual activities, she needed sustenance or she'd never last through Nelson's advances.

Nelson crossed to the table and set a cup of coffee by her plate, then moved back to his own seat. "Shel?"

"Umm hmm," she toned over a mouth full of food.

"I have something I need you to read."

Nelson extended his hand across the table and Shelby took the white envelope, her brown eyes puzzled as she slit the letter open with a knife. Her mouth moved as she read the words, but no sound came out. *Senior Vice President? Milan, Italy?* The executive perks and stock options were listed line by line and the amount of money was staggering.

Shelby's hands trembled as she lowered the letter and the full implication its meaning became clear in her mind.

A worried look tinged Nelson's eyes as he watched Shelby reread the offer. "Sweetness, what are you thinking?"

"I don't know what to think. Is this for real?"

"As real as it gets if the partnership goes through. Milan is still in question. Their government has to okay the project and FCC approval is still pending. However, the promotion goes through regardless."

"Well, what do you think? I mean do you want to go to Milan?"

Nelson rose from his chair. He leaned against the counter, crossing his legs at the ankles. "I don't know, Shelby. I've been with Techno-tronics since graduation. The company has been good to me and, until lately, the work interesting. But the system's up, the numbers are looking good, and a good junior engineer could handle any problems that might arise. I'm bored, Shel. I've never wanted to be a boardroom executive. I guess I just feel like it's time to do something else."

Shelby tried to keep the waver out of her voice as she responded. "Something else? What do you mean by something else? Your entire career has been spent in the cable industry. Surely, you're not talking about chucking ten years down the drain."

Nelson hurried to the table. He pulled Shelby from her chair, took the seat and placed her on his lap. "No, I'm not talking about anything that drastic, unless the Milan deal falls through. And if the partnership is approved, then there's your boutique, the house, your feelings about moving to another country and a host of other things to consider."

"Nelson. Milan is..." Shelby struggled to find the right words, but could think of nothing that would accurately express her thoughts, and so said, "so far away."

Nelson gave her a little squeeze. "I know that, sweetness. Which is why I've also been checking into other options. The state needs an engineer. Now the money's not that great and I'd have to commute because most of the work involves projects in the upper foothills, but I can do it, Shel. All I need is your support."

Shelby's mind was whirling. Reunited with Nelson. Milan. Her boutique. Engineer for the state. The house. FCC approval. Nelson's bored. The foothills. Techno-tronics. Nelson's career. Moving?

At that moment, nothing made any sense and Nelson wanted her support. Shelby knew she couldn't give him her support, not now. She couldn't make any decisions until she had some time to think things through. "When do you have to make a decision?"

"Not for a while. As I said, the Milan partnership is still waiting approval on both ends. Until then, I'd continue acting in the same capacity at Techno-tronics that I've always held." Nelson kissed her and held Shelby close to his chest. "I will tell you this. If the approvals come through, I'd like to take the job in Milan. It's a chance to do something really exciting. If it doesn't, then we'll discuss our options again. But I won't do anything unless you back me one hundred percent. I want you to think this through, Shel. Take all the time you need, and if you decide that

Milan is out or have misgivings about the engineer position with the state and want me to stay at Techno-tronics, then tell me. We do nothing unless it's what you want, too."

Later that morning, Nelson was puttering around in the garage. He wasn't doing anything particularly important, straightening the gardening tools in the corner, sorting through his nails and screws, checking the oil in Shelby's car.

Earlier he'd tightened the hinges on the kitchen door and fixed the loose knob on the downstairs bathroom door. Nelson was enjoying the freedom of roaming his home again, and it was his mind that was at work more than his hands.

There was one other thing he had neglected to mention to Shelby this morning and this request was the most important.

Nelson wanted to marry his wife again and he wanted to do it today. He'd already placed the call to the county. So recently divorced, all they needed was a marriage license, which could be obtained at the counter in the DMV.

But Shelby was already overwhelmed and Nelson wasn't sure how she'd react. He looked at his watch. To make this happen, he couldn't put off asking Shelby any longer. There was no telling how long the lines would be at the DMV.

He went into the house. "Shel?"

"In the kitchen, baby."

Nelson moved through the rooms and stopped in the doorway. He knew he had a specific purpose for being there, but Shelby's bottom, clad in tight jeans, momentarily arrested his thoughts.

Rising from loading the dishwasher, Shelby stood and lithely twisted from side to side, then lifted her arms over her head, raising the siren pink top. Nelson's breath strangled to a halt and his pants gradually constricted across the front of his hips.

Since he'd been home, Shelby had worn loose-fitting garments that seemed more off than on her fragile frame. Today, somewhere in that big old closet they shared, Shelby had managed to find an outfit that hugged her snugly, and in all the right places. A sucker for blue jeans, especially when they contained his wife's rounded curves, he waited for Shelby to turn around, eagerly anticipating the image that would include her full breasts and slim waist.

Then he scowled. Almost since he'd stepped through the front door, they had been making love. At some point, he had to curb his appetite for his wife. Wife! That was it, Nelson thought, remembering why he'd strolled into the kitchen. He wanted to ask Shelby to become his wife again.

Shelby knew something was on his mind as soon as she looked at Nelson. *What now?* she wondered. She closed the door to the dishwasher, carefully folded and placed the flowered dishtowel on the counter, then crossed to the kitchen table.

Whatever Nelson was about to tell her, Shelby knew she would need something solid beneath her.

Nelson waited until she was seated. Then he moved to the table and. lowered himself to one knee in front of Shelby. "Sweetness, I don't know what you're thinking, but I hope that what I'm about to ask won't send your mind into a tailspin."

Shelby reached out her hand and ruffled her fingers through the soft waves on Nelson's head. "Just give it to me straight and I'll deal with the aftermath later."

Nelson caught her hand and placed a kiss in her palm. "Okay. Shelby, you know how much I love you, and you know how hard I fought to keep from giving you that divorce. I never wanted to lose you, Shelby, even though I acted like the biggest jackass in the world. Please, if you'll have me again, I'd like you to be my wife."

Whatever Shelby had been expecting Nelson to say, it certainly hadn't been a marriage proposal. "What?"

He lifted her left hand and kissed the ring. "Shelby, you've accepted me back into your life. You're wearing my ring. I know that you love me and I love you, but I want the whole package, Shel, just like we had before. I need to know that, legally, you're mine again."

"You want to get married?"

Nelson nodded. "Yes. I want to marry you and I want to do it today."

Could she be anymore stunned? Shelby didn't think so. She'd spent the past two hours grappling with all the other shocks Nelson had laid on her that morning, and now he was back with another to add to her load.

She loved this man, this wonderful, handsome man who filled her heart with so much joy. She knew Nelson so well, as well as she knew herself. But her husband's unpredictability was something Shelby knew she'd never get a handle on.

This was not something Nelson would give her time to think about either. He wanted an answer and he wanted it right now. In a play for time, she said, "Nelson, how do you expect to pull off something like this?"

A pleased, dimpled grin spread across his face. "Does this mean you're going to marry me, Shelby Julian Reeves?"

Shelby returned the smile. "Of course, I'll marry you, Nelson. But how do you expect that to happen today?"

Nelson rose and shouted, "Yes!" He pulled Shelby up from the chair, then lifted and swung her around while hugging her to him in a powerful hold. He kissed her again and set her on her feet. "Get dressed, little woman. We have to get out of here."

"Nelson—"

"Don't worry, Shel. I'll take care of everything." He shooed her from the kitchen and after she'd gone up the stairs, hurried to the telephone. By the time he'd placed all his calls and gotten dressed himself, it was almost one o'clock. Nelson hustled Shelby to the car and tried to keep his elation in check. His wife was going to marry him again! The thought kept running through his mind. Everything was in motion. Manette had been almost as excited as Nelson when he called her to handle some of the arrangements. It would not be a fancy wedding, a small guest list, few decorations and a simple meal catered by a friend afterward, but when it was over-he would have his wife back.

Shelby kept sneaking furtive glances at Nelson. She had several reservations about what he was doing. She quickly brushed them aside, knowing that if Nelson wanted them to be married today, that's exactly what would happen.

However, as they rolled to a stop for a red light, another thought struck her. Shelby turned in her seat to face him, dreading his response to the request she was about to make.

"Baby, I know you said we were in a hurry, but can we make one stop?"

"Sure." Nelson ran his eyes lovingly over her face. "Anything for you, sweetness."

Shelby took a deep breath, hoping Nelson truly meant what he'd just said. "I'd like to visit Lamar."

Nelson's heart thudded once, twice, then stopped altogether. His hands clutched the steering wheel and a curtain of fear descended like a sudden fog. He stared at the traffic light, concentrating on the small red circle until it switched to green. Even then, Nelson sat fighting to stop the flood of thoughts trying to break through into his mind.

A horn honked behind them, jerking Nelson from his trance. His entire body shook as he forced his foot down on the gas pedal.

Shelby touched his arm. "Baby, pull over. There's a parking lot right over there." Nelson turned the steering wheel to the right. He pulled into a space, shut off the engine and slumped back in his seat.

A few minutes passed before Shelby ventured to break the silence. "This is important to me, Nelson." She ran a nervous hand through her hair, then folded her hands primly in her lap. "The last few days have been crazy and circumstances beyond my control have made it impossible for me to visit my son. I need to do this, Nelson. And today, I'd like you to go with me."

Propping his elbow on the door handle, Nelson massaged his forehead. His voice was gruff with emotion when he spoke. "I can't."

Hurt, angry tears burned to be released from Shelby's eyes. She gulped them back. "Nelson, please?"

He couldn't even consider the possibility. "Ask me to do something else, Shelby. Anything else, just not this."

Shelby pressed her lips together to hold in her pain. Why was it still so hard for Nelson? Why couldn't he understand that visiting his son would help him? Lamar liked her daily visits; Shelby knew her baby did, and he liked the things she did for him.

Physically, Lamar was no longer with them, but she always felt so much better after talking to him. She wanted to tell Nelson that his son missed him. She wanted to tell her husband that visiting Lamar would make him feel better, too. Shelby voiced neither thought. She sighed and resigned herself to accepting that Nelson just wasn't ready.

Nelson chanced a glance at Shelby. He saw the plea in her eyes, just before she turned away to stare out the window, and anger surged through him. The emotion spread like a wildfire, but it wasn't Shelby that had him incensed. He was furious with himself. His wife needed him by her side and he had promised never to let Shelby down again. This was his first test and he'd already broken that vow.

But how could he do this? Nelson hadn't been to the cemetery since the funeral. How could he make himself go now? Shelby was hurting and he was the cause of that hurt, something else he'd promised never to do again. Knowing what he had to do, Nelson sat up and reached for Shelby's hand. He kissed each of her fingers, then tipped her chin upward and, smothering his fear, drew strength by placing a kiss on Shelby's trembling lips.

"We'll go," was all he said as he started the car.

Nelson placed his hands in the pockets of his tan camel-hair coat and hugged the garment tighter around his body. Hanging back, he watched Shelby use a hand shovel to dig away the snow and place the colorful bouquet of flowers they'd bought at the foot of Lamar's headstone. He heard the scraping noise made by the shovel as Shelby tried to remove the rest of the snow

Nelson focused on those flowers. Then he looked around him at the snow-covered ground, thinking it was a good thing they'd worn boots. Nelson shivered as he glanced at the other headstones, hating that his son had to stay in such a cold place. The scraping noise stopped and Shelby's words reaching his ears brought Nelson out of his reverie.

"I'm sorry, Mommy can't get this snow off you, Lamar. There's just so much and I should have brought a bigger shovel." Shelby laughed softly. "I guess that was kind of silly, since I knew there would be snow. I know you're cold, little man, but don't you worry, the sun is shining and all this snow will soon melt." Shelby stood up and rested her gloved hand on the cold stone. She looked in Nelson's direction. "I have surprise for you today, Lamar. It's something we've both waited for, for a very long time. Your daddy's here and he's come to talk to you, too."

Shelby beckoned for Nelson to come closer. Nelson clenched his jaw and stood rooted to the spot. He'd come to the cemetery, even left the car, but he wasn't going any closer. He'd watched Shelby as she talked to her baby. He'd observed the exuberance in her face and the radiance in her eyes. Her voice sounded so full of happiness it made him wince. Shelby had spoken as if she thought Lamar could really hear her, as if she thought their son was still alive. Was this the way other people grieved for loved ones? Nelson didn't know, but something about Shelby's behavior bothered him, very deeply.

The smile dropped from Shelby's face. She moved to his side and wrapped her hands around Nelson's arm. "Baby, Lamar wants to say hello, but you have to move closer."

His eyes closed, then opened to stare at Shelby. Nelson stilled her attempts to draw him forward. "Shel, stop. Lamar is…" He couldn't finish the sentence.

Shelby tugged his arm again. "It's okay, Nelson. You just have go over there with me."

Still hesitant and very unsure of what was happening, Nelson allowed Shelby to pull him forward. His booted feet dragged a trail through the mushy, white ice beneath them. At the edge of the grave he stopped and his eyes misted over.

Shelby watched him intently. "Just say hello and that you're glad to be here."

Nelson pushed a shaking hand through his hair. It fell heavily to his side and he turned to Shelby. "We have to go,

Shelby." Then he walked off, away from the grave, away from the cemetery, away to the car.

Shelby's eyes stayed on Nelson's retreating back until he disappeared inside the car. She turned back to the headstone and whispered, "See, Lamar. Mommy told you your daddy would come and visit you, and he came. Next time, you'll get to talk to him." She bent over and straightened the flowers, then followed Nelson's steps to the car.

They picked up the license at the city-county building and returned to the car. How was he going to help his wife? The question rolled through Nelson's mind as he drove the car toward their house. The events of the last few days were enough to shake anyone. What had happened back at the cemetery was something else again.

Nelson's uneasiness grew when Shelby began humming, and looking at her, he knew that she was happy. It was the source of that happiness that concerned him. He couldn't bring himself to talk about it with her, feeling that somehow this was his fault, too. He just knew that Shelby needed help, and so did he.

Unsure where to start, there was only one person Nelson could think of to point him in the right direction. Martin Smith had flown home as soon as Nelson called to say that Shelby was in the hospital. If it hadn't been for Poppy, Nelson would have lost his mind. Now, he needed his father-in-law's help again. He was going to remarry Shelby, nothing could change Nelson's mind about that, but they could wait one more day.

Lamar's death was the reason their marriage had fallen apart and it was time to face that fact squarely and resolve their feelings about what had happened. Until they did, Nelson knew in his heart that he and Shelby could never truly be happy together.

Nelson had meant to call his father-in-law as soon as they returned home. However, when they pulled into the driveway, they found their house the scene of a festive commotion.

All of their friends had come to celebrate Shelby's safe return and their remarriage. As soon as they saw Shelby and Nelson, the air swelled with shouts of delight and the couple was mobbed. There had been an immediate bustle of activity when Nelson led the way into the house. Jordon had gone to the patio and fired up the grill, others had delivered food and drink to the kitchen and the designated DJ got the music going.

While making calls about the wedding, Manette had also arranged an impromptu party to celebrate. Now they were gathered in the living room. The sound of music and laughter stimulated the party atmosphere as Nelson and Shelby sat on the couch opening surprise wedding gifts.

Shelby stood to unwrap the last present handed to her by Jordon. They had already received a few kitchen appliances, a couple of really neat vases, a very sexy nightgown and foaming bath beads for their second honeymoon night. Those at a loss for what to buy a couple that had already been married for eight years had opted for the reliable gift certificate.

This present, though, excited Shelby. It was from Starris and it was obviously a painting. She knew her friend was an exceptional artist and could hardly wait to see what lay beneath the wrapping. Shelby pulled off the last piece of paper and gasped. The entire assembly grew quiet. Stunned, Shelby turned to Nelson, whose own eyes were glued to the life-size rendering of the first portrait he and Shelby had taken with their son. Shelby laid the painting down and ran from the room. All eyes followed her to the door.

Lonnie Gilmore stood, drink in hand, and glared nastily at his wife. "I told you to leave that ridiculous piece of crap at home. Now, look what you've done, Starris. Leave it to you to ruin everybody's good time."

Lonnie was so loud that Nelson felt the need to say something before he went in search of Shelby. At the doorway, he turned back and crossed to Starris. He took her in his arms and hugged her. "Thank you for the gift, Starris. You'll never know how much your painting means to Shelby and me. And because you are the artist, the painting is all the more precious to us."

Nelson left the room and a low murmuring of conversation began. Starris saw Lonnie heading her way again and turned her back. Her husband had been drinking heavily, but drunk or sober, Lonnie never failed to find a public medium in which to degrade her and her talent.

Lonnie moved up close behind her. "I don't care what Nelson said. You are a loser, Starris," he sneered in her ear, "and a pitiful mate. Maybe, if you'd stop wasting your time at these unprofitable pursuits, for which you have no talent, you might find the time to be a better wife to me."

When Starris didn't reply to his taunting, Lonnie's speech turned vulgar. Her shoulders trembled, but still Starris did not respond.

Watching from the corner, a tight muscle worked in the cheek of Jordon Banks. He'd heard every despicable word uttered from Lonnie's filthy mouth. Holding himself in check, Jordon stayed right where he was. He didn't know the couple, but as long as the man's insults remained verbal, he would refrain from interfering in the marital dispute. After all, Shelby and Nelson were the exception. Most marriages, to his way of thinking, including his own, were never the happy, loving affairs everyone made them out to be. Nonetheless, he felt himself relax when the woman finally walked away and the man did not follow.

Nelson came back into the room with Shelby a short while later. She went immediately to Starris for a quick hug, then went to get the painting and returned to stand beside her friend. "This is the greatest gift anyone could have given to us. Thank you, sister-girl. Nelson and I will find a special place to display your talent in our home. But how?"

Starris managed to smile. "I painted it from the photo-graph."

They hugged again and sensing that all was well, the party revved back into full swing. A man standing by the television set suddenly hollered for silence. He adjusted the volume on the big screen, high-definition set, then moved so that they could all see the screen.

They saw Christopher Mills being accosted by a large throng of local and national reporters and photographers on the steps outside the police station. A woman with wild blond hair stepped in front of him. "We understand that if not for you, Shelby Smith would have died in that car crash a few days ago," she shouted over the din. "Care to make a statement?"

Remaining silent, Christopher started down the steps. He did not grant interviews because he did not consider the media his friend, but they had been hounding him for the last two days. The mass surged forward and followed him.

"Detective Mills? We know how much Martin Smith loves his daughter. Have you been offered a reward for saving her life?"

Christopher pushed the microphones out of his face and kept moving.

A burly-looking man tried to cut off his progress. "Look, Detective. We're just trying to do our jobs and the public has the right to know. Can you confirm reports that Shelby Smith was riding in an unlicensed cab and that the driver had been cited for several DUIs over the past six months?"

Christopher turned and stared at the gathering. Microphones rose in anticipation of his statement. "Her name is Mrs. Shelby Reeves." Then he pushed through the crowd and walked away to his Jeep.

In the Reeves' living room, colossal hurrahs broke out and high-fives were passed all around. Everyone cheered Detective Christopher Mills and his handling of the press hounds.

"We need to get that brother over here," someone yelled. "He should be part of this celebration, too."

"That's a great idea," another person remarked.

"Does anyone have his number?" still another asked. "We'll call the police station. They'll hook us up," came the answer. Manette rose from her chair. "I'll do it," she volunteered.

It was the last anyone saw of Manette Walker for the remainder of the evening. It wasn't until much later that Nelson was able to slip from the room with Martin Smith for an undisturbed talk in his study.

# CHAPTER NINETEEN

Christopher threw a handful of peanuts into his mouth and twisted the cap off his bottle of Coors. He downed half the bottle, then looked at the group of people surrounding him, shaking his head in amusement.

"I told that idiot not to do it, but did he listen? Not on your life. The fellas had thrown out the dare and despite my instructions to the contrary, Nelson Lamar Reeves, Jr., decided, come hell or high water, he was going to jump on the back of that milk truck. So, he crouched low and waited for the truck to roll by, then he leaped through the air. When the truck moved away, Nelson lay on the pavement, holding his head and howling in pain. After that, whenever the kids saw him, they called him Milkhead."

Christopher howled with laughter, then tipped the bottle to his mouth. The group cracked up in sidesplitting hilarity.

"Being hardheaded is a trait Nelson has perfected," Jordon chimed in. "Never could tell that brother anything, and if you told him not to do it, it only made him more bullheaded."

Hearing the laughter, Nelson, his face hot with embarrassment, walked over. He looked Christopher dead in the eye. "Look, Mills. I know you're getting a kick out of telling that story, but would you mind not repeating it to everyone in the room. We were boys at the time and these people are my friends. Cyrus here works for the *Denver*

*Post* and you are in effect giving him an exclusive that may plaster my name in its headlines."

Martin Smith laid a hand on Nelson's shoulder. He was laughing at Nelson, too. "Son, calm down. I know it's difficult for you to see the humor in the situation. But you must admit that your attempt to jump on the back of a milk truck fell a little short of the mark. Well, son, you just stick to cable television and leave the stunts to the daredevils of this world."

"Thanks for your support, Poppy," Nelson grumbled with sarcastic undertones.

Nelson, Senior, chuckled loudly. "Junior always did want to be a stuntman and it was his talent for building things that him got into trouble time after time. Why, I remember this one day, and I believe Junior was ten or so at the time, when he built a wooden ramp from the ground to a large branch of a maple tree in our backyard. The boy called himself 'Bikerman' or some such nonsense. Anyway, Junior proceeded to pedal his bike up that ramp and fly through the air. It was a miracle all the boy got for his trouble was an arm broke in two places and a large bump on his head. I thought his Mama was gonna have a stroke. I know other stories, but his brothers tell 'em better." Nelson, Senior, looked around the room. "James, come over here and tell these good people about the time Junior climbed on top of the roof…"

Hearing the doorbell and glad for the chance to escape the ridicule being directed at him, Nelson went to answer the front door. Amazement shone in his eyes, and opening the door wider, he stepped aside to admit the woman standing on his porch. Christopher's eyes zeroed in on the woman and narrowed in appreciation.

The clingy, long-sleeved, mint green, knit number outlined a pair of full breasts before tapering to the waist and flaring out slightly from the shapely hips. She had curves, curves he felt would just fit his hands, should he ever get close enough to size them. Black hair fell in waves around a heart-shaped face enhanced with a makeup job so professional, one could hardly tell she was wearing any.

Nelson walked up behind Manette and placed his hands on her waist. He leaned over and placed his mouth at her ear. "Manny Walker, you are a vision of loveliness."

"Thanks, Nels," Manette replied. "Now let me go. You already have a woman. I'm taking your advice and creating my own romantic tale. If things go according to plan, I won't be available much longer." Twinkling brown eyes found and linked with those of Detective Mills, and when her lips curved in a smile aimed directly at his heart, Christopher felt a hand clench inside his chest.

"Where in the hell is Manny?" Pamela asked, looking around the bedroom. She colored a little when her eyes met those of Henrietta. "I beg your pardon, ma'am. But as maid of honor, shouldn't she be here helping us?"

"She'll be here soon," Shelby said, her voice wavering slightly.

"I'm here," Manette said, walking into the room. The women stared as she crossed the floor to Shelby. "Here are the earrings, girlfriend."

Maxie whistled. "What, no fur this time? What happened, you get hit by a van from the beauty school?"

Manette twirled. "No. I've been hit by the love van."

"Well, I think you look great," Jacqueline remarked. "And so will the driver of that van." "But not too great," Starris said. "After all, Shelby is our bride."

"I'm not trying to steal Shel's thunder, but I am keeping a flash of lightning for myself."

Shelby rolled her eyes. "Just give me the earrings, Manny." "Well, if you'll hold your hand still, I will." Shelby looked down. Her hand and the rest of her body were shaking badly with nerves she hadn't been able to control all day. When Manette passed her the jewelry, it took three tries before Shelby was able to hook one of the pearl earrings to her lobe.

"Here, let me," Starris offered.

"Okay, ladies," Pamela said when she was done. She looked down at the paper in her hand. "Now, according to the list, I think we've covered everything. Borrowed?"

"My pearl earrings," Manette replied.

"And my diamond tennis bracelet," Jacqueline added. "Old?"

"Nelson's old."

Pamela propped a fist on her waist. "Maxie, will you please get real?"

"Well, he is," Maxie protested. "I don't mean age-wise, I mean husband-wise."

"Oh, never mind, Maxie," Pamela returned. "Nelson doesn't count. What's old here?"

Henrietta, who'd been sitting in a chair watching the six women and the camaraderie that flowed between them, stood up. "I'm old."

Shelby crossed the room and took Henrietta's hand. "In that beige wool you look younger than any of us. Marna, I'd like you to meet Manette Walker, my maid of honor and best friend. Manny, this is Mrs. Henrietta Reeves."

"I'm proud to meet any friend of my daughter."

"Thank you, ma'am," Manette replied. "Shel, you do have something old, the pictures inside your locket."

"And isn't Junior about to put your wedding ring back on your finger where it belongs?" Henrietta asked.

Shelby nodded.

"Okay, that takes care of the old. Now, what about the new?"

"My locket is new, Pam, and Mama bought me the hat. For the blue, Poppy has a handkerchief for me."

"That's it then," Pamela said. "Except for Shel's hat, she's ready."

"Ladies, why don't we go and check on things downstairs," Henrietta suggested wisely. "I think Shelby needs a few minutes alone." She passed each woman a single white orchid as they moved toward the door.

"Wait," Shelby called. She looked at each of her friends all dressed in mint green, each style uniquely their own. "You guys are the best. Thank you."

"You're welcome," they replied in unison, and headed out the door.

*Why am I so nervous?* Shelby wondered, staring at herself in the mirror. She was remarrying Nelson and this was something she wanted most in the world. By the time the clock struck midnight and the new year began, she would again be Mrs. Nelson Reeves. The way Nelson had it figured, if they re-wed before midnight, technically they could count the past year as part of their married life. She felt there had to be a flaw somewhere in his thinking, but had decided not to counter the Reeves' rationale.

Shelby rose from the dressing table, the heels of her rose pumps sinking into the carpet as she crisscrossed the floor trying to understand the deep tension that had engulfed her body.

In one year, she'd divorced her husband, narrowly escaped losing her life in a car accident and she was about to remarry her husband. It was almost as if her life had turned into a soap opera. To top everything off, she now faced the prospect of possibly uprooting her life and moving to Milan, Italy, and, if not that, supporting Nelson as he adjusted to a new job with the state.

Living abroad wasn't something she'd ever contemplated and after much thought last night, Shelby still wasn't sure how she felt about the idea. Milan was important to Nelson and saying no to the offer could be detrimental to his career. Could she deny him this opportunity, especially when he'd already stated that he wanted to go? She might have the chance to work with some the world's most celebrated fashion designers, possibly even open her own house. But the thought of leaving her home was scary, and the relocation might draw more attention to her.

As good as Milan sounded, Shelby was leaning toward saying no. Despite what he'd said, she knew Nelson would be disappointed, but the notoriety she'd garnered in national fashion circles and being related to Martin Smith had placed the news of the car accident in newscasts and headlines around the world. The blanket "no interviews" statement Nelson had issued through their lawyer didn't seem to be working, and Shelby was very uncomfortable with the spotlight focused on her. She wanted her relative obscurity back and fervently wished for the hubbub to go away.

Knowing she had to come to grips with what was really bothering her, Shelby stopped in the middle of the floor. Her fingers found and played with the locket hanging around her neck. She sat on the bed, picked up a picture of her son and tried to hold back the tears, knowing that to cry now would ruin her makeup.

What kind of mother would leave her baby? If she left the country, Lamar would be all alone. Who would visit him, bring him flowers, talk to him? Shelby replaced the picture on the nightstand and folded her hands in her lap.

She couldn't do it. She had to be here, where she could be close to her son. "Come in," she said softly in answer to the knock on her bedroom door.

Martin Smith entered the room. "Everyone's waiting for you to make your appearance, pumpkin. Most of all Nelson, who I believe is about to bust a gut, as they say." He crossed to the bed where Shelby still sat and after lowering himself beside her, placed an arm around her shoulders. "What is it, pumpkin?"

Shelby leaned on her father, resting her head against his shoulder. "Oh, Poppy, I can't do this. I can't leave my baby here."

Sighing deeply when he heard his daughter's tears begin in earnest, Martin's other arm enclosed Shelby against his chest. He patted her back in a comforting gesture and let her cry. Few times in her life had Shelby shown outwardly that she needed anyone to lean on emotionally, and he could count on one hand the number of times Shelby had reached out to him for comfort. His daughter was a strong and determined woman. Strong enough to reach for her dreams and attain them, and sometimes too strong for her own good.

In his mind's eye, Martin still saw the image of five-year-old Shelby, without a trace of tears, standing stoically at his side, watching her mother being laid to rest. After the guests departed the house, Shelby had climbed into his lap and said, "Mommy doesn't want us to cry, Poppy. She wants us to live good and 'member her."

Those words, from the mouth of a babe, had given him the strength to go on. And until Shelby fainted during the burial of her son, Martin hadn't been sure how deeply the death of his grandson had affected his daughter. He also knew leaving her husband had to be the hardest decision Shelby had ever faced. Nelson was her world, and that world had crumbled around her feet. Yet his daughter had hidden her feelings and gone on with her life.

But Shelby needed help. In raising his daughter, he had neglected to teach her an important lesson. At times, everyone needed help and it was okay to hurt and lean on the strength of others. He nudged her away from his shoulder, then reached into his back pocket for his wallet. He withdrew the business card he'd carried around for almost two years and placed it in her hands. "Pumpkin, you know that I love you and will always be here for you any time you need me. But I want you to take this card and when you and Nelson return from your trip, I want you to sit down together and call this number."

Shelby looked down at the white card. It read: NSIDSF, National SIDS Foundation, Colorado Chapter. She lifted her head and frowned at her father. "I don't need a support group, Poppy," she stated forcefully. "I have accepted the death of my baby and am fully capable of continuing to do so on my own. What I need is to stay here, in this country, so that I can be close to Lamar."

"What you need is to learn how to grieve for your son. He was taken from us so young and by something which has no explanation as to its cause. Now, in our hearts, we will always remember Lamar, Shelby, but Lamar is dead and he doesn't need you any longer. I think it's safe to say that my grandson and your mother are at peace and if it helps you to think of the two of them together, then do

so. But it is time for you to let go and these people can
help.

"You are a strong woman, Shelby. I'm very proud of
you and what you've accomplished, but you have to
accept Lamar's death. Last night, Nelson and I spoke at
length about this situation. He told me about the nightmares, Shelby, the visit at the cemetery yesterday and the
guilt he feels for leaving you alone... Both of you need
help. Talking to other parents who have experienced the
same type of loss and learning about the disease that
ended my grandson's life will help you and Nelson come
to terms with his death and with each other."

Every word her father spoke struck a chord in Shelby
and deep down, she knew he was right. She and Nelson
had talked about their baby, but neither had spoken of
their feelings regarding his death. And coming to terms
with the loss of her son was something she'd never really
done. Oh, she knew Lamar was gone; she just didn't
understand why. And rather than seek out answers, she'd
made the necessary adjustments in her life and gone on.

Her son's room had not been touched and it finally
dawned on Shelby why. The bedroom was a shrine, an
external memorial to Lamar's short life on this earth. She
shuddered through the emotional realization and groped
for her father's hands. "Poppy, I don't know. What if
Nelson and I can't do this alone? Will you help us?"

Martin pulled his daughter into his strong hold.
"Little girl, I will do whatever you and Nelson need for
me to do. Now I've already talked to a colleague of mine
at the Nebraska State Department of Health. The doctors

and staff members there have been studying SIDS since 1975. While there is no substantial evidence or explanation for the occurrence of Sudden Infant Death Syndrome, they have made remarkable progress in understanding the effect the loss of a child to SIDS has on the parents and family. When you are ready, he has agreed to speak with you and Nelson; I will be there, too."

Martin chucked Shelby's chin with the knuckle of his forefinger and kissed her cheek. "Now you repair that lovely face of yours and finish dressing. Your husband is downstairs waiting for you to marry him."

Martin laid the wedding bouquet of white orchids, baby's breath and pink tea roses in Shelby's arms, then stood back to admire his daughter. With no time to make anything, Shelby had chosen a two-piece suit of soft rose from her wardrobe. The top, with its decorative gathered stitch across the back, fell like a mini-cape to her rounded hips and featured a satin-edged hemline that matched the deeper shade of rose lancing the long sleeves. Five small rhinestone buttons adorning the front picked up the color and added a touch of elegance. The only feature marking the slim skirt falling two inches above her knees was the darted slit in the back. A thinly veiled, rose-colored hat sat at a jaunty angle on hair that floated in a dark, billowy cloud of curls around her face.

Shelby took hold of her father's arm and for the second time began her bridal walk to stand at Nelson's side. Bathed in candlelight, the room glowed and the light sprinkling of snow outside the large picture window gave the setting an almost fairytale-like appearance. Shelby focused on Nelson. He looked so handsome in his black tuxedo and white silk shirt. His image swam before her eyes, distorted by the tears which threatened to overflow down her cheeks.

There was no red carpet, no white dress of satin and lace, and her tears were tears of happiness. With the help of her husband and her father, Shelby knew she would learn to show her emotions and learn to live with the death of her son on a more realistic basis. As she walked, her eyes looked heavenward. "Are you watching, Lamar?" she asked silently. "Mommy and Daddy are getting married again and this time we will stay together because no matter what, Daddy and I are inseparable."

Nelson was so antsy he couldn't stand still, and not even the restraining hand of Jordan could stop him from moving. He left his place and went to meet Martin and Shelby at the arched doorway. When he reached them, Nelson pulled Shelby into his arms. "You're beautiful, Shel," he said. "You're beautiful and you're mine."

Martin relinquished his hold and passed his daughter forward, then followed as Nelson and Shelby walked together to stand in front of the fireplace and the minister. He stepped to the side, his eyes misted with tears. Soon Nelson and Shelby would start the healing process and he could stop worrying about his daughter and son. Martin held one other thought close to his heart, his hope that one day he would again be a grandfather.

At two minutes to midnight, Nelson pressed his lips to Shelby's, sealing the marriage vows they had just spoken. When the clock struck twelve and the merrymaking and shouts ringing in the New Year began, Nelson still hadn't let Shelby up for air.

*Three months later...*

Shelby laid her hand in Nelson's, seeking his warmth and strength, and stared around at the group of people seated around their living room.

Everyone there had lost a child, too. Some faces looked ravaged, as if they were living in a war zone. Others were serene, as if they'd somehow come to terms with the death of their child. Still others had bewildered, frightened looks, as if they hadn't yet woken up from the nightmare. Shelby and Nelson put on their brave faces and tried to draw strength from each other.

Two weeks after returning from their second honeymoon in Hawaii, they had made the trip to the Colorado SIDS Program office and had also spoken again with Lamar's doctor. Through those visits and the information they had gathered and read on Sudden Infant Death Syndrome, they had learned about the malady that had taken their baby.

Three weeks ago, they had flown to Nebraska with Poppy and met with his friend. For no reason she could think of, when they'd approached Dr. Mendoza's door, fear had welled up inside her and she'd tried to pull away.

Nelson had held her until she stopped shaking and tenderly led her inside the office. She recalled that meeting now...

Dr. Mendoza watched the young couple enter his office. They looked like so many others he'd seen over the years. The wife was scared. He could see the look of stark fear in her eyes. The husband was doing his best to stay strong. He might make it through the session and he might not. Sometimes the roles were reversed: the wife strong and the husband scared. Jose Mendoza removed the wire-rimmed glasses from his eyes and tossed them on the desk. He uncrossed his legs and rose from his chair, placing his hand inside the pocket of his brown tweed pants. These were Martin's children and he'd do what he could to help them.

His head nodded in approval as he watched the group move farther into the room. He'd seen it, felt it, and knew it was the one thing Martin's children would need to complete the healing process. The Reeves loved each other and Dr. Mendoza considered their love the essential element. So many couples didn't have the wherewithal to survive the tragedy that ripped families apart. These two could make it, and this step toward understanding, if not accepting, was the first step toward healing.

"Martin, my friend," Dr. Mendoza exclaimed. He shook the hand Martin extended.

"It is good to see you, Jose, and thank you for seeing me and my family." Martin turned. "This is my son and my daughter, Nelson and Shelby Reeves."

Jose gave them a kindly smile after seeing their apprehensive glances around his office. "Hello, Shelby, Nelson. Please have a seat." Jose indicated the chairs and waited until they had seated themselves before lowering himself to his chair.

Dr. Mendoza made a temple of his forefingers and propped his chin on the tip. "First of all, let me say that I am glad to talk to Martin's children. We have been friends for many years and I am a great admirer and have much respect for Martin and his work in genetics.

"Having said that, Shelby and Nelson, it is entirely up to you how this meeting is conducted. I can relate what is known about Sudden Infant Death Syndrome or if you'd rather ask questions, I will answer to the best of my ability." Jose leaned forward and rested his arms on the desk. "But know this, I will shoot from the hip and won't pull any punches with my answers. And everything you hear in this office today is under intense dispute in the medical community. That is because after more than thirty years of research, we still have no idea of what causes SIDS and because we have no answers to these questions, we also have no procedures to predict or prevent the illness from occurring."

Nelson looked at Martin. Knowing his son needed help getting started, Martin cleared his throat. "Shelby and Nelson have read many books and articles on the subject of SIDS, Jose. However, they have just started their study and they are eager to learn anything you can tell them. If they have questions, they will ask as we talk."

"Very well, Martin." Dr. Mendoza took a deep breath. "Nelson and Shelby, as I've already mentioned, the malady of Sudden Infant Death Syndrome is a mystery to the medical community. We don't know why it happens, why it's so sudden, or what causes it. However, there are a few things we do know.

"SIDS is neither predictable nor preventable. It is also unexplainable at this time, though many theories abound. It is the most common cause of death for babies between the ages of one week and one year, usually occurring between one and four months, and estimates range from five thousand up to ten thousand deaths annually in the United States alone. More boys are affected than girls and most deaths occur during the early spring, fall and winter months. The disorder crosses all lines. It knows no racial, ethnic, economic or social barriers, and is also not hereditary or genetic, as Martin can attest.

"Death occurs due to cardiac and/or respiratory failure, though how the actual event unfolds is still a mystery. As you are probably already aware, there was nothing you or the doctors could have done to prevent your son's death.

"Some in the medical community believe that brain stem disorders play a role; others believe that sleeping position is a factor. Some have thrown up their hands in frustration that we'll ever discover the reason why an apparently healthy infant, such as your son, Lamar, dies so unexpectedly. However, sleeping position has recently come under close scrutiny and it has been documented in some countries-England, Australia and Norway to name few-that placing infants on their backs or side to sleep has some effect on reducing the risk of SIDS."

Shelby gripped her bottom lip between her teeth and sat up a little straighter. Jose glanced at her. "You have a question at this time, Shelby?"

"Go ahead, pumpkin," Martin encouraged. "We are here to get answers to all the questions you and Nelson may have."

"Doctor Mendoza—"

"Jose, please."

"Thank you. Jose, Nelson and I know that SIDS is not hereditary or genetic. On the other hand, we've also read that SIDS siblings have a slightly higher risk of succumbing to the disease." Shelby's bottom lip trembled as she continued. "Doctor? I mean, Jose. I'm two months pregnant and I'm scared. Nelson is terrified. We don't know what to believe."

Jose was thoughtful for a moment. The problem with a disease like SIDS was that all the available information was controversial. "Shelby, do you remember what I said when we first began? All current thought processes about SIDS can and will be disputed, and what you've just said is a prime example of the dialogue.

"However, there are studies which indicate that SIDS families have no more risk of losing another child to the disease than families who have not lost an infant. In fact, some studies indicate that the risk is less than one percent. My position is to go with this theory."

"What about home monitoring systems?"

Nelson leaned forward, eager to enter the discussion. "I've read that they keep tabs on the baby's breathing and heart rate and if they drop below a certain level, an alarm will go off as a signal that something's wrong."

"If it will ease your mind, then I recommend that you get one and install it in the baby's room. However, a home monitoring system will not prevent SIDS from occurring."

Jose left his chair and moved around the desk. He hiked his hip and leaned on the edge in front of Shelby and Nelson. "I have to be honest with the two of you. There is nothing we can do to stop SIDS because we don't know the cause and without a cause, we can't find a cure. You have suffered the unfortunate tragedy and trauma of losing a child to this horrible disease. I will pray for you, as I will for my friend, Martin, and also continue to pray that one day we stop the occurrence of SIDS.

"In the meantime, I would like the two of you to focus on these things. You are having another child. While this baby, boy or girl, will never replace Lamar, you owe it to yourselves and to the baby who will one day be yours to accept and go forward. Continue to read and educate yourselves about the malady of SIDS. At this point, knowledge and awareness are the most helpful tools we have available.

"Consider what I've said about sleeping positions and get the best pre-and postnatal care you can. Talk to your doctor and enlist his help in making sure that your baby is thoroughly examined and monitored during its first year of life.

"Most importantly, I would urge the two of you to join a support group and, if necessary, seek sessions with your religious benefactor or a professional therapist. I do not believe that a parent who has ever lost a child can fully recover from that loss, but you can put the experience in perspective and not let fear rule your lives or that of your child."

Shelby looked around at the group gathered in her living room again. Sessions with a therapist they had decided against, for now anyway, but they had talked to their minister.

Earlier that day, Nelson had brought home a stack of cardboard boxes and together they had packed up the things in their son's room. It had been a painful experience, packing away the belongings and evidence of their son's existence, and both had broken down several times. But when they needed strength, they leaned on each other and took comfort in the thought that while they were putting away the visual reminders the memories and love they had for Lamar would always remain in their hearts. It had taken a long time, but they had finally filled the boxes and stored them in the attic. One day, when they were stronger, they would go through those boxes again, and they would tell their coming son or daughter about the brother they never knew.

Feeling much better knowing about the disease that had killed their son had led to their decision to hold the next meeting, and their first, of the NSIDSF, Colorado Chapter, in their home.

Nelson closed his arm about Shelby's shoulders and drew in a deep breath. "We are the Reeves," he began. "Nelson and Shelby. Our son, Nelson Lamar Reeves, III, was three months old when we lost him to SIDS."

# EPILOGUE

An alarm sounded, jerking Nelson awake in the rocking chair. He jumped up from the seat and rushed to the crib, his chest heaving with heavy pants.

Shelby ran into the room, the veins in her hand showing as she clutched the front of her nightgown. Her eyes closed in thankful prayer when she heard the loud wail.

Nelson held his daughter close to his heart and looked at Shelby. "She's all right, Shel. Our baby is just fine."

Six-month-old Lauryn Nicole didn't like the position in which her father held her. She added wiggling and squirming to her loud cries of protest. Nelson lifted her away, raising her to kiss the tiny, damp mouth. "Okay, little bit," he cooed. "Daddy's very sorry for holding you like that."

Shelby walked over to her family. She ran her hand over Nelson's back. "Baby, I'll take her. It's time for Lauryn to eat."

Shelby sat in the rocking chair and Nelson laid the baby in her arms. He waited until Lauryn was happily nursing, then went to the crib to check the wiring on the home monitoring system. He didn't find anything wrong, and was glad he'd been in the room when the alarm sounded. Otherwise...

Nelson didn't finish the thought, glancing at Shelby instead. She smiled and he went to her, sitting on the floor at her feet.

"You don't have to say anything, sweetness. I know. But something told me that I needed to be in here tonight."

Shelby filtered her fingers though his hair. Nelson was doing better. This was the first time in two months that she'd found him in the nursery during the night. Lauryn had spent the first weeks of her life sleeping in their bedroom.

They had taken turns sitting through the night and watching over their child. But Shelby and Nelson had soon realized they couldn't operate on minimal sleep and high stress and still keep up with the demands of work and daily living. Slowly, it had gotten better, especially when the fourth month had passed.

Milan wouldn't happen; the deal had fallen through and they had decided that Nelson would stay with Technotronics for the time being, although he was exploring the possibility of starting his own engineering firm.

Lauryn gurgled and Shelby looked down at her baby. Their second tacit benchmark was a year. So many things could happen, but both felt that once their daughter reached one year of age, they could breathe a little easier.

"I know exactly how you feel, baby. There are times when I sit with her at night, too."

"She's strong, Shel, and the tests say she's healthy. I'm glad that Jose made arrangements to check Lauryn over next week when he visits Poppy. I know he said there are no guarantees, but the older our baby gets, the better I feel."

"All we can do is keep loving her, Nelson, and enjoy every day we are granted with Lauryn. We'll love her and we'll keep loving each other."

"Inseparable, Shel?"

"Inseparable, baby."

Nelson laid his head on Shelby's knee, extremely content to be sitting with his family and grateful for all of his blessings. They still carried a measure of regret, on both sides.

After what they'd been through, how could they not?

For a time they had lost their way, but the one constant through all the heartache had been their love. That love had brought them back together and would carry them forward to face whatever life had left to throw at them. Now all was right, Nelson thought. He had his wife back and his daughter would grow into a beautiful, young woman.

"Shel?"

"Hmm," she responded, letting the thick patch of Lauryn's soft black curls slide through her fingers.

"I'll always love you—endlessly forever and a day."

## 2007 Publication Schedule

### January

Rooms of the Heart
Donna Hill
ISBN-13: 978-1-58571-219-9
ISBN-10: 1-58571-219-1
$6.99

A Dangerous Love
J. M. Jeffries
ISBN-13: 978-1-58571-217-5
ISBN-10: 1-58571-217-5
$6.99

### February

Bound By Love
Beverly Clark
ISBN-13: 978-1-58571-232-8
ISBN-10: 1-58571-232-9
$6.99

A Love to Cherish
Beverly Clark
ISBN-13: 978-1-58571-233-5
ISBN-10: 1-58571-233-7
$6.99

### March

Best of Friends
Natalie Dunbar
ISBN-13: 978-1-58571-220-5
ISBN-10: 1-58571-220-5
$6.99

Midnight Magic
Gwynne Forster
ISBN-13: 978-1-58571-225-0
ISBN-10: 1-58571-225-6
$6.99

### April

Cherish the Flame
Beverly Clark
ISBN-13: 978-1-58571-221-2
ISBN-10: 1-58571-221-3
$6.99

Quiet Storm
Donna Hill
ISBN-13: 978-1-58571-226-7
ISBN-10: 1-58571-226-4
$6.99

### May

Sweet Tomorrows
Kimberley White
ISBN-13: 978-1-58571-234-2
ISBN-10: 1-58571-234-5
$6.99

No Commitment Required
Seressia Glass
ISBN-13: 978-1-58571-222-9
ISBN-10: 1-58571-222-1
$6.99

### June

A Dangerous Deception
J. M. Jeffries
ISBN-13: 978-1-58571-228-1
ISBN-10: 1-58571-228-0
$6.99

Illusions
Pamela Leigh Starr
ISBN-13: 978-1-58571-229-8
ISBN-10: 1-58571-229-9
$6.99

## 2007 Publication Schedule (continued)

### July

Indiscretions
Donna Hill
ISBN-13: 978-1-58571-230-4
ISBN-10: 1-58571-230-2
$6.99

Whispers in the Night
Dorothy Elizabeth Love
ISBN-13: 978-1-58571-231-1
ISBN-10: 1-58571-231-0
$6.99

### August

Bodyguard
Andrea Jackson
ISBN-13: 978-1-58571-235-9
ISBN-10: 1-58571-235-3
$6.99

Crossing Paths, Tempting Memories
Dorothy Elizabeth Love
ISBN-13: 978-1-58571-236-6
ISBN-10: 1-58571-236-1
$6.99

### September

Fate
Pamela Leigh Starr
ISBN-13: 978-1-58571-258-8
ISBN-10: 1-58571-258-2
$6.99

Mae's Promise
Melody Walcott
ISBN-13: 978-1-58571-259-5
ISBN-10: 1-58571-259-0
$6.99

### October

Magnolia Sunset
Giselle Carmichael
ISBN-13: 978-1-58571-260-1
ISBN-10: 1-58571-260-4
$6.99

Broken
Dar Tomlinson
ISBN-13: 978-1-58571-261-8
ISBN-10: 1-58571-261-2
$6.99

### November

Truly Inseparable
Wanda Y. Thomas
ISBN-13: 978-1-58571-262-5
ISBN-10: 1-58571-262-0
$6.99

The Color Line
Lizzette G. Carter
ISBN-13: 978-1-58571-263-2
ISBN-10: 1-58571-263-9
$6.99

### December

Love Always
Mildred Riley
ISBN-13: 978-1-58571-264-9
ISBN-10: 1-58571-264-7
$6.99

Pride and Joi
Gay Gunn
ISBN-13: 978-1-58571-265-6
ISBN-10: 1-58571-265-5
$6.99

## Other Genesis Press, Inc. Titles

| | | |
|---|---|---|
| A Dangerous Deception | J.M. Jeffries | $8.95 |
| A Dangerous Love | J.M. Jeffries | $8.95 |
| A Dangerous Obsession | J.M. Jeffries | $8.95 |
| A Drummer's Beat to Mend | Kei Swanson | $9.95 |
| A Happy Life | Charlotte Harris | $9.95 |
| A Heart's Awakening | Veronica Parker | $9.95 |
| A Lark on the Wing | Phyliss Hamilton | $9.95 |
| A Love of Her Own | Cheris F. Hodges | $9.95 |
| A Love to Cherish | Beverly Clark | $8.95 |
| A Risk of Rain | Dar Tomlinson | $8.95 |
| A Twist of Fate | Beverly Clark | $8.95 |
| A Will to Love | Angie Daniels | $9.95 |
| Acquisitions | Kimberley White | $8.95 |
| Across | Carol Payne | $12.95 |
| After the Vows | Leslie Esdaile | $10.95 |
| (Summer Anthology) | T.T. Henderson | |
| | Jacqueline Thomas | |
| Again My Love | Kayla Perrin | $10.95 |
| Against the Wind | Gwynne Forster | $8.95 |
| All I Ask | Barbara Keaton | $8.95 |
| Ambrosia | T.T. Henderson | $8.95 |
| An Unfinished Love Affair | Barbara Keaton | $8.95 |
| And Then Came You | Dorothy Elizabeth Love | $8.95 |
| Angel's Paradise | Janice Angelique | $9.95 |
| At Last | Lisa G. Riley | $8.95 |
| Best of Friends | Natalie Dunbar | $8.95 |
| Beyond the Rapture | Beverly Clark | $9.95 |
| Blaze | Barbara Keaton | $9.95 |
| Blood Lust | J. M. Jeffries | $9.95 |

## Other Genesis Press, Inc. Titles (continued)

| | | |
|---|---|---|
| Bodyguard | Andrea Jackson | $9.95 |
| Boss of Me | Diana Nyad | $8.95 |
| Bound by Love | Beverly Clark | $8.95 |
| Breeze | Robin Hampton Allen | $10.95 |
| Broken | Dar Tomlinson | $24.95 |
| By Design | Barbara Keaton | $8.95 |
| Cajun Heat | Charlene Berry | $8.95 |
| Careless Whispers | Rochelle Alers | $8.95 |
| Cats & Other Tales | Marilyn Wagner | $8.95 |
| Caught in a Trap | Andre Michelle | $8.95 |
| Caught Up In the Rapture | Lisa G. Riley | $9.95 |
| Cautious Heart | Cheris F Hodges | $8.95 |
| Chances | Pamela Leigh Starr | $8.95 |
| Cherish the Flame | Beverly Clark | $8.95 |
| Class Reunion | Irma Jenkins/ | |
| | John Brown | $12.95 |
| Code Name: Diva | J.M. Jeffries | $9.95 |
| Conquering Dr. Wexler's Heart | Kimberley White | $9.95 |
| Crossing Paths, | Dorothy Elizabeth Love | $9.95 |
|   Tempting Memories | | |
| Cypress Whisperings | Phyllis Hamilton | $8.95 |
| Dark Embrace | Crystal Wilson Harris | $8.95 |
| Dark Storm Rising | Chinelu Moore | $10.95 |
| Daughter of the Wind | Joan Xian | $8.95 |
| Deadly Sacrifice | Jack Kean | $22.95 |
| Designer Passion | Dar Tomlinson | $8.95 |
| Dreamtective | Liz Swados | $5.95 |
| Ebony Butterfly II | Delilah Dawson | $14.95 |
| Echoes of Yesterday | Beverly Clark | $9.95 |

## Other Genesis Press, Inc. Titles (continued)

| | | |
|---|---|---|
| Eden's Garden | Elizabeth Rose | $8.95 |
| Everlastin' Love | Gay G. Gunn | $8.95 |
| Everlasting Moments | Dorothy Elizabeth Love | $8.95 |
| Everything and More | Sinclair Lebeau | $8.95 |
| Everything but Love | Natalie Dunbar | $8.95 |
| Eve's Prescription | Edwina Martin Arnold | $8.95 |
| Falling | Natalie Dunbar | $9.95 |
| Fate | Pamela Leigh Starr | $8.95 |
| Finding Isabella | A.J. Garrotto | $8.95 |
| Forbidden Quest | Dar Tomlinson | $10.95 |
| Forever Love | Wanda Y. Thomas | $8.95 |
| From the Ashes | Kathleen Suzanne | $8.95 |
| | Jeanne Sumerix | |
| Gentle Yearning | Rochelle Alers | $10.95 |
| Glory of Love | Sinclair LeBeau | $10.95 |
| Go Gentle into that Good Night | Malcom Boyd | $12.95 |
| Goldengroove | Mary Beth Craft | $16.95 |
| Groove, Bang, and Jive | Steve Cannon | $8.99 |
| Hand in Glove | Andrea Jackson | $9.95 |
| Hard to Love | Kimberley White | $9.95 |
| Hart & Soul | Angie Daniels | $8.95 |
| Heartbeat | Stephanie Bedwell-Grime | $8.95 |
| Hearts Remember | M. Loui Quezada | $8.95 |
| Hidden Memories | Robin Allen | $10.95 |
| Higher Ground | Leah Latimer | $19.95 |
| Hitler, the War, and the Pope | Ronald Rychiak | $26.95 |
| How to Write a Romance | Kathryn Falk | $18.95 |
| I Married a Reclining Chair | Lisa M. Fuhs | $8.95 |
| Indigo After Dark Vol. I | *Nia Dixon/Angelique* | $10.95 |

## Other Genesis Press, Inc. Titles (continued)

**Other Genesis Press, Inc. Titles (continued)**

| | | |
|---|---|---|
| Magnolia Sunset | Giselle Carmichael | $8.95 |
| Matters of Life and Death | Lesego Malepe, Ph.D. | $15.95 |
| Meant to Be | Jeanne Sumerix | $8.95 |
| Midnight Clear (Anthology) | Leslie Esdaile | $10.95 |
| | Gwynne Forster | |
| | Carmen Green | |
| | Monica Jackson | |
| Midnight Magic | Gwynne Forster | $8.95 |
| Midnight Peril | Vicki Andrews | $10.95 |
| Misconceptions | Pamela Leigh Starr | $9.95 |
| Montgomery's Children | Richard Perry | $14.95 |
| My Buffalo Soldier | Barbara B. K. Reeves | $8.95 |
| Naked Soul | Gwynne Forster | $8.95 |
| Next to Last Chance | Louisa Dixon | $24.95 |
| No Apologies | Seressia Glass | $8.95 |
| No Commitment Required | Seressia Glass | $8.95 |
| No Regrets | Mildred E. Riley | $8.95 |
| Nowhere to Run | Gay G. Gunn | $10.95 |
| O Bed! O Breakfast! | Rob Kuehnle | $14.95 |
| Object of His Desire | A. C. Arthur | $8.95 |
| Office Policy | A. C. Arthur | $9.95 |
| Once in a Blue Moon | Dorianne Cole | $9.95 |
| One Day at a Time | Bella McFarland | $8.95 |
| Outside Chance | Louisa Dixon | $24.95 |
| Passion | T.T. Henderson | $10.95 |
| Passion's Blood | Cherif Fortin | $22.95 |
| Passion's Journey | Wanda Y. Thomas | $8.95 |
| Past Promises | Jahmel West | $8.95 |
| Path of Fire | T.T. Henderson | $8.95 |

## Other Genesis Press, Inc. Titles (continued)

| | | |
|---|---|---|
| Path of Thorns | Annetta P. Lee | $9.95 |
| Peace Be Still | Colette Haywood | $12.95 |
| Picture Perfect | Reon Carter | $8.95 |
| Playing for Keeps | Stephanie Salinas | $8.95 |
| Pride & Joi | Gay G. Gunn | $15.95 |
| Pride & Joi | Gay G. Gunn | $8.95 |
| Promises to Keep | Alicia Wiggins | $8.95 |
| Quiet Storm | Donna Hill | $10.95 |
| Reckless Surrender | Rochelle Alers | $6.95 |
| Red Polka Dot in a World of Plaid | Varian Johnson | $12.95 |
| Reluctant Captive | Joyce Jackson | $8.95 |
| Rendezvous with Fate | Jeanne Sumerix | $8.95 |
| Revelations | Cheris F. Hodges | $8.95 |
| Rivers of the Soul | Leslie Esdaile | $8.95 |
| Rocky Mountain Romance | Kathleen Suzanne | $8.95 |
| Rooms of the Heart | Donna Hill | $8.95 |
| Rough on Rats and Tough on Cats | Chris Parker | $12.95 |
| Secret Library Vol. 1 | Nina Sheridan | $18.95 |
| Secret Library Vol. 2 | Cassandra Colt | $8.95 |
| Shades of Brown | Denise Becker | $8.95 |
| Shades of Desire | Monica White | $8.95 |
| Shadows in the Moonlight | Jeanne Sumerix | $8.95 |
| Sin | Crystal Rhodes | $8.95 |
| So Amazing | Sinclair LeBeau | $8.95 |
| Somebody's Someone | Sinclair LeBeau | $8.95 |
| Someone to Love | Alicia Wiggins | $8.95 |
| Song in the Park | Martin Brant | $15.95 |

## Other Genesis Press, Inc. Titles (continued)

| | | |
|---|---|---|
| Soul Eyes | Wayne L. Wilson | $12.95 |
| Soul to Soul | Donna Hill | $8.95 |
| Southern Comfort | J.M. Jeffries | $8.95 |
| Still the Storm | Sharon Robinson | $8.95 |
| Still Waters Run Deep | Leslie Esdaile | $8.95 |
| Stories to Excite You | Anna Forrest/Divine | $14.95 |
| Subtle Secrets | Wanda Y. Thomas | $8.95 |
| Suddenly You | Crystal Hubbard | $9.95 |
| Sweet Repercussions | Kimberley White | $9.95 |
| Sweet Tomorrows | Kimberly White | $8.95 |
| Taken by You | Dorothy Elizabeth Love | $9.95 |
| Tattooed Tears | T. T. Henderson | $8.95 |
| The Color Line | Lizzette Grayson Carter | $9.95 |
| The Color of Trouble | Dyanne Davis | $8.95 |
| The Disappearance of Allison Jones | Kayla Perrin | $5.95 |
| The Honey Dipper's Legacy | Pannell-Allen | $14.95 |
| The Joker's Love Tune | Sidney Rickman | $15.95 |
| The Little Pretender | Barbara Cartland | $10.95 |
| The Love We Had | Natalie Dunbar | $8.95 |
| The Man Who Could Fly | Bob & Milana Beamon | $18.95 |
| The Missing Link | Charlyne Dickerson | $8.95 |
| The Price of Love | Sinclair LeBeau | $8.95 |
| The Smoking Life | Ilene Barth | $29.95 |
| The Words of the Pitcher | Kei Swanson | $8.95 |
| Three Wishes | Seressia Glass | $8.95 |
| Ties That Bind | Kathleen Suzanne | $8.95 |
| Tiger Woods | Libby Hughes | $5.95 |